GLIMMER OF THE OTHER

OTHER REALM, BOOK 1

BY HEATHER G. HARRIS

DEDICATION

For my mum, now and always. Miss you.

CHAPTER 1

I WAS PERCHED precariously in a birch tree in Mr Michael Mackenzie's back garden. It was chilly out, and I pulled my green camouflage jacket tighter. I tried my best not to shift around. I was employed for discreet surveillance and falling out of a tree didn't fit the bill.

I'd been in situ for a good hour before I saw movement in the conservatory. The freshly showered Mr Mackenzie was carrying something large into the glass-covered room. It was a human-sized fox plushie, complete with plush boobs and big eyes framed with eyelashes. The fox plushie had her mouth open as if she were surprised.

I grimaced a little. She was going to be surprised all right. Mr Mackenzie removed the tented towel from his waist and lay down next to Miss Foxy. It wasn't long before things started getting hot and heavy. I'd definitely seen enough.

I took a short video and several pictures on my phone. Fetish cases are often harder than cheating spouse cases. Mr Mackenzie wasn't actually cheating on his wife;

he just had a kink that he preferred to keep secret. Of course, I was about to blow that out of the water.

Fetishes are a murky area. The newly-wedded Mrs Mackenzie had suspected her husband of cheating on her, but technically he wasn't. Maybe she'd be okay with her husband getting it on with a fake fox, or maybe it'd be too much for her. But Mr Mackenzie hadn't done anything wrong. Maybe it's a good idea to make sure your spouse shares or understands your kinks before you rush down the aisle, but the truth is that I'm no expert. I haven't had a relationship last longer than a long weekend.

I climbed carefully down the tree. Mr Mackenzie was too busy with Miss Foxy to notice. I went over the back fence, walked down the alley and got into my car, a black Ford Focus. They're a dime a dozen and she certainly doesn't stand out, which makes her handy for a private investigator. My dog just about fits inside her too, if he takes up the whole back seat. That's okay; I don't often have passengers.

I called Mrs Mackenzie and arranged a meet in fifteen minutes at her local Starbucks. I figured I'd get there in five and would have a chance to order a latte before she arrived.

I parked up front, hopped out and ordered my drink. I was sitting in an armchair when Sarah Mackenzie walked in with a friend. She was twenty-seven, blonde, beautiful and voluptuous; even on a bad day, she was still out of Mr Mackenzie's league. He was forty-six, mousy and also voluptuous, but not in a good way. He was also pretty wealthy. I couldn't say what their emotional connection was like, save that she had cried her eyes out when she explained all the reasons she suspected 'Mick' of having an affair. The cynic in me wondered how much Mr Mackenzie's money contributed to her tears.

Mrs Mackenzie's friend was a brunette, svelte and athletic, and she had a hardness in her eyes that told me she was a no-bullshit type. Mrs Mackenzie had struck me as nice but vapid, and I wondered how they had become friends. I'm nosey like that.

I stood up to greet them. 'Jinx!' Mrs Mackenzie wailed. 'Just tell me … just tell me straight.' She slumped into the armchair opposite me. I thought, perhaps rather ungenerously, that she was milking the scene somewhat. Some people live for drama.

During my seven years as a PI, I've learnt that pictures really are worth a thousand words. I pulled up a well-angled shot on my phone and made sure to show it only to Mrs Mackenzie.

She stood up and let out a dramatic shriek. 'Oh my God, oh my *God*! What the hell is he doing to that … thing?' She sank back into the armchair. 'I'm going to faint. I'm going to throw up. I don't know which way to go.'

Her friend pushed Mrs Mackenzie's head between

her legs. 'Push against my hand and breathe,' she instructed. Mrs Mackenzie obeyed.

I waited in silence while Mrs Mackenzie tried to wrap her mind around what she'd seen. She waved her friend's hand away. 'I'm all right, Lisa. I'm okay.' *Lie*, my internal radar pinged. She wasn't okay, and I didn't blame her.

She shook her head. 'I'm just – hell!'

'You're in shock,' I offered helpfully.

'No shit, Sherlock,' Lisa snarled.

I guessed I wasn't her favourite person. Deflection – I get it a lot.

'Show her the picture,' Mrs Mackenzie said. 'She's my cousin. I need someone to know.' *True*.

Now their relationship made a little more sense – they weren't friends, they were family. I showed Lisa the picture. She blinked several times before she paled and sat down. 'Well,' she said. 'Well then.'

'He's fucking a fox,' Mrs Mackenzie said flatly.

'A plushie fox,' I explained. 'It's not real.'

'I've always liked Mick,' Lisa said. *Lie*, my internal radar told me. 'But this is a bit … different. You really had no idea?' she asked dubiously. She was trying to be diplomatic, trying not to let her dislike of Mr Mackenzie show.

Mrs Mackenzie shook her head, her eyes glassy and wide. She stared at her hands and picked at her peeling nail varnish. 'No. He doesn't even have a soft toy from his

childhood. I had no idea he … with … that… Christ!'
True.

It was time for me to make my exit. 'I'll leave you to talk things over.' I stood up. 'I'll email through the evidence and my invoice, as discussed.'

Mrs Mackenzie looked up. 'Thanks, Jinx. It's not what I expected, but I needed to know. I love him.' *True.* Huh, I guess she really did love him. It takes all kinds.

'No problem. I hope things work out for you.' I nodded politely to Lisa and made my way out. Another day, another dollar.

It was 4 p.m. I had a debtor trace on the books, but I wasn't feeling fresh, so I called it a day and headed home. Home is a three-bedroom, semi-detached house on a good street in an even better area. I was born and raised in Buckinghamshire, and I'd inherited my house from my parents when I was eighteen. I'd done very little with it since.

I run my business, Sharp Investigations, from the house. I had toyed with the idea of renting office space, but my operation is too small to need it. I do my job well, but I don't advertise and I'm run off my feet. I have a basic website and a PO box. *Keep off the radar* – it was my parents' watch phrase, and I try to obey it.

I parked outside my house and walked over to my neighbour's. Mrs Harding looks after my dog when I'm on a job and can't take him with me. Gato is a three-year-old enthusiastic Great Dane. I've had him for just over a year and a half. He's sleek, black and has a distinctive white blaze across his face. He is a simple creature who loves nothing more than cuddling on the sofa. He's easy going and friendly, but he despises walks in the rain. The most important thing about him, though, is that he loves me unconditionally; he is one of two creatures left on this Earth that do – though I think Mrs Harding has some affection for me too.

She opened the door, dressed immaculately as always with painted nails that matched her outfit. Today she was in floral coral. Her lined face had sweeps of careful make-up, and she didn't look her age.

Gato pushed his way past her. 'Be careful!' I admonished, as he nearly took out the sixty-two-year-old woman in his hurry. I gave him an enthusiastic body rub in greeting, and he licked my face.

For a moment the grass he was standing on flickered turquoise. I blinked and it returned to its normal shade. Maybe I was more tired than I thought.

'Hey, pup,' I greeted him. 'Did you have a nice day with Mrs Harding?' He wagged his tail enthusiastically.

Mrs Harding has lived next door for as long as I can remember. Her husband, Sam, died a few years ago, and her daughter, Jane, visits infrequently. Jane is about ten years older than me. She has never married or had kids, and seems to have no inclination towards either. She's a consultant in A&E, and her job is her life. Again, I can't comment. My job is my life too – I'm just significantly less successful at it.

'We've had a lovely day. He was no trouble,' Mrs Harding assured me. *Lie.*

I raised an eyebrow and sighed. 'What did he do this time?'

Mrs Harding let out the smile she was trying to keep in. 'He chased the postman a little. I told the postman not to run, then it wouldn't be such a good game, but he didn't listen. When Gato caught him, he licked him and came right back. So, really, there was no harm done.'

I rolled my eyes. 'I'm going to get another stern letter from Royal Mail,' I huffed to Gato, who looked at me wide eyed as if he would never do a bad thing in his life.

'Thanks, Mrs H. I appreciate it.' I handed her a paper bag. Today's offering for taking Gato was two mangoes. Mrs Harding refuses to accept payment for helping me out; she says she does it because she enjoys the company. She claims she is too old to commit to a dog of her own, but she's more than happy to care for mine. I enjoy giving her weird and wonderful thank-you gifts. To be honest, mangoes were a pretty poor effort. I'd have to up my game tomorrow.

I waved goodbye and unlocked my front door. Once inside, I slid home two deadbolts, a chain and a Yale lock. The house hasn't really changed since my parents were alive, save for the added security, and I know I should redecorate. Some shrink or other would say it is indicative of my issues, that I haven't significantly altered the house since their death. I painted the lounge after their murder to cover the blood stains, and, eventually, I redecorated the master bedroom, but only because of my best friend Lucy's non-stop pestering. It was another year before I actually moved into that bedroom.

Despite Gato's play with the postman, he was still frisky, so I swapped my camo jacket for a leather one, grabbed some poo bags and headed out. We had a brisk walk to the park, where Gato peed on virtually every flower he could find.

I tensed as a little white Westie careened towards us, yapping playfully. When the dog got to within three metres, she stopped as if frozen. A low growl emerged from her throat and she started to back away slowly. When she was a little further away, she turned tail and ran.

'It's okay,' I told Gato firmly. 'We don't need any other dogs to like you. I like you more than enough for anyone. You're my best boy.' I patted him and his tongue lolled out in a doggy smile. He isn't bothered that he's a pariah to other dogs but *I* mind. I feel like the other dogs are bullying my baby in the playground, but there's nothing I can do about it. Even the finest treats have never enticed another dog close to Gato.

Ignoring the Westie incident, we walked on. An area in the park was cordoned off by the police, and CSI was there. I walked closer and called Gato to heel. I recognised one of the policemen as Detective Steve Marley who had dated one of my friends in high school; the juvenile relationship was brief, so we weren't bosom buddies. Our paths had crossed during the last few years as I'd given witness evidence in several court cases.

I gave him a nod and a small smile, and he came over. He is tall and willowy, with prematurely greying hair and an open face. I bet he's a runner. 'Jinx,' he greeted me with a friendly smile.

'Hey, Steve. What's up?'

He frowned. 'A stabbing.' *Lie.* Why would Steve lie about the nature of a crime? The news report would be out soon enough. Curious.

I whistled. 'Damn, this neighbourhood is going downhill. Fatal?' I kept it casual but my heart was racing. However tenuous the connection, I always hoped a new attack might provide clues about my parents' deaths.

He shook his head. 'Nah, a few slices to the arm and neck.' *True.* 'The victim said he owed some money to a few different sharks. I'd say one of them got sick of waiting.'

That rang true as well but I didn't understand why the victim was sliced and not stabbed. What was the difference? Weirder and weirder. 'Any idea which loan shark?' I asked.

'Too early to say.' *Lie.* Now that lie I *could* under-stand; it was an open investigation, so Steve wasn't supposed to divulge details of suspects. Besides, people lie all the time. Some people do it for fun. It probably meant nothing, but I noted it all the same.

I wished Steve well and headed back home, a little on edge. Stabbings, even pseudo-stabbings, make me jittery. The image of my parents' ruined bodies flashed into my mind. You couldn't call what had happened to them a stabbing – it was a violent and vicious rending of their flesh to the point that I wasn't able to identify them properly. Identification had required dental records. And yet their deaths had been chalked up to a home invasion gone wrong. My ass.

I pushed it away. Not now. Later. Later I'd dream of them and the tang of blood.

Gato seemed spooked too. Normally he dashes away from me and then runs back, but tonight he was walking close to me and looking around. He stayed by my side until we were nearly home then abruptly turned, hackles raised, and let out a low, menacing growl.

I couldn't see anything that could be upsetting him and the hairs on my neck stood up. 'Come on,' I coaxed, feeling unnerved. 'We're nearly home.'

Gato followed me, growling the whole time. He was freaking me out. His eyes were fixed on something that I couldn't see, but it wasn't outside the realms of possibility that there was something – someone – out there that couldn't be seen.

I drew my small knife out of my pocket and flicked out the blade. 'Whatever you are,' I said calmly, 'you can fuck off. We're not an easy target.'

Gato barked twice to emphasise my words. I watched him move his head as if watching something walk away. He stopped growling. I swallowed hard, shaken but trying to pretend I wasn't.

Mrs Harding opened her door. 'Everything okay, Jinx?' she asked with concern.

I forced a smile onto my face. 'Fine, Mrs H. Gato just got a little spooked.'

'Did he?' She looked around. 'That's not like him.'

I shook my head.

Mrs H looked around one last time. 'Nothing here, Gato,' she reassured him. He trotted to her and gave a little whine. She stroked his head. 'All gone. Good boy.' She patted him and gave me a wry smile. 'Well, that's given me the wobbles. I'll be sure to lock my front door tonight.'

I rolled my eyes. 'You should lock the doors every night, Mrs H!' I said, exasperated.

She laughed. 'You're right, of course. Good night, Jinx. Sleep well.'

'You too, Mrs H.'

I switched on all the lights as I went inside, then went into the kitchen and started to make dinner. I also made myself a coffee; caffeine or not, I knew sleep would be a long time coming tonight. All the meditation in the world wasn't going to chase away the nightmares that would haunt me.

CHAPTER 2

I WAS SWEATING, panting and tangled in my sheets when I sat bolt upright. My phone was ringing. I checked the time with bleary eyes: 6:37 a.m. Who thought 6:37 a.m. was a reasonable time to call? Whoever it was, I was grateful that they'd pulled me from that particular nightmare.

My heart was still thundering and I debated not answering, but – in the end – curiosity got the better of me. It always does. 'Good morning, Sharp Investigations,' I said, using my soft phone voice.

'Good morning,' an imperious voice replied. 'You have come recommended for your discretion. I need you to find someone. Is that within your ambit?'

'Yes, ma'am,' I assured her.

'Good,' she said abruptly. 'My name is Lady Elizabeth Sorrell. My address is Foxwood Manor. Do you know it?'

'Yes, ma'am,' I repeated. It was the nearest stately home that I knew of that had not yet been passed to The National Trust. Still privately owned, it was often used for weddings and corporate events.

'Eight a.m. Don't be late.' She hung up without so much as a goodbye.

Sleep had been elusive until at least 2 a.m., and I felt gritty and tired. I thought seriously about grabbing an extra thirty minutes, but my sweat-soaked sheets dissuaded me. Besides, I was awake now.

I heaved myself into the shower to wash away the last of the cobwebs. I grabbed the jeans I'd been wearing the previous day from the floor and threw on a fresh T-shirt. This client was going to be a suit client for sure, but a suit isn't really dog-walking attire.

I took Gato for a brisk, incident-free walk and grabbed a slice of toast for breakfast. Mrs H would fetch him from my house when she was ready, so there was no need to disturb her at the crack of dawn.

I changed into a nondescript grey suit and a white shirt. I left the suit jacket unbuttoned; it looked worse buttoned, like my chest was straining to get out. I applied basic make-up and swept my dark-brown hair into a messy bun. I checked my appearance in the mirror: I was about as smart as I'd ever be. Satisfied, I fed Gato, kissed his head and climbed into my Ford.

Foxwood Manor was only twenty minutes away, but I was leaving thirty minutes before, just in case. I hadn't driven in that area yesterday, so I wasn't sure if there were any roadworks to contend with – and I didn't think Lady Sorrell was the type to forgive tardiness.

I was there by 7:50, but I waited an extra five minutes in the car. Lady Sorrell wouldn't appreciate me turning up too early either. Punctuality is a skill. At five to the hour, I knocked on the ancient wooden door. Barely a moment passed before it was opened by a gentleman in a fine-looking suit. He had salt-and-pepper hair and his ageing skin put him in his late fifties. I guessed Lady Sorrell had an honest-to-goodness butler. Who knew that was still a thing?

'Jessica Sharp, I presume,' he intoned. I wondered if they taught the butler stereotype in butler school.

'Jinx,' I corrected. He blinked; I guessed that people didn't normally correct him.

He stepped back to let me in and shut the heavy door behind us. The weak October sunlight barely penetrated the wood-panelled hall. He inclined his head for me to follow him.

I stared as I walked. Pictures were missing from the walls and there weren't many ornaments on display. Were the Sorrells having financial difficulties? I made a note get a deposit and to agree a figure for the retainer and disbursements up front. I prefer to think that my attitude makes me a good businesswoman rather than a cold-hearted bitch. Potato, po-tah-to.

The butler paused in front of a mahogany door, knocked and opened it. 'A Miss … Jinx to see you, ma'am.' He gave a moue of distaste as he said my name.

'Thank you, Jackson. That will be all.' I wondered if Jackson was his first name or his surname. Either way, he had a stick up his ass about something.

I stepped inside. No missing paintings or ornaments here – this must be the receiving room. It was obscenely large; I was pretty sure the whole footprint of my house could have fit into it. Three matching sofas were set around a large fireplace; behind them was a modest table with four chairs and a vase of fresh flowers. There were six large windows, all on the same wall. The room was painted a soothing sage green, but the carpets were floral and chaotic. Thankfully, the room was lit by lamps, which helped chase away the dark ambiance of the corridor.

Elizabeth Sorrell was perched on one of the sofas, dressed in a peach suit and a white blouse. Her legs were crossed modestly at the ankles. Her face was ageless, and I'd bet good money she'd had work done, but her neck gave her away. I'd put her at mid-seventies. She made no move to stand to greet me.

I crossed the room. 'Lady Sorrell,' I greeted her, not taking a seat until she offered me one. Mum had taught me my manners, and I suspected Lady Sorrell was going to be a stickler for them.

A flicker of approval passed over her stern face – blink and you would have missed it. 'Do take a seat, Ms Sharp,' she invited.

I sat. I waited. This was her show. She didn't offer me refreshments; I was here as the help.

'My granddaughter Hester is missing,' she stated. 'She's a good girl but she's only eighteen. She recently went up to Liverpool University to study psychology.' She virtually spat the last word, so I guessed it wasn't a respectable degree in her eyes. My mum was a psychologist, and she'd spent her adult life trying to help people. It was respectable degree to me.

'It was a rebellion against the family's wishes. Thankfully, Liverpool University is a redbrick, but still… She is living in student halls.' Lady Sorrell couldn't suppress a shudder. 'Hester has been there for five weeks, and she phoned every single day until two days ago. She hasn't attended classes or posted on social media. We have filed a missing person's report with the police, but it is clear that they think she has gone away willingly on an alcohol-infused break. We are told there is some suggestion she's been using drugs.'

Interestingly, she appeared to find the study of psychology more distasteful than the idea that her granddaughter was using drugs. 'The police investigation has been unsatisfactory. I am told they haven't even attempted to access her room.' Her disapproval was obvious. Someone somewhere was going to be getting a complaint letter.

'You come recommended by a family friend, Lord

Samuel. He assures me of your discretion. Whatever Hester is doing, we don't want it becoming public knowledge and ruining her chances of securing a good marriage. Although we have arranged a tentative betrothal with Lord Samuel's son, nothing is secured. And, while Wilfred is a dear friend, even he would not want a partner for his son who comes with scandal attached.' Her lips tightened.

Christ, these people lived in the Stone Age. At least that answered the question of where she'd found little old me. I had done several discreet retrieval jobs for Lord Wilfred Samuel; despite having huge wealth, he had a habit of betting family heirlooms during poker games.

I nodded my understanding. 'Do you have details of Hester's accommodation in Liverpool and the friends that she's made so far?'

Lady Sorrell nodded. 'We have compiled a dossier for you. Details of her local friends here, the friends she has mentioned in Liverpool, and of her accommodation and study schedule.' She was impressed with herself.

'Excellent, thank you. As I will be travelling to Liverpool, we need to discuss a retainer and expenses.'

Lady Sorrell waved it away. 'We have wired 10,000 pounds to your bank account. Lord Samuel has confirmed your hourly rate. Please advise me when you require more and it will be sent.'

I had found Lord Wilfred Samuel early in my career

when I was young and a bit desperate for cash. He had a title and so I'd quoted him an exorbitant hourly rate, which he'd agreed to without blinking. The family heirlooms were worth vast amounts. Despite his gambling addiction, he still had a fortune.

I remained calm even though I was doing a happy dance inside. 'May I see Hester's bedroom?'

Lady Sorrell grimaced but nodded reluctantly. 'Very well. Jackson will show you up. I trust that will be all?'

I wasn't quite ready to be dismissed. 'Can I speak to Hester's parents?' I asked.

'Her father is out of the country and her mother is indisposed,' Lady Sorrell said sharply. She softened a little. 'My daughter-in-law is taking this badly. She is wracked with worry. She has been taking sleeping pills.' *All true.*

The family's reaction seemed a little over the top to me, but I guessed Hester had been sheltered for most of her life. Now she had gone to Liverpool of all places. I love Liverpool, but it does have some rough edges which can cut a naïve young girl.

Lucky me; it looked like I was going on a road trip. Hopefully I would find Hester slumped over in a bar somewhere.

As I stood, Lady Sorrell rang a bell and Jackson opened the door. 'Give Ms Sharp the dossier and show her to Hester's rooms before you escort her out.'

'Of course, my lady.' His gaze turned to me. 'If you'll follow me, ma'am.'

I suppose he preferred ma'am to Jinx. I followed him up some stairs to a suite of rooms, and he stood inside the door while I started to rifle through Hester's belongings. His nostrils flared in outrage, but he said nothing. I didn't bother with small talk; I'd broach the subject of Hester with him in a second.

Hester's rooms were opulent, decorated in a floral wallpaper that made my eyes hurt. The bed was a four poster complete with gold canopy and bed coverings. It was a little too Disney for my tastes, but to each their own. Next to the bedroom was a dressing room, and through that, an en suite the size of my lounge. It had a free-standing iron bath with carved lion's-claw feet. A modern double shower stood in one corner, with a toilet and sink in the other. There was an airing cupboard filled with towels and a cabinet with all the usual girl paraphernalia. No drugs, not even paracetamol. I even lifted the toilet cistern lid, but nothing was hidden in there.

Hester's dressing room was lined with built-in wardrobes and floor-to-ceiling mirrors. Suffice to say she had enough shoes to shoe a small army. Although she had great taste in shoes, the rest of her clothing was pretty modest: knee-length dresses, jeans and tops. Nothing racy. I laboriously checked through her pockets, but there was nothing in any of them, not so much as a receipt. I checked the cupboards carefully – no false bottoms.

No drugs, no sex toys, no fun. I moved into her bedroom and looked under her bed. Nothing. I looked through her drawers. No diary, no sentimental photos. The only thing I found that was vaguely interesting was a photo of a handsome young man aged about eighteen. He was smirking at the camera, and he had an arm around Hester. He was good looking and he knew it.

'Who is this?' I asked Jackson.

'Lord Samuel's son,' he said reluctantly. 'Archibald Samuel – Archie. He is a friend of Miss Hester.' Now that he said it, I could see the resemblance.

I took a picture of the photo with my phone and put the keepsake back where I'd found it. I suspected Hester had been a good girl before she'd gone to university. The good girls always hit university hard; the freedom after so much cloistering is overwhelming. The good girls don't know their limits because they haven't drunk at home; they get excited the first time they get shitfaced, and it's all downhill from there.

'Did Hester ever drink wine with her friends or family? At meals and the like?'

Jackson thought about it. 'Rarely,' he admitted. 'But she would try a glass now and again with a meal.'

'Did she smoke?'

'Heavens, no!'

'Did she have any hobbies?'

'Reading,' he said slowly.

'There aren't any books in this room.'

'Of course not,' he said, aghast. 'They're in the library.'

I sighed; I'd better look at the library too. I glanced over the room one last time. It didn't have anything else to tell me. 'Take me to the library,' I ordered.

He balked. 'Those are not my instructions.'

I studied him. 'By all means, let us interrupt Lady Sorrell to get permission to visit the room Hester spent most of her time in.'

He grimaced. 'Follow me.' He led the way back downstairs and along a corridor. Like the rest of the manor, the library was dark and smelled faintly musty. It had more books than I had ever seen in a private collection. Some looked old, but there was a modern section too. 'Where would you usually find Miss Hester?' I asked.

Jackson led me to the back of the library where there were some comfy armchairs around a fireplace. The bookcase next to it was full of modern novels – urban fantasy, science fiction and books about the paranormal. Well, at least I knew a little more about her headspace now: she liked the romance of vampyrs and werewolves and ghouls.

'How would you describe Miss Hester?'

Jackson pressed his lips together.

'No one else will hear what you tell me,' I reassured him. 'I just need to find her. To do that, I have to know about her. The more I know, the easier I can think like her and work out where she'd be likely to go.'

His jaw clenched, but nevertheless he nodded. 'She's a good girl, never strayed far from this library. She doesn't have many friends. She is ... enamoured of Master Archie. Archie is popular and often makes time for her, but I believe he views her as a plaything. He is not a kind individual. I was grateful when she went to university, away from his influence. He uses drugs and I know he has offered her some in the past, but she said no. There has been some suggestion between his parents and Miss Hester's family that they marry one day, but there isn't a formal betrothal at the moment. That's why I don't feel it's likely she would use drugs at university – it's just not her. She would have taken them with Archie, if anyone. Miss Hester is very respectful of her parents and their boundaries. To my knowledge, she has never had an amorous relationship.' Jackson's tone warmed as he spoke; it was clear he had a lot of affection for the girl.

'Her best friend?' I queried.

'Sybil Arlow. She lives at Arlington Grove. They attended boarding school together.'

I nodded. Another posh trust-fund kid. Everything Jackson said rang true – as he believed it, anyway.

'I'm sure she will be found alive and well,' he said

confidently. *Lie.*

The question was, did Jackson believe she wasn't alive and well because he was involved in her disappearance, or was he just a cynic? My gut said the latter, and I'd learnt long ago to trust my instincts; they never lead me astray.

CHAPTER 3

TIMING IS EVERYTHING in missing persons' cases, especially if foul play is suspected. I had already texted Lord Wilfred Samuel and requested an interview with his son in relation to Hester's disappearance. He replied immediately that he would rouse his son and I could come as soon as I liked. He also said he had a surprise for me, which made me a bit apprehensive. Wilfred is ... eccentric. There was no saying what he would think constituted a surprise – or whether I'd like it.

Jackson handed me the dossier that Lady Sorrell had compiled as he pushed me out of the front door. I unlocked my car and climbed in. I cranked on the engine, turned up the heating and decided to sit for a moment and flick through the papers before I decided on my next course of action.

There was a paltry section entitled *Local Friends*. All it listed was Sybil and Archie, with their respective addresses and contact numbers. If they were all the friends she had here, Hester had probably been a lonely girl. The list of friends at university was longer. There were quite a few names, though there were no boys on the list.

Her class schedule wasn't demanding – morning lectures most days, but only two or four hours at the most. She had a tutor-group session on a Friday. Maybe psychology was a topic that required a lot of reading around in your own time, something Hester would thrive on.

The final page included details of Hester's address at the new build at Greenbank Village. I'd spent a fair amount of time visiting my best friend Lucy at Liverpool University. She'd lived in Lady Mountford Halls in Carnatic, and we'd had a mournful drink the day Carnatic was demolished. Greenbank Village was the new, swanky student accommodation. Hester had a top-of-the-range room, complete with en suite and her own kitchen. Lucy had shared a kitchen with thirteen people. Wealth tipped the scales – though perhaps Lucy had had more fun and friendships than Hester. Hester could effectively self-isolate if she wanted, and the picture I'd got of her so far was that isolation was all too likely.

I decided to call Sybil Arlow from my car while I drove to Lord Samuel's residence. I put Wilfred's address in the satnav. I'd been there often enough but my focus would be diverted while I was talking to Sybil. I dialled her number and hooked the call up to the car's Bluetooth.

Despite the hour, she answered on the second ring.

She hadn't heard from Hester in the last two weeks and assumed her friend was having a lot of fun. It was obvious that Sybil was a bit jealous; her parents wouldn't let her go to university and were packing her off to a finishing school.

Sybil told me that Hester enjoyed horror movies and the macabre. She also told me her friend was hooked on Archie and hoped to marry him one day. But she knew that day wasn't now, and she'd been looking forward to spreading her wings at university. Hester had told Sybil she was going to start over, re-invent herself. Sybil thought Hester had done just that, and that was why she was leaving her friend behind.

Hester had turned wild, Sybil told me, jealousy pouring out with every word. She had joined a skydiving club and a mountain climbing club. Her parents would flip if they knew. Hester was going out to bars and enjoying rock music. She'd even mentioned getting a tattoo. There was some guy she fancied; she hadn't told Sybil his name but called him 'My Mr Mystery'. Sybil didn't know anything about drugs, but she was dubious that Hester would use them, even with her reinvention.

The chat was helpful, but I was glad I hadn't wasted time visiting Sybil in person. Wrapped up in her own misery, she hadn't come across as caring about where Hester was. There was no danger on her radar. Maybe she was right – but something was telling me she was wrong.

It looked like I'd been wrong about Hester being isolated at university. If what Sybil said was true, Hester was having the time of her life. About time, too.

I pulled up outside Lord Samuel's mansion. It is an Edwardian build in pristine condition, with rolling landscaped gardens that must cost a pretty penny to maintain. There was a brand-new black Range Rover parked in the drive and I pulled in next to it. I beeped my car locked – you can never be too careful – and bounded up the steps to the front door.

Lord Samuel's housekeeper, Mrs Dawes, opened the door. Short and plump, she was always ready with a biscuit and a smile. She has the patience of a saint and I have a faint suspicion that she holds a small candle in her heart for Lord Samuel. He hold her in great regard, but I doubt he's given her a moment's thought in *that* way. 'Have you come to fix another problem for Lord Samuel, Jinx?' she half joked with a knowing smile.

'Someone else's problem this time,' I assured her.

She led me to the receiving room. Airy and light, it was a real contrast to the Sorrell's home. Pale yellow adorned the walls and there were several mismatched sofas set opposite each other.

There were three men in the room: one was Wilfred Samuel, the second was Archibald Samuel, and the third was not known to me. He was older than me, perhaps in his late twenties, with light-brown hair, warm brown eyes and a square jaw. His skin was tanned as if he'd just come home from a holiday. He had the muscular build of a wrestler, which looked somewhat awkward in a charcoal grey suit, despite it obviously being tailored to fit him. His black cufflinks were embossed with silver triangles. He was classically handsome – and I suspected he knew it. He was appraising me with just as much interest, though he kept his expression carefully blank.

Archibald was lounging on the sofa in tracksuit bottoms and a polo shirt. He had an arm flung over his eyes and he looked tired or hungover, or both. Like his father, he had sandy blond hair, blue eyes and milk-pale skin.

Lord Samuel rose and came to greet me. 'Jinx!' he said warmly. 'I'm so glad to see you.' *True.* He gave me two air kisses.

'Wilf,' I said. It had taken about five heirlooms before he'd insisted that we were friends and I should call him Wilf. I'm not sure I would define our relationship as a friendship, and it still feels odd to have an acquaintance called Wilfred.

Wilf is fifty-one, toned and strong. He works out regularly, dyes his grey hairs blond, and he moisturises. Technically speaking, he is married, but his wife moved to France when Archie was thirteen. Since I've known him, Wilf has had a string of mistresses. He once asked me to be one of them but thankfully didn't take it badly when I refused.

I had never met Archie. If I'm honest, my first impressions weren't great.

'Archie!' Wilf said in a stern tone I'd never heard before. 'Stand up and meet Jinx.'

Archie let out a loud huff and stood. As he held out his hand for me to shake, he displayed all the hallmarks of teenage antipathy. His handshake was limp and unimpressive and, once I'd released his hand, he sniffed it. Wilf elbowed him and Archie stopped sniffing and coloured slightly.

The third man had already risen. He offered his hand. 'Zachary Stone,' he said in a warm baritone voice.

'Jinx,' I replied. As we reached out to shake hands, I swear I literally felt a spark of electricity run through me as we touched. I thought he felt it too because one of his eyebrows rose minutely in an unconscious expression of surprise. He gripped my hand firmly; there was nothing limp about *his* handshake.

'Stone is the other investigator,' Wilf explained.

It was my turn to raise an eyebrow. 'The other investigator?'

Wilf grimaced. 'Elizabeth has hired two of you.' My radar pinged. *Lie.* If Elizabeth Sorrell hadn't hired Stone, who had? Wilf? If so, why was he lying about it? 'She thought that at least one of you would be able to find Hester.'

I sighed aloud. 'All that will do is piss everyone off

that they're being asked the same questions twice.' I was exasperated. If I'd known someone else was investigating Hester's disappearance, I would have turned Lady Sorrell down. But now … well, I had 10,000 pounds in my bank account and a mystery to solve. I'm the type to always read to the end of a book, even if I'm not enjoying it; I've started, so I'll finish. The same ethos applies to my cases; I *always* see them through.

Wilf nodded. 'Quite. That's why I had the two of you come here at the same time. Saves repeating matters. He was my little surprise for you.'

I'd been expecting something worse. I turned to Stone. 'Let's talk after this,' I suggested.

His gaze measured me. 'Sure thing.' His accent was nondescript British. He could have been from anywhere in the UK.

Archie had slumped back onto the sofa. I decided to give him a break and question Wilf a little first. 'Lady Sorrell indicated that Hester is good friends with Archie.' She hadn't, but Wilf didn't need to know that. 'I trust you know Hester as well?'

Wilf smiled. 'Of course. Dear Hester.'

Archie snorted. 'Dear, plain, boring Hester.'

Wilf glared. 'Have some respect. You're going to marry her one day.'

Archie glared right back. 'No one has arranged marriages these days. You're from the Stone Age. I don't want to marry Hester. She'd be a lousy mate, in bed and in life.'

I could almost see Wilf counting to ten in his head. It was interesting to see him in a paternal role; usually when I saw him, he was flirting and a bit drunk. Responsible, authoritarian Wilf was a new one on me. I think I liked him more like this.

His jaw clenched and his nostrils flared. Counting to ten hadn't helped and anger was written on every line in his face. I was impressed with his control when he didn't lamp his son as he so clearly wanted to do. Instead, his words were hissed. 'Frankly, Hester doesn't deserve to be saddled with an insolent pup like you.'

He turned to me, taking a deep breath, trying to defuse the tension. 'Hester is a kind soul. Elizabeth said something about her using drugs, but I can't believe that. She's not the type to let loose. She hardly has a drop to drink, let alone drugs. She's a good girl, often found with her head in a book, even at a party. I can't see her dropping out of classes – she's always been studious. And she has a very close relationship with her mother, Margarete. She wouldn't let Margarete worry. I'm concerned something has happened to her.'

Archie snorted again. 'She's just discovered the fun of drinking and she's hungover somewhere. You're all being ridiculous.'

'You don't think she's in trouble?' Stone asked.

'Nah, she's with friends, I reckon.' *True.*

'Would you care if she was in trouble?' I queried softly.

Something flashed across his eyes before he shrugged indolently. 'Nah.' *Lie.*

Stone was looking at me strangely. I met his gaze challengingly, and he gave me a faint smile in return. I turned back to Archie. 'Has Hester been in touch since she went to uni?' I wanted him to answer. I needed a lead, so I leaned on him.

Archie looked at me steadily for a moment before a 'what the hell' expression came over his face. 'Fine. Yes, we've spoken a few times. Most days. She's having fun and I've encouraged her. She's made a few friends. A girl called Maeve seems to be her best bud, and Hester is into a guy called Nathaniel. He's a rich kid like us, into skydiving, so she's signed up. She's having the time of her life.' He believed everything he said, and I wondered if there wasn't a twinge of jealousy in there. Hester was supposed to be his future wife, after all. He looked a little surprised at how much he'd opened up to us.

I dialled it back a touch. 'Do you know which bars she hung out at?'

Archie shook his head. 'No. I know she was going out dancing. She was enjoying the rock scene. That's all I know.'

'You don't know where she is?' Stone asked.

Archie rolled his eyes. 'No, I don't know where she is.

All this fuss over nothing – talk about over-protective parents.' He turned to his dad. 'If I disappear for a day or two, you don't freak.'

Wilf gave his son a chilly smile. 'That's because you are quite likely to disappear in a drug-induced haze. I know your dealer and I know your haunts. If I needed to, I could find you in an hour. You're predictable, if nothing else.'

Archie flushed a little, uncomfortable at the thought that his wild rebellion was something that Wilf allowed and even controlled to a degree. Poor Archie, even his rebellion was sanctioned.

I stood. There was nothing else to be gleaned here, but at least I had a few more names to work with. Maeve was in the dossier; Nathaniel hadn't been.

Stone stood up too.

'Thanks,' I said to Archie. 'You've been really helpful.' There was only the faintest trace of sarcasm.

Wilf caught it and smiled wryly. 'I'll see you both out.' He took us to the front door and opened it, gesturing Stone out first. I started to follow, but Wilf caught my arm. 'Be careful of him,' he warned, his voice low. 'Stone is dangerous.' I could tell he wanted to say more, but something was holding him back.

I took his warning seriously. 'So am I,' I said.

I gave Wilf an air kiss and headed out after the delectable Zachary Stone.

CHAPTER 4

S TONE WAS LEANING against the black Range Rover. He pushed off as I walked towards him. 'Not here,' he said abruptly. 'There's a café a mile or two away – Rosie's. You know it?'

I nodded. I had met Wilf there once; I remembered it was a distinctly odd meeting. Wilf had bought me every drink from the café menu. Stone didn't need to know any of that.

Stone's expression told me that my knowledge of Rosie's had some significance that I didn't understand. Maybe it was a place for swingers to meet, or a place where dealers pushed drugs, or maybe Rosie's car park was a famous dogging site. I'd learnt a lot about the underbelly of humanity in the last few years, though I had to admit I hadn't caught a bad vibe when I was at Rosie's. I was missing something, and I didn't like it.

'Let's go.' Stone hopped into his Range Rover and started the engine. I watched him drive off. I had half a mind to drive to Liverpool without him, but I needed to pack and sort out Gato. Besides, Stone might have information. His manner was rubbing me the wrong way, but I knew he wasn't better than me. I'm a damned good investigator; I was going to find Hester Sorrell with or without him – preferably the latter because I've never been much of a team player.

I followed him reluctantly to Rosie's. It was at the end of a small row of shops including a Co-op, a Chinese takeout, a dry cleaner's and a funeral director's. Everything a community needed. I parked outside and grabbed my handbag. Stone was already inside.

Rosie's was empty except for a young woman with a baby and a small child who didn't appear to appreciate the croissant the harassed-looking mum had bought for her. The baby was happily breastfeeding. The mum was looking with longing at the hot chocolate she had put down too far away to reach. I moved it closer to her, and she flashed me a grateful smile. 'Thank you so much.' She tucked her hair behind her ear with one hand while the other arm held her baby close, then she picked up her drink. 'Yum.' She beamed at me.

I smiled back. 'No problem.' I turned to the blue-eyed child who was on the verge of a tantrum. 'You want jam with that?'

The girl wrinkled her nose. 'Yes,' she said. 'Strawberry jam.' I grabbed a packet of jam from the counter and cut the croissant in two, smearing it liberally. 'There you go,' I said. 'Now be good for Mummy,' I ordered.

The mum was grinning at me. 'Do you babysit?' she asked jokingly.

I smiled back. 'Sorry, I'm only good with kids for a few minutes at a time.'

'Me too,' she sighed.

I went up to the counter where Stone was waiting with visible impatience. 'Making friends?' he asked archly.

The owner of the café snickered a little. I ignored them both and looked at the menu. I ordered a toasted tea cake and a chai latte. Stone ordered a black coffee.

Rosie's owner was tall, with bright-red hair and a smattering of freckles. He was surprisingly muscular. I know that it's a bit of a stereotype, but you expect café owners to look as if they eat their own cakes, not like they could bench press all five feet eight inches of me without breaking sweat.

When everything was ready, Stone paid and carried the tray to our table. I hung my handbag on the back of the chair and sat down. My mum always made a big deal out of manners, and I didn't want to be churlish. 'Thanks,' I said.

Stone nodded. The silence stretched out, but this was his party, so I would ride it out. I started to eat my teacake. By the time I was done with one half, Stone was smiling a little. 'Most people fill silence,' he commented.

'I'm not most people.'

'No,' he agreed. 'You're not.' He held my gaze. The silence, thick and heavy, rolled on. Then Stone laughed. Maybe that meant I'd won, though I wasn't quite sure what.

'You're a truth seeker.' He whispered it, but his tone was flat, almost accusatory. He said 'truth seeker' like anyone else would say doctor or plumber.

I blinked. 'I'm a – what?' Fuck, was there a name for what I was? Was I a *thing*?

His eyebrows raised in surprise. 'You don't know?'

'Know what?' Frustration bled into my tone. I wasn't lying; I had no idea what a truth seeker was – though whatever it was, I was probably it. I've always been different; my internal 'ping' has never let me down. But I wasn't going to tell him that. I took another sip of my drink and kept my face blank.

He was searching my eyes for knowledge I knew wasn't there. 'You've been hidden this whole time,' he said wonderingly. 'You really don't know.'

'You're beginning to annoy me,' I said evenly. I pulled my handbag off the chair and put it on my shoulder. I was getting ready to leave. Mum and Dad had told me to *stay off the radar*. I didn't always understand what they meant; mostly I'd thought it was a figurative phrase for staying out of trouble. But now ... I wasn't sure if there was an actual radar. And if there was, with Stone looking at me like that, I thought I was on it.

Dammit.

As I stood up, Stone reached out and grabbed my hand. He motioned for me to sit. 'I'm from the Connection,' Stone explained, a little more loudly. He said 'the Connection' as if it should mean something to me. There was no buzz of a lie, but I didn't understand what the truth was.

'Like a Wi-Fi provider?' I asked finally. The café owner guffawed. Clearly no one had taught him that eavesdropping was rude.

That cracked Stone a little and he grinned. 'No, Jinx, not like a Wi-Fi provider. It's easier to show you. Do you trust me?' The question seemed important to him, and he laid emphasis on the last two words.

I opened my mouth to tell him that hell no, my trust is hard won, but I felt weird and hazy. 'Yes.' That wasn't what I intended to say, but it was true – I did trust him. My 'yes' rang with truth. My mind cleared and I frowned at him. 'What the fuck did you do?' I snarled. I hated being on the back foot.

'I compelled you,' he admitted. 'Like you compelled Archie. I'm sorry, but now you know how it feels. If ever you feel that haze again, you need to get to a seer to remove the compulsion. You know how to truth seek, but that's only one facet of your skills. You need to learn both sides of the coin.' Stone slumped a little; it looked like compelling me had taken it out of him.

I – what? I had wanted Archie to answer, and I'd leaned on him a little, though I couldn't explain exactly what that meant. Archie had seemed surprised at the words that had come out of his own mouth… Holy hell – what was this? What was *I*?

I didn't know what to say, so I didn't say anything. Finally, I cleared my throat. 'You compelled me to tell the truth about whether or not I trust you? Why?'

Stone shrugged. 'If we're going to be working closely together, it's good to know you've got my back.'

I narrowed my eyes. 'I'm trustworthy. If I say I've got your back, then I've got it.' I frowned. 'It's weird that I trust you, though. We've only just met.'

'Gut instincts count for a lot,' Stone said. I couldn't disagree. Identifying the truth was only one facet of my skillset; my gut instinct was another.

Stone pushed back from the table and stood up. 'As I said, it's easier to show you. Follow me.' He went past the shop's counter. Nodding at the ginger owner, he opened a door to a back room and walked through. He didn't look back to see if I was following. My gut instincts might trust him, but he was an arrogant son of a bitch all right.

I knew I should leave – my parents would want me to leave – but my insatiable curiosity was getting the better of my caution. I was *something*. I wasn't just a weird aberration. What I could do had a name: *truth seeker*. I wanted to know more. This was only the first page, and I needed to finish the book.

I followed Stone through the back room – and I walked back out into the café. Huh? Then I walked past the owner and felt my jaw drop. The friendly, ginger-headed shop owner was now smouldering. Literally. His ginger hair had been replaced by dancing flames and heat was rolling off him. His head was on fire, but he seemed unconcerned. And he had a tattoo of a single triangle in the middle of his forehead.

The mum and her family had forest-green skin. Their blonde hair and bright-blue eyes looked odd against their skin tone. Stone looked the same, except he now bore a runic tattoo of three triangles inside each other on his forehead. What the actual hell?

It was only my own truth-gleaning abilities that stopped me losing it. I had grown up knowing that I could sense truth and lies in a way that no one else could. I had wondered many times if there were others like me. Now the question I'd been asking my whole life was finally being answered. I closed my gaping mouth with a clack.

The little green girl was looking at me. 'First time in the Other?' she asked with a sympathetic smile. I nodded dumbly. 'The Other is a cool realm,' she reassured me. 'But I still like the Common best. Everyone is the same in the Common. Though the trees are so much warmer in the Other.'

I nodded again, trying to keep my face relaxed. 'Sure.'

The mum was watching me carefully, waiting for me to freak out.

'So,' I said calmly, 'green skin?'

'Dryad,' she replied evenly. She was still assessing me, wary if I was going to make a scene or frighten her children.

'No triangles?' I asked, gesturing to her forehead.

'Dryad,' she repeated. 'Magical creatures don't have the symbol, just the humans.'

I nodded again. Magical creatures. Sure.

I went back to the table Stone and I had been sitting at. Half of my teacake was still there, so I sat down and ate it. Stone sat opposite me, watching me like the mum, waiting for me to blow. I rolled my eyes. 'If I haven't freaked out by now, I'm not going to.'

Stone chuckled. 'I've never seen an introduction go so well. Normally there's shouting or vomiting.'

'Or fainting,' the dryad mum chipped in.

'I'm not doing any of that,' I said firmly. God, I hoped not. I had a tight lid on my inner crazy.

The café owner handed me a fresh chai latte. 'We noticed,' he quipped. 'I'm Roscoe. I'm a fire elemental.'

'I've met you before. Wilf brought me here once.' A dawning realisation crept over me. 'Wilf ordered loads of drinks and they were all cool. You handed me one and it was red hot. You used your elemental magic to heat it up,' I accused him.

Roscoe nodded. 'Got it in one. Wilf was trying to see if you knew about the Other. He said you smelled off, not like Common.'

I was a bit insulted. 'I smelled off?' I objected. Something clicked and I felt like I was the last one to the party. 'Wilf is Other,' I said dumbly.

Stone nodded. 'He's a werewolf.' He said it matter of factly, like it was commonplace. I guess it was to them, but it wasn't to me. It took everything in me not to spit my latte everywhere. 'Wilf is a wolf?' I asked incredulously.

Stone nodded. 'His parents had a whimsical sense of humour.'

'And Hester?'

Stone shook his head. 'She's Common. She's just an ordinary girl who has gone missing. The Other might have something to do with it – or not.'

'I'm in the Other, eating a teacake that was in the Common. Explain that to me.'

'Normal objects exist in both realms. Buildings are the same, cars are the same. It's only people who change. In the Other, you can see people's true forms. They don't change spatial location, just appearance and the ability to use their powers.'

I let that soak in for a long moment. 'So do people live in the Other all the time?'

The café owner shook his head and the flames bobbed and surged. 'Some do, some don't. It depends on your classification. The magical creatures can be in the Other all the time. For the human side of things – that's your witches, wizards, seers, pipers and the like – they must leave the Other to recharge. The stronger your power, the longer you can exist in the Other. The magical creatures can stay in the Other permanently, but the rest of us need to recharge regularly. When it's time to go Common, your skin starts to itch. If you don't leave voluntarily, the Other will expel you. Believe me, you don't want the backlash.'

'So what about elementals like you? Are you classified as humans?'

Roscoe nodded. 'Of course.'

It wasn't quite so clear cut to me – I mean, the man was literally on fire. 'So who are the magical creatures?' I asked. 'The werewolves?'

Roscoe shook his head. 'The werewolves are a bit of an oddity. They're still on the human side of the line, and they still have to recharge even though they have a creature form.'

'We're classed as creatures,' the Dryad mum explained. Her voice was flat and I could tell she wasn't thrilled about her categorisation. I wouldn't be either.

I searched around for a subject change. 'So whatever powers you have, you can't use them in the Common?'

Stone cleared his throat uncomfortably before he answered. 'The strongest of us can use a small amount of power. Like a teardrop to our usual waterfall.'

I took it all in. I could use my truth-seeking abilities in the Common. Apparently, I could even compel. So what would my powers be like here in the Other?

CHAPTER 5

I HATE FEELING uncertain. Knowledge dispels fear, that's my motto. More questions were needed, or rather more answers. 'Are Other powers inherited? Or can anyone be born to them?'

'It depends on the powers,' Roscoe answered. 'A dryad is a species, so it's hereditary. So is being an elemental. A werewolf is born or made. Vampyrs are made.'

'Vampyrs.' My tone was flat. 'You're shitting me.'

Stone shook his head; there was no trace of humour in his expression. 'No. Vampyrs, daemons, witches are all on the human side, all real.'

'Of course they are. What are you?' I asked curiously.

'I'm a wizard,' Stone answered. 'Like you.'

'I'm a witch?' I said, rolling the idea round my head.

'No, you're a wizard and an empath.'

I didn't want to touch the empath part. I am the least empathetic person I know; I'm from the school of tough love. I focused instead on the wizard part. 'I thought women were witches and men were wizards.'

Stone smiled. 'Forget anything the Commons have whispered to you about the Other. It's all twisted and half-truths. The Verdict compels everyone from the Other not to speak of the Other to anyone or anything in the Common. So anything leaked to the Common – knowledge about werewolves, vampyrs, witches – is twisted. The full truth couldn't be told because the Verdict binds us all.'

I hadn't run away screaming or fainted or thrown up, but I was seriously contemplating checking myself into a mental institution. I was a wizard. And vampyrs were real. 'Unicorns?' I asked.

Stone nodded. 'They're nasty bastards.'

That shattered one of my childhood illusions. Wait… I remembered Mum looking a little green when I played with my unicorn toys as a child. Had my parents been Other? If that was true, why hadn't they told me about the Other? Was it a lead? If my parents were Other, could their killer have been Other too? That was a question for another day; first I needed to confirm that my parents really were Other. Still, my heart was beating too fast and hope was blossoming for the first time in so long. It could be a lead, an honest-to-goodness lead. I had become a PI to find their killer; seven years later I was still drawing a blank. Now I was drawing unicorns and vampyrs. It wasn't much, but it was something.

I blew out a breath and re-focused. I didn't want

everyone knowing my inner demons; my motivation was my own. I cast about for other mythical creatures I could ask about. 'Dragons?'

Stone nodded. 'Deadly and dangerous creatures, but they tend to keep themselves to themselves.'

'Ghosts?'

He shook his head.

'Aliens?'

Stone shrugged. 'Not as far as we know. But I wouldn't write them off.'

I pulled my scattered thoughts together, analysed the new data, reviewed everything Stone had said. 'What's the Connection?'

Stone tapped the second triangle on his forehead. 'The triangle is the symbol of the Connection.'

The dryad raised her eyebrow at Stone. 'Two triangles mean you work for the Connection. The Connection is the police and the government, the judge and the jury. There is no separation of the powers in the Other. You don't want to get on the wrong side of the Connection.'

'They rule the Other in the UK?'

She shook her head. 'They rule the Other in the *whole world*. There's a Connection Symposium for every country, but the Unity rules over all the Symposiums.'

Stone frowned at the dryad. 'It's a bit more complicated than that. There is a representative of every faction, human and creature, within each Symposium and in the

Unity. It is the governing body of the whole realm. They seek to keep us hidden and to maintain the balance, both here and in the Common.'

The dryad rolled her eyes. 'That's all very well, as long as your faction representative actually represents *you*. Power tends to corrupt, and absolute power corrupts absolutely.'

Stone narrowed his eyes at her. 'Would you prefer the Chaos?' He held her gaze until she looked away uncomfortably. Stone continued. 'All politicians have their own agenda. I'm just saying that the Symposium is the best way to maintain order and balance in the Other. Without the Verdict being enforced, the creatures would decimate humans in the Common. Without the Unity there would be no Verdict.' Everything he said was true as he believed it.

A whole new government I had no idea existed helped rule our world. I felt like someone had pulled the carpet out from under me; I was not even sure what was under my feet. I continued with my questioning. Asking questions always makes me feel better. 'Does anyone in the Common government know about the Other?'

Stone shook his head. 'Only Others that we have placed in those positions. There are Others in all walks of life – we call them cross-overs. They serve both functions in both realms. It helps smooth things over and keep us hidden. There are cross-overs in every major position you can think of, and we all have the same obligations under the Verdict to help things run smoothly. Say you witnessed a vampyr slicing a human. A human would see an ordinary man with a knife because they can't see Other. You'd tell the police you saw a man with a knife run away, then you'd contact the Connection and make a report. They would send a team to check over the scene and run interference. The Connection would send a detective or an inspector to track down the rogue vampyr.'

Abruptly, I remembered Steve Marley and the stabbing in my park. He'd lied when he said it was a stabbing, but later he'd said the victim was sliced, and that rang true. A vampyr had attacked someone in my park, and Steve Marley had known about it. He was Other. I'd known him most of my life, and he was something else – like I was. Holy shit. I was one more question away from having my mind blown.

I had to ask. 'My parents?' I swallowed hard. 'Do you know anything about my parents?' I hated the vulnerability I felt.

Stone shook his head, his eyes curious. 'I don't. If I'd known you were Other, I would have run a background check on you, but I thought you were Common. I didn't know you were hidden.' That rang true.

'My parents were killed – stabbed, I thought. But maybe there's more to it. I never found the culprit.'

Stone was looking at me carefully, his gaze measuring me. 'It might have been Other, it might have been Common. There are some heinous crimes in Common.'

I nodded. I'd seen all kinds in my years as a private investigator. I needed to change the subject; this was too raw for me. 'You said I was hidden. What does that mean?'

'You've never been to the Other, even though you're *of* the Other. You're human, so once you go you'll be marked for all Others to see.' He picked up the metal box which held the knives and forks on the table. In the reflection I could see my forehead now bore one triangle. I raised my hand to feel it. The skin wasn't raised or sore.

I glared at Stone. 'Don't you think you should have explained a little more before you forced me to get a tattoo on my head?'

He shrugged. 'I don't normally do introductions. But if I'd told you there was a world where there were griffins and elves, are you telling me you wouldn't have wanted to see it?'

I was side-tracked. 'Griffins *and* elves?'

He smiled. 'See?'

'Are they both creatures?'

'Griffins are, and they're as deadly as they come. Elves are on the human side of things.'

I couldn't help but notice he was describing most creatures as deadly, but the human types didn't get the same label. The Bronx Zoo had once had an exhibit which was simply a mirror behind bars; underneath it read: *The most dangerous animals in the world.* It had been true then and, even with all the other magical creatures in the mix, it felt like it was still true now. The dryad mum and her kids didn't exactly strike me as deadly.

I switched things up. 'Now I'm marked, what does that mean?'

'When you're in the Common, you'll look like you always did. As a courtesy, we often wear the sign of the Other somewhere so we can be recognised. Some get tattoos. I wear my cuff links.' Stone gestured to the tiny triangles on his wrists. 'Wilf's T-shirt had a triangle on the collar.'

He took a sip of his coffee and continued. 'When you're in the Other, your mark on your forehead will be visible. That shows you're in the Other. So you and I could meet in the Common realm and both of us would be unmarked. You'd know I didn't have access to my full powers. If we met in the Other, we'd see each other's marks and know we had access to our powers.'

I took it all in. 'So the magical creatures have a real advantage. If you have an Other enemy, you're vulnerable in the Common. They can see you're not in the Other, that you can't access your powers.'

Stone nodded. 'That's why I wear cufflinks. If I need

to, I remove them and pose as Common. That way, I'm not drawing Other attention to myself. But mostly I try to minimise my time in the Common.'

'And you're also powerful enough that you're not wholly vulnerable. You still have powers in the Common,' I pointed out.

Stone looked uncomfortable.

The dryad smirked. 'It's not really the done thing to ask about his powers in the Common.' She covered her daughter's ears with her hands. 'It's like asking about his cock size.' She uncovered them.

I felt my face warm and redden. 'Oh,' I said archly, riding out my embarrassment. 'I'll ask about that another time.' Roscoe let out a booming laugh and the dryad snickered.

Despite Stone's secrecy about my truth seeking, this felt like a safe space to ask all the questions about the Other I could think of. But time was ticking on, and Hester still needed us to find her. 'We need to refocus,' I said firmly. 'We must find Hester. You can teach me about the Other as we work.'

Stone gave a faint smile. 'I got the impression you're a lone wolf.'

I let out a fake howl.

'Don't let Wilf hear you howling.' Stone's eyes had a wicked glint. 'He'll be telling you all about his powers in the Common.'

The dryad snorted with laughter. 'I never knew you had a sense of humour, Stone.'

'You all know each other?' I asked.

'Everyone knows Stone,' the dryad said with a shrug.

'It's a relatively small local community,' Stone explained. 'Most of us visit the Other from a young age.' He gestured to the dryad children. 'We get to know each other.'

'You're local?' I asked.

He shook his head. 'I'm sent wherever they need me.' He stood and nodded to Roscoe and the dryads. 'We'd better go,' he said to me.

I held out a hand to Roscoe but he smiled and shook his head. 'We don't shake hands, honey. I'm about three hundred degrees centigrade. You'd get burnt just touching me, unless you're runed up. We do this to each other.' He touched his right hand to his heart and gave a small bob of his head like a shallow bow.

I copied him. 'I'm Jinx.'

'Roscoe Flavian,' the café owner said.

'Nice to meet you, Roscoe.'

'The honour is all mine. It is my honour to meet you.' He paused. 'You will always be welcome here in the hall of your introduction. I will answer your call.' He gave the little bow again.

I smiled my thanks, even though I had no idea what he was talking about. I turned to the dryad family and bowed to them. 'I'm Jinx,' I repeated.

The mum smiled. 'Joyce Evergreen, and these are my daughters, Rose and Wren.'

Wren was the three-year-old. She stood, touched her hand to her heart and gave me a solemn bow. 'My honour to meet you, Jinx,' she intoned. Then she sneaked a sideways glance at her mum to check she'd done it right. Joyce nodded encouragingly.

'My honour to meet you, Wren,' I repeated, bowing. She gave me a smile brighter than the sun and did a twirl of happiness. I waved goodbye to the baby and she gurgled at me.

Stone held the door open for me and we went outside. I blinked. The world looked different; the grass was almost turquoise, and the sky looked a soft shade of lilac.

'I'll drive,' said Stone firmly. 'Hop in.'

'The grass isn't green,' I muttered faintly. Grass is supposed to be green, and the sky is supposed to be blue; these things had been taught to me as absolutes. They weren't supposed to change colour willy-nilly. I'd seen flashes of this realm before but I'd put it down to tiredness or a brain tumour. Nope – I'd been seeing into a whole other realm.

I blew out a breath. I considered objecting to Stone playing chauffeur, but I was going to be staring at the new normal for quite some time, and driving didn't seem like a good idea. I hopped into his Range Rover. 'What about my car?' I asked.

'I'll get someone to move it to your house.' I rattled off my address. He tapped out a message on his phone, pressed send, then programmed my address into the car's GPS.

'How will they get into my car to move it?'

He raised his eyebrows in a 'duh' expression. 'They'll use magic to move it.' *Lie.*

'Really?' I arched an eyebrow in disbelief.

He grinned. 'No. They'll break in and hotwire it – but they'll fix it up before they leave. Magic is good, but technology has its place.'

I stuck my tongue out at him. 'Jerk.'

Stone winked.

CHAPTER 6

IT WASN'T FAR to my house and Stone seemed perfectly content with silence. I'd absorbed a lot of knowledge in a short time, and I needed to sort through my thoughts and come to terms with what was happening. 'Do I have to keep going between realms forever?' I asked.

Stone nodded.

'What about gnomes?'

'Real.'

Silence.

'What about gargoyles?'

'Real.'

Silence.

'Zombies?'

'No.'

More silence.

'What about porn?' I asked innocently. The car swerved.

'Christ,' Stone muttered. 'What about porn?'

'Is there like ... vampyr on dragon action?'

He squeezed the bridge of his nose. 'God, I hope not.

For one thing, they're sworn enemies.' He slid me a glance before looking away quickly. 'Cross-species relationships exist in the Other.' He cleared his throat. 'So there is cross-species porn. Not that I've seen any.' *Lie.*

'Truth seeker,' I said in a sing-song voice.

He reddened. After a minute he said, 'I investigated an illegal porn ring. I had to watch it to review the evidence.' He sounded extremely awkward, but his words rang with truth. *Hmmm.*

'But did you ever watch it on any other occasion?'

He didn't answer, and I snickered. He turned the music on, and I laughed louder. 'You know, having a partner is kind of fun,' I teased.

'Is that what we are, Jinx? Partners?' He turned on the smoulder, his gaze hot and heavy.

As usual, I backpedalled. 'Sure. Team Find Hester partners.'

He flipped me an amused glance, but he didn't say anything and he quit smouldering, thank goodness. I reminded myself not to piss off the only guide I had to this crazy-ass realm. I was marked as Other; if I stumbled on a vampyr, I could accidentally insult it into mortal combat or something. I guessed I was going to have to stick to Stone like glue for the foreseeable future.

We drew up to my home. 'Nice digs,' he commented.

'Thanks. It was my parents'.' I try to view my house impartially but with little success. I don't see the flaky paint on the front-window ledge, or the rose bush on the drive. It's just home; it has been my whole life. It is my sanctuary and my purgatory. My parents lived here – but they also died here. I can never forget that.

We got out. Before I put the key in the front door, I turned to Stone. 'Any ramifications about inviting you in?'

He smiled. 'No. That one is just for vampyrs and ghouls.'

'Really?'

He nodded. 'Don't invite them in. Once invited, they can come and go as they please, and a lock won't stop them.'

'Ten-four. Do vampyrs really have fangs, drink blood and only come out in the dark?'

'They do have fangs and they do drink blood. They hunt at night, which is where the night-time reputation comes in, but there's nothing stopping them walking in the sunlight as well.'

'No horrific burning up in the sun?' I asked, disappointed.

'Nope. And they have reflections too.'

'Damn,' I muttered. I unlocked my front door and let us in. As I walked into the lounge, I stopped dead. My parents' photos had changed. I knew these photos; I'd seen them every day of my life, for the last seven years at least. To see them changed momentarily floored me.

My parents now bore three triangles on their foreheads like Stone. In some of the pictures, there were other creatures that I had never seen. My mum was next to a dragon; I'd always thought she looked off-centre in that picture, and now I knew why.

At least that answered the question of whether they knew about the Other. 'You sons of bitches,' I swore at their photos. 'In eighteen years you couldn't have found the words to tell me about the Other?' I stifled the urge to throw something. I wanted to, but Stone was there, and Mum taught me not to air my dirty laundry in public. *This isn't over,* I said to them silently. *We're going to talk about this.*

Of course, the reality was that I was going to talk and they would never answer.

I swallowed past the huge rock in my throat. Most of the time, my grief is manageable. I don't believe it heals with time like people say, but it becomes part of your world. The constant ache in your heart and head become the norm, but you're better able to deal with it. Even so, moments like these always kick me in the gut, like when something arises that I want to ask them about and can't. I'd missed the chance to ask them about the Other, and now I never could. So many questions unanswered.

Stone picked up one of the pictures. 'Do you recognise them?' I asked, half hopefully and half with dread. I was relieved my voice came out level.

He shook his head regretfully. 'Sorry. They were before my time.'

'What do the three triangles mean?'

He slid me a glance. 'I can't answer that truthfully,' he said reluctantly. 'Suffice to say it's a symbol that they were either inspectors or high up in the Connection.' Like Stone.

'More questions.' I sighed. Unanswered bloody questions. They haunted me.

His gaze was level. 'I've known you for all of two hours, but I have no doubt you'll find the answers you seek.'

I forced a smile. 'Thanks. So which are you? An inspector, or high up in the Connection?'

'Both.' He looked a little uncomfortable, so I left it alone.

I excused myself to go and pack for our trip to Liverpool. Truthfully, I needed a minute to collect myself. I sat on my bed and buried my head in my hands, trying to pretend the sting in my eyes wasn't there. God, I'd cried so much over the years, but the tears still kept coming. Shouldn't they have run dry by now? Shouldn't I be over it? I bit my lip. I'd never be over it. I knew myself well enough to realise that.

I took a long breath, then ordered myself to get my shit together. There was a hottie downstairs and I looked splotchy after a good crying jag. *No tears, Jinx.*

I looked up. By my bedside was a picture of me and Gato. I swore loudly. Gato now had obsidian spikes up and down his spine. 'What the actual fuck?' This was the cherry on top of the cake. Luckily, anger and annoyance were kicking in, my best defenders and friends.

Stone hurried up the stairs. 'You okay?'

'What the hell is wrong with my dog?' I demanded, showing him the picture.

He looked genuinely shocked. 'You have a hound!'

'He's a Great Dane,' I said. 'He's *supposed* to be a Great Dane.'

He looked at me sympathetically. 'He's a hell hound.'

I sat down heavily on my bed. 'My pup is a hell hound?' *Really? Did my fur baby have to be involved?*

I shook my head. I could freak out later. We needed to get to Liverpool – Hester needed us. I shoved a few more things into a duffle bag and packed my trusty black bum bag. Hands-free object carrying is essential when you're being sneaky. I packed a photo of my parents, my knife and my lock-picking tools. 'I need to sort out the arrangements for Gato,' I said to Stone.

He laughed out loud. 'You've called your hell hound "cat" in Spanish?'

'It seemed funny at the time.'

'We should take Gato with us, he'll be an asset. He's a creature of the Other, and he can go between the realms without using a portal. If you're touching him when he

62

turns, you'll be transported with him. Hell hounds are incredibly rare. It's rarer still to bond with one.' He said it admiringly and a tad jealously.

I had so many questions but, for the first time I could recall, I was sick of asking them. 'Let's go and speak to Mrs H,' I suggested. 'She's my neighbour.'

Stone picked up my duffle bag, I grabbed some supplies for Gato and we loaded up the car. I bobbed back into the larder and fridge for today's offerings for Mrs H: a coconut and a whole chicken. That was more like it.

I knocked on her door. She opened it and my smile faltered. Her skin was purple – bright purple – and she had three triangles on her forehead like Stone. Her three triangles had a circle round them.

Mrs H's eyes darted to my solitary triangle. 'Oh my,' she said faintly.

'You're purple,' I said dumbly. 'She's purple,' I said to Stone.

Stone elbowed me sharply. 'It's Lady Harding,' he hissed. 'Show her some respect.' He did the bowing thing. 'Inspector Stone. My honour to greet you, my Lady Seer.'

Amanda Harding smiled at Stone. 'My honour to greet you, Inspector. Your formidable reputation precedes you.' She turned to me. 'Jinx.' Her tone was pleading; she didn't want me to be upset with her.

I held out the chicken and the coconut. Stone made a strangling noise; I guess he didn't think they were good gifts for a high-and-mighty Lady Seer, or whatever she was.

Mrs H smiled warmly and took my offerings. 'Thank you, dear. He's been no trouble this morning.'

Gato trotted out; sure enough, he had sharp black spikes running down his spine. He came up to me and licked my forehead – on my triangle. 'Huh,' I said. 'You know Mummy can see you properly, now?' He wagged his tail vigorously. I stroked him as I normally do and his sharp spines automatically retracted under my fingers. They reappeared after my fingers had passed them. Cool. No spiking Mummy. Something in me eased; Gato might be a hell hound, but he was *my* hell hound.

'Who's a good boy?' I cooed, kissing his head. He gambolled around my feet, happy to be reunited after a few hours apart. He was always perfectly happy with Mrs H, but I was his home.

I looked up from Gato to Mrs H, the woman I'd known all my life. She'd babysat me, comforted me when my parents had died. 'You knew my parents. You knew what they were.'

There was sympathy in her eyes. 'Yes, Jinx. But now is not the time for this conversation. Hester needs you. You need to go.'

I wanted to argue, but I felt the truth in her words, so I nodded reluctantly. 'When this case is done, you'll tell me everything I need to know?' I asked desperately.

Maybe I could ask her some of the questions I wanted to ask my parents. She might not know everything, but she would know *something*, and that was a whole lot better than the black hole of nothingness I was staring into.

Mrs H smiled kindly at me, with more understanding than I liked. 'I will tell you everything that I am free to tell you. And I will tell you this now: I don't know who was responsible for their deaths. I am not keeping that from you.'

True. 'Thank you for that,' I said softly. I cleared my throat and cast about for a change of subject. 'Hey, what happened last night? Was it something Other?'

Mrs H frowned. 'I didn't see anything, but something upset Gato. He was in protection mode. Something meant you harm and he scared it away. I cast a protection rune over your house last night, just to be safe.'

All true. I blinked. 'Well, thanks.' Runes: more shit to learn about.

She rubbed my arm. 'I'm purple,' she said, 'but I'm still the same person.'

'Purple looks good on you,' I assured her. 'It was just a surprise. I'm sorry, it's been a bit of a whirlwind. Apparently, *I'm* an empath.' We both snickered at that; Mrs H knew first hand about my lack of empathy. A thought occurred to me. 'Is your daughter Other too?'

Mrs H shook her head. 'No, my husband Sam was a witch, but Jane is Common. Seers rarely breed true. Witches sometimes do, but not in this case.'

'Does she know about the Other?' I asked.

Mrs H lost her smile and let out a soft sigh. 'No. The Verdict forbids me to speak of it to her. And some things can't be explained, not without seeing them for yourself.'

'So what does she think you do?'

'Everyone in the Common believes I'm a housewife.'

Stone was gaping. 'Your daughter thinks you're a housewife? You?'

'It's refreshing, actually. Jane never asks after my Symposium work, never asks for favours for her or her friends. I'm just her mum.'

Gato barked and turned around. 'You're right,' Mrs H said to him, 'we do digress. Off with you to Liverpool. I'll be going there myself in a few days' time. Perhaps I'll see you there.'

'Can you tell us anything about Hester that will help? She's Common, right?' I asked.

'She was,' Mrs Harding said slowly. 'But now I sense the Other encroaching. I fear someone or something has broken the Verdict. She is in between.' *True.*

Stone frowned like Mrs H had said someone was going to drop an atomic bomb. 'We'll find Hester,' he asserted, 'and track down whoever is breaking the Verdict.'

Mrs H nodded. 'Of that I have no doubt. You take care of my Jinx. Off you go.'

I rolled my eyes at that. I can take care of myself.

We piled into Stone's car. Gato climbed into the boot

and settled down for the ride.

I love a good road trip. I fiddled with the radio settings until some music I was happy with blared out. Stone reached over and turned it off. 'You know Lady Seer Harding?' he asked incredulously.

'Obviously,' I said flatly.

'She is a *very* important person.'

I grinned. 'I gathered that from the bowing and scraping.'

He coloured slightly. 'Cut me some slack. I wasn't exactly prepared to meet Lady Seer Harding. I'm not even in my good suit…' He groaned.

'She knew who you were, and I'm sure she didn't care about your outfit, pretty boy.'

He flashed me a grin. 'You think I'm pretty?'

I felt my skin warm. 'You know you're good looking. It's unseemly to pretend otherwise.'

'I wouldn't want to be unseemly now, would I?' he teased.

I didn't have an answer to that, so I retreated into silence. We drove a good fifteen minutes without speaking before Gato barked. I turned to face him. 'What's up?' He barked again. 'He wants music.' I turned on the radio again. I had no idea what Gato wanted, but *I* wanted the radio on. Gato settled down again. Maybe I could secretly speak hell hound. At that point, anything seemed possible.

CHAPTER 7

BUCKINGHAMSHIRE TO LIVERPOOL was a three-and-a-half-hour drive on a good day. Stone was a competent driver, and I felt safe in the car. The best thing to help me get to grips with my emotional turbulence and this Other crap was to have a nap. I leaned against the headrest and cleared my mind. My mum taught me meditation when I was young and it always helps. I pictured myself walking along a beach and listened to the waves rolling in. A seagull cawed and the sun warmed my face. It wasn't long before I was out for the count.

STONE SHOOK MY shoulder near Warrington. 'Sorry to wake you,' he said. 'But I think we should talk a little before we hit Liverpool.'

My heart was pounding. I'd been having a nightmare that I was being chased by my parents' killers. I stretched and yawned casually, hoping I hadn't cried out. It's hard to maintain a tough exterior if you whimper in your sleep. 'No problem, Rocky,' I said flippantly. He cut me a hard look. 'Not a fan of the Rocky franchise?' I asked cheekily.

'My name is Stone,' he said with no humour in his tone. Jeez, some people can't take a joke. He took himself too seriously; I decided it was my job to help lighten his day. 'Basalt? Igneous?' I suggested irreverently.

'No,' he said decisively. 'You can call me Stone or Zach.'

'But not Rocky, Basalt or Igneous?'

'You think you're funny, don't you?'

'Hilarious,' I admitted.

A smile tugged at his lips against his will and he shook his head. 'If you'd just been a Common investigator, I could have cleared your memories. But no, you had to be hidden.'

'You can wipe memories?'

Stone nodded, like it was a normal concept. 'It's not done lightly or often, but it's an option. Most of the time we modify memories. Most Common minds naturally blank out weird occurrences that don't conform to their world view – seeing someone fly, for example. Some need help to do it.'

'Don't EVER fuck with my head,' I said firmly. 'I mean it. That will be a deal-breaker.' I didn't know what deal I was talking about, but if he ever messed with my head, that would break something for sure.

'I will never mess with your memories of my own volition. If I'm ordered to do it…'

'You disobey the order.'

'As much as I like you, I've been working my whole career to move up the ranks. I'm not throwing it all away by disobeying a direct order. Look, it will probably never happen. Let's not borrow trouble.'

A heavy silence fell. He liked me?

Stone cleared his throat. 'Anyway. We're not far from Liverpool. I want to deputise you.'

'You want to what?'

'Make you part of the Connection. It will afford you some protection and I can introduce you as my partner, Detective Sharp. You'll be able to question others with legal authority. If you compel someone by accident, you won't get into trouble. Your role will be temporary, just for the duration of the case. Do you agree to those terms?'

'I'll be an inspector too?'

'No, you'll be a detective. Inspectors are the elite. We are few and far between, and two inspectors together on a case is virtually unheard of. Detectives are far more common.'

'What are the drawbacks?' I asked seriously.

'If I give you an order, you need to follow it or you'll be court-martialled and could end up in jail.'

I chewed on that for a moment. 'I occasionally have authority issues,' I admitted.

'No shit,' Stone smirked. 'Look, all joking aside, I won't give you an order unless it's life or death, okay? We're a team. I need you to trust me and have my back. Deal?'

Stay off the radar. Dammit, I was in so deep, I was tap dancing on it.

In for a penny, in for a pound. Besides, I was feeling rebellious. My parents had kept all of this from me. I knew there was a reason, hopefully a damned good one, but I needed to do this for myself. 'Deal,' I agreed. I hoped I wouldn't come to regret it. I felt a sharp zing in my forehead as I said the word. 'Ow! What the hell?'

'Oh, yeah – be careful what deals you make in the Other. They can be binding.'

I glared. 'Oh really? Anything else you forgot to mention?'

'You look good with two triangles?'

I pulled down the sun visor and looked in the mirror. Sure enough, two triangles.

'Two triangles mark you as part of the Connection,' Stone explained.

'If you keep tattooing me with triangles without my consent, I could sue you.'

Stone slid me an amused glance but didn't answer. He cleared his throat. 'We'll stay at a Connection chapterhouse while we're in Liverpool. Liverpool is a big Other site – it's our capital. The Scouse friendliness extends to all manner of oddballs, and the Other presence here is even bigger than London. You need to act casual. I can't pass you off as my partner if you gape every time a ghoul walks by.'

'Are there lots of ghouls?'

'There's a lot of everything,' he assured me. He spent the next twenty minutes talking me through some essential dos and don'ts, then pulled out his phone and displayed a slide show of the weird and wonderful.

'What's that?' I asked as he swiped to show a particularly handsome man with the usual triangle on his forehead.

'Vampyr.'

I blinked. 'Where's the fangs and the pale skin? He's tan!'

Stone laughed. 'We're in Liverpool. Everyone's tan. Vampyrs can go out in the daytime. They have fangs, but they can retract them at will.'

'Are all vampyrs that good looking?'

Stone nodded. 'It's one of the main signs that they're vampyr. When they turn, something burns out all the asymmetry and imperfections.' He paused. 'Quite a few celebrities and actors are vampyrs.'

'No way! Do they age?'

'They can change the appearance of age like we can change our hair colour. Normally, when they've had enough time in the spotlight, they will "overdose" or something, change their age back to eighteen or whatever, and start again. Immortality – but not with one fixed age. They can even appear as really beautiful children. Sometimes they pretend to be their own children.'

'Do they drink blood?' I asked, expecting him to scoff.

Instead he nodded. 'Yes. The Connection purchases blood from blood donation centres and hands it out to the clans. Apparently, real blood direct from the jugular tastes better – or so I'm told. That's why some vampyrs go rogue in contravention of the Verdict. Then we hunt them down.'

'Stake in the heart?' I asked flippantly.

Stone shook his head. 'Decapitation.'

'Gross.'

Stone shrugged. 'You get used to it.'

I drummed my fingers on the car console. 'So, shall we go to Hester's halls first, or get checked in at the chapterhouse?'

'Halls,' Stone voted. I agreed; it was time to get some investigating done.

We headed for Greenbank Student Village. 'Hey!' I said excitedly. 'Penny Lane!' I pointed to the street sign.

'In our ears and in our hearts,' Stone responded tunefully.

'Beatles' fan?' I was somewhat surprised: Stone struck me as more of a rock guy than a Beatles guy. We had been a Beatles household. My dad once told me that his parents' home had been silent, then the Beatles had arrived and there was music. It had been a profound change for him and I'd had a soft place in my heart for them ever since. Besides, how couldn't you love someone called Ringo?

Stone shrugged. 'I don't like all of their songs, but they made some amazing records.' He paused. 'Did you know that one theory is that Penny Lane was named after a slave trader called James Penny?'

'No way!'

'Yeah. One of the city councillors tried to campaign to change the name, but people accused her of white-washing Liverpool's history.'

'You learn something new every day.' I paused. 'In my case, today I've learnt about a whole other realm, but your Penny Lane fact takes the cake.'

'You're pretty unshakeable, aren't you?'

I shrugged. 'I'm just an ordinary girl who became a PI and has seen a lot of things in the last seven years. I saw some weird stuff yesterday, for example. Have you ever heard of plushies?'

Stone nodded but his skin warmed a little. 'There isn't much I haven't heard about.'

'You've got the jump on me in terms of Other weird-ness, but I'll catch up,' I said confidently.

'No doubt,' he agreed, giving me an amused look.

We parked up at the student campus and let Gato

out. He stretched dramatically and promptly found a tree to wee on. I grabbed my bum bag full of useful things and clicked it on, buckled a collar on Gato and hooked on his lead. He looked at me reproachfully.

'Listen,' I said to him, 'I know you're a great hell hound, but sometimes people don't like dogs, let alone massive dogs, and you can look a little scary. *I* know you don't need a lead, and *you* know you don't need a lead, but *they* don't know that. Besides, dogs aren't really allowed in halls. Now be a good boy.' Gato gave me a lick; he was on board with the plan. I turned to Stone. 'So, being a witch...'

'Wizard,' he corrected reproachfully.

'Wizard, right. Being a wizard, can you get us into locked rooms and stuff?'

'If you don't mind blasting the doors off their hinges, yes. If you're looking for subtlety, no. My natural tendency is to use force. I'm sure I could do subtlety if I really tried, but that's not my forte.'

'Okay, my show then,' I declared.

It was just after 4:30 p.m – students were streaming in from lectures and the common areas would be busy. I waited until a student opened the main door with her electronic pass, and we followed her in. 'You're not allowed pets, you know,' she said pointedly, looking at Gato.

'Oh, we're just visiting.' I gave her a friendly smile.

'Hester Sorrell, do you know her?'

The girl brightened. 'Sure, I know Hes. Everyone knows Hes! She's so much fun, isn't she?'

'She's great!' I enthused. 'Have you been to a rock club with her yet? She's great on a night out.'

'Yes!' the girl agreed. 'We went to Zanzibar the other night and it was totes amaze!'

'Cool. When was that?' I asked.

'Three days ago? Monday night. Yeah, it was defo Monday because I had a psychology lecture the next morning but Hes wasn't there. She partied too hard!'

'Ahh. Shame I missed it. I only got to Liverpool on Tuesday. Maybe I can persuade her out tonight.'

The girl frowned. 'Actually, I haven't seen her since Monday. I think she must be shacked up with Nate. She was *so* all over him Monday.'

'Ooh,' I cooed, 'the infamous Nathaniel. Is he as hot as Hes says?'

The girl glanced at Stone, wondering if he was my boyfriend and if I should be talking about another guy's hotness. I saw her dismiss the idea. 'He is so hot!' she gushed. 'Look.' She pulled out her phone and scrolled through the gallery until she came to a shot of Hester Sorrell wrapped round a very handsome guy with a triangle on his head. Vampyr?

I burst out laughing. 'Oh my God, look at Hes's face in that.' I snapped a quick photo of the girl's photo before she could move away. 'She will die when she sees that picture.' I continued to laugh like it was no big deal that I'd copied her photo.

Stone was a bit further back. He shook his head a little – he couldn't see the photo. I'd show it to him later. I guessed vampyrs could be photographed.

'I'm Jess,' I introduced myself in my best perky voice.

'Rhiannon,' the girl replied with a friendly smile.

'Can you show us to Hes's room? I'll just give her a knock. If she's not there, I'll try to track her down with Mr Sexy.'

'Sure, this way.' Rhiannon led us up two flights of stairs and opened the door onto a hallway. 'She's 3F.'

'Great. Thanks, Rhiannon. Maybe we can all go Zanzibar one night.'

'Totes!' said Rhiannon. 'Catch you later, Jess.' She gave us both a wave and went up another flight of stairs to her floor.

'Keep watch,' I said to Gato. He turned and faced the stairwell, ears pricked. Stone faced the other way and used his body to hide my movements. This floor was empty, but I knew we wouldn't have long before another student came along. I dug into my bum bag and pulled out my lockpicking tools. Hester's lock was basic. I applied some pressure, raked it and it clicked open in under thirty seconds.

We went inside and shut the door behind us. The

room was dark. Stone clicked on the light and let out a low whistle. 'Damn,' he said. 'Either she's messy as hell or this room has been tossed.'

It had definitely been tossed. Lady Sorrell had been right – the police obviously hadn't been to Hester's room. If they had, they'd have suspected foul play.

'The latter,' I huffed. 'Obviously. Her room at the manor was immaculate, a place for everything and everything in its place.'

'That could have been the staff tidying up for her,' Stone countered, playing devil's advocate.

'Maybe,' I conceded, 'but I just got a fastidious vibe, you know?' I shook my head. 'Obviously this wasn't her, this was someone else. Someone really fucking angry. Raging.' I frowned. 'How do I know that?'

'That's the empathy in your weapons' arsenal.'

I rolled my eyes. 'How is empathy a weapon? I'm going to care a vampyr to death?'

Stone cracked a smile. 'I'd like to see that.' He sobered. 'Empathy is a powerful tool. Your truth-seeking skills come from your abilities as an empath. I don't know what degree of empathy you have; some can just feel what others are feeling when they touch them, others can read a whole room without any physical contact. Some can use their emotions to manipulate others. That's considered rude, so don't do it in polite society.'

'But it's fine if we're interviewing deadbeats?'

Stone grinned. 'You catch on fast.'

'Have you got any empathy?' I asked curiously.

'Only the Common kind.'

Gato was sniffing around, bringing me back to task. I looked at the room. Hell, you couldn't call it a room, it was a studio apartment. There was a kitchen and a sitting area, an en suite and a bed – not bad digs at all. I guess the Sorrells forked out for the best for their baby girl.

The sofa was trashed – it had been knifed and pulled apart. Similarly, all the cushions had been ripped into. The kitchen cupboards were open, and someone had emptied the cutlery drawer onto the floor. The chest of drawers was open, and Hester's clothing had been dumped in a pile. 'Someone was angry and looking for something. They didn't find it.'

'How do you know?'

I shrugged. 'I have no idea. But I know they didn't. They left as angry as they came.' He was studying me. 'What?' I asked. 'Is knowing that not normal?'

He said nothing, so I couldn't detect a lie. Dammit, even in the Other I was weird. When he had explained about empathy earlier, he'd suggested that physical touch was needed for a lot of empaths, so presumably people needed to be present at the very least. These echoes I could read – that wasn't normal. I shelved it. We didn't have time for my questions. We needed to look for clues.

I was certain now that we weren't going to find Hester happily propped up in a bar. Something more sinister was going on. The echo of rage that I felt in the room… A shiver ran down my spine. I didn't want that fury directed at me.

Stone and I divided the room and started working our way through it methodically. I found some cannabis, only a small quarter bag. Okay, so it was drugs, but it was hardly the smoking gun that crack cocaine or a bag of speed would have been. There was enough drug paraphernalia in the room for me to think it was hers: there was a grinder with a pretty purple-and-pink flower painted on the lid, and there was a red floral bong. There were papers, some loose filters and three lighters. She was using the bong and rolling her own joints. Hester really was cutting loose.

I looked through her psychology notes. A quarter of her notebook had been filled in; she might be smoking weed, but she was still studious. I checked the date she'd taken her last notes; sure enough, there were no notes for Tuesday's class. She'd disappeared on Monday night. 'Anything?' I called to Stone.

'Condoms, lube, small vibrator.'

Hester had been expanding her horizons. 'We've got cannabis here, but not much,' I said. 'There's a bong too. I'd guess it's a social thing she does with mates. No hard drugs.'

I dug out my phone and brought up the picture of

Hester with the dude from the Other. I showed the picture to James. 'Vampyr?' I asked, already confident of the answer.

He nodded, his eyes grim. 'Oh yes. That's Nathaniel Volderiss, Lord Gabriel Volderiss's son. He's the head of the vampyr clan in Liverpool. This investigation just got dicey.'

CHAPTER 8

AFTER WE WERE done in Hester's room, we tracked down her new BFF, Maeve, by knocking on all the neighbouring flats. We found six Common humans, a dryad, an elf and a water elemental. I had kept a careful smile on my face for all of them. No gaping, no country-bumpkin gawping; I was playing it cool – I hoped. But in the same way that Roscoe had flames as hair, the water elemental had translucent dreadlocks made of water. They looked awesome and it took me a couple of blinks to offer my usual polite smile. I really wanted to touch those watery locks. What would they feel like? Was the water hot or cold? I was too nosey for my own good.

During the door knocking, I did the whole 'friend from home' routine, but nothing salient came up. Everyone liked Hes; she was fun, the life and the soul of the party, not the Hester that Archie and Sybil knew. In five weeks she had reinvented herself; add in a dash of some Class C drugs and a sprinkle of a vampyr boyfriend and *voilà*, a new Hes.

Maeve didn't have much to add. She wasn't worried

about her friend, she was envious. Hes had snagged the elusive Nate, who apparently hadn't been seen since Monday night either. Maeve knew that they were both rich kids, and she figured Nate had hired them a fancy hotel and they were shacked up. She told me Nate was a second-year student who knew all the cool places. He was a keen skydiver and Hes had been excited about giving it a go. Maeve figured they might have even gone off for a skydiving trip together.

Alarm bells were ringing in my mind. Nate was missing too – but was he the kidnapper or also the kidnapped?

By the time we finished knocking on doors, it was 6 p.m. We decided to head back to the chapterhouse to grab some food and settle in Gato. Later we would hit up Zanzibar, Hes's last-known location.

Gato peed on the same tree again. Once his tank was empty, we climbed into the Range Rover and set off. 'So,' I said, 'what does a water elemental's hair feel like? Is it just water, or does it feel like hair? Would you get wet if you touched it?'

Stone shook his head. 'That's your focus? Hair?'

'You can just say you don't know,' I replied snippily.

He laughed. 'I don't know. I've never felt inclined to touch an elemental's hair. I know if you touch Roscoe's skin, you'd get burnt, so I'm assuming if you touch the water elemental's hair, it would be wet – but that's conjecture.'

'You've never arrested a water elemental?'

'Arrested? No.' He said it tightly. There was a story there.

I twisted in my seat to study him. There had been too much meaning in those two words. 'Tell me,' I said softly.

Stone's jaw clenched and his hands tightened on the wheel. He let out a harsh breath. 'He was trying to flood a village in Shropshire. You'll have heard about it on the news. Hundreds of homes were destroyed by the time I was sent in. He'd been enthralled. He wanted to kill his ex and her new lover, and he didn't care about taking a whole village with them. I couldn't break through to him, so in the end, I threw a lamp post at him and it struck him on the head. I intended to knock him out, but my throw was too strong. I killed him.'

There was a lot to unpack in that. 'Enthralled?' I asked.

'Too caught up in his own magic. When that happens, all you can feel is the magic, the power pouring out of you. If you can't put a cap on it, you can burn yourself out. When you're enthralled, all reason goes – it's extremely dangerous.'

I took that in. 'How did you throw a lamp post?'

He looked at me wryly. 'You don't think I could pull one out of the ground through sheer physical strength?'

I rolled my eyes. 'You're strong, I'm sure, but you're

not Arnold Schwarzenegger. You're deflecting. Tell me how.'

'Like a dog with a bone,' he muttered. 'I used the IR.'

'Ire? You have rage issues?'

'IR. I. R. Intention and release.'

'And that is…?'

'It's a wizard's main magic.'

'I'm a wizard, right? Does that mean I can do it?'

Stone nodded, his eyes on the road. 'Yes, you can do it. Like anything, though, it's a matter of degree. Some can barely use it; others can do it as easily as they breathe.'

I studied him. 'You're on the breathing side of the spectrum.' He said nothing. He didn't need to. 'You used this IR to pick up a lamp post and fling it at a rogue elemental.' He nodded. I chewed my bottom lip. 'Can you teach me?' I asked casually, as if learning actual magic was normal. Like it wasn't a big deal to me.

Stone's caramel eyes gave me a sideways glance before he nodded again.

'Cool.'

That made him smile and the tension eased out of him. I guess he was worried I would think badly of him for the elemental's death. I was beginning to understand that an inspector wasn't just an investigator like me. Stone was a fixer, sent in to eliminate a problem, no matter how. Wilf had warned me Stone was dangerous; if he decapitated vampyrs and killed elementals, I could see why he would get that reputation.

Despite that, I trusted him – I had from that first moment in Rosie's. It's unusual for me to trust so quickly, but I have great instincts and have yet to be wrong. It took me years to let down my guard with Mrs H, but with others, like Lucy, it's such a strong gut reaction that I'd be mad not to trust it.

'We're here,' Stone commented, bringing me out of my reverie. We pulled up to a hotel, Hard Day's Night.

I blinked. 'This is a hotel? I've stayed here before. I thought we were going to the chapterhouse.'

'We are.' He pressed a button on his car fob and a wall of the hotel shimmered and became translucent. He drove right into it.

'Holy shit!' I yelled, bracing myself as he drove into the wall. Of course, we drove straight into an underground car park without so much as a hair displaced. An illusion. I took a deep breath. 'There's no parking at Hard Day's Night,' I said flatly.

'Not as far as the Common knows,' Stone agreed. 'But we're in the Other now and there's parking for the chapterhouse. Half of the hotel is Common, half of it is the chapterhouse. The two sides are entirely separate. There are even separate bars.'

I brightened. 'The chapterhouse has a bar?'

'Sure. It has everything, even a pool.'

'Man,' I sighed. 'I didn't pack a bikini.'

'You can skinny dip.' Stone gave an exaggerated leer.

As I hit him, my cell rang. It was Lucy. 'Hi, Luce.'

'Jessie! I have the best news ever! I got the job!' Lucy is the brightest person I know. After school she came to Liverpool to study accountancy, and I visited her sometimes during her three-year degree. Then she did a master's and the ACCA qualification while working part time in an accountancy firm. She is now qualified, and last week she'd interviewed for a role at her dream firm.

'Ahhh!' I screamed. 'That's amazing! Well done, Lucy. I'm so proud of you!'

'Me too!' Lucy laughed. 'I can't actually believe it. We need to celebrate. Cocktails?'

'Aw, I'm sorry, lovely. I'm on a job. I'm in Liverpool tracking down a missing person.'

Lucy sighed. 'Jess! As if you went to Liverpool without me. You better have a dance in Heebies or Alma for me.'

I laughed. 'I will one hundred percent dance somewhere for you,' I promised. 'I'm so sorry I can't celebrate with you.'

'It's okay,' Lucy said easily. 'I'll hit on some of the work girls instead – as long as you know you were my first choice.'

I grinned. 'You're always my first choice too.'

Lucy snorted. 'I'm your *only* choice!'

'I'm selective,' I agreed.

'You're misanthropic,' she countered.

'Yeah.'

'I'm getting through to you!' Lucy said triumphantly. 'When you're back, come out with me and my work girls.'

Lucy is always trying to get me to expand my friendship circles, but I have her, I have Gato and I have Mrs H. I don't need more friends. The more people you have in your life, the more likely they are to die and leave you.

'I'll definitely have a drink with you, but I'm not sure about your friends. I've got to go, Luce. I'm supposed to be checking in at the hotel. Love you.'

'Love you, Jessie. Have the best time.'

'You betcha!' We rang off. 'Sorry,' I said to Stone. 'My bestie.'

He grinned. 'You're what – twenty-five? And you still have a "bestie"?'

'Lucy will be my bestie when we're a hundred.'

'Not such a lone wolf, then.'

'I'm not completely solitary, I just have a very small pack.' Gato barked. I turned to smile at him. 'Of course you're in my pack, sweetie.'

Stone laughed. 'Let's get this show on the road.' We grabbed our bags and let Gato out. Stone led us confidently to a reception desk. He dug out a leather badge, which had two triangles, some digits and a barcode underneath, scanned it on the desk and a faint bell sounded.

A door opened and the receptionist walked in – blonde, tanned, with fake nails and fake eyelashes. She was stunning. She was what I would term a typical Scouse ideal of beauty – a size eight with DD boobs. Her cup overflowed. Literally. She also had a shimmer around her, which told me she was a siren. She had been one of the first in Stone's slideshow. She smiled when she saw Stone. 'Zach,' she greeted him with a thick Scouse twang.

'Esme. Two connecting rooms, please.'

She raised a perfect eyebrow as she typed. 'No problem. 2B and 2C.' She handed Stone the passkeys – then she caught sight of Gato. 'Oh my God,' she gushed. 'A hell hound. You are so lucky!' she said to me. 'I've always wanted one!'

'He's pretty awesome,' I agreed. I was having to work at friendly, and I wasn't examining the reason why too closely.

'This way.' Stone held the door open for me.

'See you later,' I said to Esme.

She smiled at me, but her gaze lingered on Stone. 'Sure you will, honey.'

I tried not to glare.

I followed Stone down the corridor into a suite of rooms with a connecting door. The door had a lock on both sides. 'Leave it unlocked,' Stone advised. 'Then I can come and help you if anything … unexpected visits.'

'Like Esme in the night?' I suggested.

He gave me a flat look. 'She'd better not,' he muttered. 'Bloody sirens. They hate being told no.'

Instantly, I felt brighter. 'So, what's the plan? Shower, room service, Zanzibar?'

'How are you feeling?' Stone asked.

'As in my mental or my physical health?'

'Why can you never answer a straight question? How are you feeling? Physically, mentally, spiritually, whatever.'

'Peachy,' I replied with a flutter of my eyelashes and a shoulder tilt.

'You're hard work, you know that, right?'

'Why do you think the pack is so small?'

Stone rolled his eyes. 'Showers, room service, then we'll train you a little on the IR. Then Zanzibar. It won't heat up until 10 p.m., so there's no point going before then. I've arranged for us to meet with Lord Volderiss tomorrow at 10 a.m., his first free appointment. His staff didn't seem eager for an appointment with an inspector.'

'Is he coming to us, or are we going to him?'

'We are definitely going to the mountain. He owns Exchange Flags.'

I pictured that in my head. 'Where Fazenda and Philpotts is?'

Stone smiled. 'Do you know everywhere with reference to food?'

'A girl has to eat!'

'He owns all of Exchange Flags. We have an appointment in the central office. Ostensibly, it's a law firm – GV Law.'

I'd heard of GV Law; it was a big firm but not one I had worked for. A company like that tends to hire big PI firms, not small outfits like Sharp Investigations. Other than the fact they are heavily into defencing people, I didn't know much else. I would do some googling later; I don't like going in blind.

Stone and I went to our rooms. Mine had a double bed, a wall-mounted TV and a small chair and dressing table. There was a decent sized en suite with a shower, and a full-length mirror. The hotel had already provided a dog bed for Gato, which was impressive and a bit freaky, unless every room came with a dog bed in case of hell hounds. It was on the floor next to the bed. I pointed it out to Gato and put down a bowl of food and some fresh water for him.

My dad would have lost his shit to stay here. And then it occurred to me: he was Other, so maybe he had. The discovery of my parents' Otherness picked at a wound I had thought long since scabbed over, but here I was, bleeding all over again. My parents had lied to me, even though it was by omission. A huge part of their lives had been closed to me and now was lost forever. It felt unfair to be grieving the loss of something I hadn't known I was missing.

I scrubbed at my face and refused to let tears fall. I'd feel better after a shower, as long as it wasn't a shitty, drizzly, hotel shower. Those always left me disgruntled.

Thankfully, the shower was hot and powerful, and it washed off my dirt and my funk. I came out wrapped in a towel. As I'd expected, Gato hadn't touched his dog bed; instead, he was sprawled out on my double bed.

I sighed. 'You know that's not your bed. You are not sleeping there.' He lifted his head, looked at me, then settled back down.

I huffed a little and rang room service to order a burger and fries. As I waited for it to arrive, I dried and straightened my hair. I selected a dress and some heels for later and slung on some black jeans and a loose T-shirt for now.

I wasn't sure what to expect for my IR training. I was mindful of the need to dip in and out of the Other, but I wasn't sure how long I needed to be out to recharge. Now seemed like a good idea to plug in the battery.

I spoke to Gato. 'Stone said you can do portals, so can you take me back to the Common? And then bring me back to the Other later?' I should have felt ridiculous talking to my dog, but intelligence gleamed in his dark eyes. He was no mere dog; he was a hell hound.

Gato sat up, climbed slowly off the bed and stretched

out his back legs. He came and jumped towards me. I caught him easily – we'd done this trick a good few times. Standing on his back legs he is close to six feet tall, so his forelegs rested on my shoulders. He touched his wet black nose to my forehead, then climbed back on the bed and curled up.

I looked in the mirror: no triangles. I looked at Gato: no spikes. Cool.

'Thanks,' I said.

He wagged his tail once. I turned on the TV for some background noise and started googling GV Law. I checked out the information on Companies' House. GV was a multinational law firm headquartered in Liverpool, with twenty-nine offices worldwide. Its value was currently a cool 350 million pounds. It was listed on the Stock Exchange, but information about the owners was surprisingly sparse. On paper there were lots of them, of whom Lord Volderiss was one. His status as a lord wasn't on there, but he was down as a Sir – he'd been knighted by the Queen in the Common. That must have been a nervous day for the Connection – a vampyr in close proximity to the Queen of England. Stone had said the government was clueless about the Other; I wondered if the Queen was too.

There was a knock on the door and I looked through the spyhole. Room service. I opened the door, took my meal and gave the waiter a small tip.

By the time I'd finished eating, it was 7:30 p.m. I'd had an hour or so in the Common, though I had no idea whether that was a sufficient recharge or not. 'Gato, can you pop me back to the Other?' I asked.

He heaved himself off the bed like it was a huge imposition, placed his forelegs on my shoulders and touched his nose to mine. *Voilà* – my dog had spikes again. I checked the mirror: two triangles. Good to go. Stone knocked on the door jamb. Perfect timing.

As he entered the room he asked, 'Ready to try some IR?'

'I reckon it should be okay. I've always got some ire.' I winked.

Stone rolled his eyes; apparently, he wasn't a fan of puns. 'Put some shoes on and follow me. It's time to get our magic on.'

CHAPTER 9

S TONE LED ME down the stairs to an underground room. He had to use a fingerprint scan to gain access, which seemed like overkill to me. We entered a huge space, largely empty, except for cabinets all along the back wall. The wall that ran the length of the room was mirrored. There were no windows, no carpets and no furnishings except for a very large digital clock. It was hard to see why the fingerprint scan was necessary.

'Minimalist,' I commented.

Stone ignored me and walked to one of the cabinets. He typed in a code, a locker opened and he pulled out a black-and-red football. Definitely overkill security for some sporting equipment. He handed it to me. 'Examine it so you know it's just a normal football.'

I checked it over. There was nothing special about it, as far as I could tell, but I was in the Other right now, so it honestly wouldn't have surprised me if the ball had sprouted hands and legs and called itself a flobberwam. I handed it back to Stone. 'It's just a football.'

Stone set it down on the floor. 'I'm going to make it

float. First, I gather my intention, then I focus on the object and think about what I want it to do. When I'm ready, I release my focus towards the object. I use words – some people use gestures.'

I stared at him blankly and he read my confusion. 'It's easier to show you.' That seemed to be his go-to teaching style. 'Float,' he commanded sharply. As he said the word, the ball rose up to his eye level and stayed there. 'Examine it so you know there's no strings. For IR to work, you need to *believe* it will work. The slightest doubt and it won't. Belief is key.'

I waved my hands over and under the floating ball. No strings. I tried to pick it out of the air, tried to push it down – nothing. An immovable force held it in the air. Stone waved his hand dismissively; it dropped to the floor and bounced on the concrete. I bit my lip. 'It's that simple?'

Stone nodded. 'It's not rocket science, it's magic. You need faith and intention. The reason I use a word as my release is that it is too easy to lose focus at the last minute. You're thinking of floating, then you wonder if you turned the oven off. You make a gesture and off the ball goes to try to find your oven.'

I grinned at that. 'Did you cook a few footballs?'

'Not me. I learned IR as I was growing up. My father made my introduction when I was a few weeks old, so I grew up in both realms – most human parents wait until their children are older to introduce them to the Other. Once you've been introduced, you have to continually move between the realms. That's too much for most young families – juggling naps and nappy changes and magical recharging. But not my father; he wanted my IR to be innate.'

He shrugged. 'Anyway, to me the IR is like opening a door or switching on a light. One of my friends got introduced much later, like you, and he cooked a few footballs when he was first learning IR. So – words. If you're thinking float, float, float, over and over again then you're not thinking oven. Then you *say* float, and it will.'

I wondered if my parents had had lessons like this or if they'd been introduced when they were young, like Stone. I looked at the black-and-red ball. I wanted it to spin so I could see the colours whirl. 'Spin,' I said. The ball gave a slow rotation. I stifled the urge to jump up and down and squeal in delight, though I did allow myself a little smile.

'Good,' Stone said. 'Now put some force behind it. Order the release, like you would Gato.'

'Spin!' I ordered. The ball did nothing.

'You didn't gather your intention first. Focus: what do you want it do? Then release.'

I looked at the ball. I wanted it to spin, like a basketball player would spin a ball on his finger. 'Spin!' I snapped.

The ball immediately started to rotate quickly. I watched, amazed, while it spun and spun. I couldn't tear my eyes away from it. I fed it more energy to keep it going, though I couldn't tell how the heck I did that. As the ball continued spinning, I could feel my energy levels dipping.

It could have been a moment or a year before Stone broke the silence. 'Now you need to stop it,' he said firmly. 'You can use a word or a gesture. Focus on it stopping, on undoing what you did.'

I focused on the blur of the ball. Red. Black. Red. Black. Did I want it to stop? It was so pretty. The colours were mixing. I wondered if I could get it to turn forever.

'Stop it, Jinx. Now,' Stone repeated decisively.

I complied reluctantly. 'Stop,' I ordered grudgingly. The ball stopped instantly. As the connection between me and it was severed, my energy levels plummeted. I felt sick and dizzy, and my vision went sideways. I dropped to my knees and brought a hand up to my head. What the hell? I blinked several times and slowly my vision came into focus.

'That's what it's like to be enthralled,' Stone said softly.

I blew out a shaky breath and nodded my under-standing. That had been thrilling and terrifying in equal measure, and the loss of control scared me. I wasn't going to be using IR for fun, that was for sure, and not without

Stone there to help snap me out of it.

Stone said nothing for a few minutes while I concentrated on breathing. When the nausea and dizziness had passed, I looked at the huge clock on the wall. 8:55 p.m. I'd been watching the ball spin for well over an hour. 'What would have happened if I hadn't snapped out of it?'

'You need conscious intention for the IR,' Stone explained, 'even if it's just a hint of it. If you pass out or fall asleep, the IR stops. If I couldn't break you out of the thrall by talking to you, knocking you unconscious was the next step.' He said it calmly, like knocking people unconscious was an everyday occurrence.

I looked at the cabinets. 'Have you got a baseball bat in there?'

'Something like that.'

I felt vulnerable, a feeling I dislike intently. Knowledge dispels fear; I needed to ask more questions. 'How do you know which word to use?' I questioned.

Stone was checking me over carefully; there was concern in his eyes. 'The word doesn't really matter, it's the release that's important. The word just gives it focus. You can just use a gesture if you like. When I'm fighting, I use gestures so my opponent doesn't know what I'm trying to get an object to do. If you're really good at IR, you can even use a gesture and then say a different word aloud to trick your opponent; that's called misdirection. Only the most skilled IR users can do that because it's hard to train your brain and mouth to work differently.'

I nodded. 'So what kind of things can you use IR for?'

'The important thing to know about IR is that it can't create from nothing. If you want a fireball, keep a match or a lighter handy. You can make a small flame grow but you can't create fire from air.'

Stone continued his lecture. 'Every wizard has a talent – some have more than one. Everyone can move one object to another place, and for some that's the totality of their IR skills. No floating, no transportation, just moving an object from one place that you can see to another place you can see. We call that a level one IR user. The highest-level user is a level five.

'Some wizards can use their IR to heal, to draw the skin together, to duplicate blood cells. There's a whole sect of wizards dedicated to offering the healing arts – they're known imaginatively as "healing wizards".

'Primer wizards can use the IR to manipulate fire, wind, earth or water. Their magic is not dissimilar to an elemental's magic. However, an elemental like Roscoe can create their element from nothing, whereas a wizard needs something to prime it before it can be used.

'I'm a warrior wizard, so my main talent is combat – kicking open a locked door, ripping out a lamp post, that kind of thing. I'm trained in a variety of weapons and martial arts. Most warrior wizards find their way to the

Connection. We're the enforcers of the Other.

'The last subset of wizards are known as subterfuge wizards. They can make themselves hard to be seen or heard. People don't tend to advertise subterfuge skills because they're considered a little underhand. They're known, a little unfairly, as "sub-wizards".

'There are only really three limits to the IR: you can't create from nothing; you can't bring back the dead, and you can't heal yourself. I could use the IR to heal you, but you can't use it on yourself. Although, if I'm honest, I can't heal much past a paper cut. Most of us can do a little of each branch of wizardry, but our skills outside our main talent are *de minimis*.'

I snorted. 'Good to know you're not healing me if we get attacked by a rogue vampyr.'

'If we get attacked by a rogue vampyr, his head will roll before he can touch you,' Stone promised fiercely. *True.* Well, wasn't he the macho one? He cleared his throat a little awkwardly. 'Any questions?'

'Stone, there are so many questions.' I blew out a breath. I was still feeling woozy, and we didn't have time for an extended Q&A session right now. 'Where does my truth seeking fit into all this?'

'Truth seeking is part of your being, not part of the IR. Like an elemental is an elemental, you're a natural-born empath with strong truth-seeking talents.'

I considered that. 'But you compelled me in Rosie's.

Does that mean you're an empath too?'

He shook his head. 'Compelling is part of a sub-wizard's skill set. Compelling involves using your strength of will to manipulate someone against their will.' He paused. 'That's how I knew you were a wizard as well as an empath, because you could compel and truth seek. Any other questions?'

A million. I shook my head.

Stone nodded. 'The only other thing you really need to know is that using the IR burns through your energy levels far more quickly than using your innate skills like truth seeking. You used the IR for one hour and nineteen minutes. You were enthralled, pouring energy into the IR, and now you feel as weak as a drowned kitten. Everyone enthrals the first time they use the IR, but it gets easier with experience. The best practice is always to charge up in the Common before using the IR, if you can.'

'How long do I need to recharge?'

'It depends on your reserves. It's just like a recharge-able battery – if it's half full then it charges quicker than if it only has five percent of its power left. Most people try to recharge little and often, and remain in the Other as much as possible. The stronger you are, the faster you'll recharge. Given that you could use your truth seeking and compelling in the Common, I'm betting you're going to be a strong magic user in the Other.

'You have a huge advantage in Gato. Most people have to go to a portal to recharge. The richest have their own portals, but the hoi polloi must make their way to a portal station, which are set up in places like Rosie's. There are a few portals in the parks for kids to use. But with Gato near you, you'll always be able to recharge quickly. That's why hell hounds are so sought after. Don't worry, he's bonded to you for his life, so he won't run off with a new owner.'

Stone hesitated. 'Just be careful. There are those who will want to fight you to prove their supremacy, and those that will want to use you. If it becomes common knowledge that you can truth seek… Before the Verdict, truth seekers were often enslaved. They were seen as a handy tool. Keep your skillset to yourself. Also, if someone knows you're a truth seeker, they know to phrase their responses carefully, and that can hide a wealth of lies. For now, keep your strength to yourself.'

'Supposed strength,' I corrected. 'We don't know if I'm magically strong. That's just conjecture.'

Stone nodded. 'Right.' He pressed his lips together. He wasn't sure if he should tell me something.

'Tell me,' I entreated.

Stone hesitated again, then met my eyes. 'While you were showering, I looked up your parents on the Connection database. George and Mary Sharp were both inspectors, Jinx. Decorated ones. I saw their file and the pictures of the crime scene. Whatever killed them was very powerful – a daemon, a dragon, or maybe something else. It's an unsolved murder in the Other as well as the Common. And they were both in the Other when they died. They had access to their magic, but something still killed them. Their killer is still out there. Don't advertise your parentage.'

I'd seen the crime-scene photos from the Common's police files, but Stone's words tipped me over the edge. I felt like my world was unravelling. My parents had been inspectors. Dammit, my mum was supposed to be a psychologist, and my dad a music teacher. What the fuck?

I drew in a sharp breath and let it out slowly. 'Keep off the radar,' I said softly.

Stone nodded. 'Exactly.'

CHAPTER 10

I WAS FEELING solemn as we made our way back to our rooms, lost in my own thoughts. Stone left me to them. As we approached my door I asked absently, 'Do you want to come in?'

A strange expression crossed his face and I realised my comment was open for misinterpretation. I blushed. 'To recharge. With Gato, I mean.'

Stone's expression cleared. 'Yeah, thanks. That's a good idea.'

It was gone nine, but we could have an hour's downtime before we headed out to Zanzibar. God knows, I needed some energy to get me through the night; I was still as weak as a day-old kitten.

Gato wagged his tail from the bed in greeting. 'Lazy pup,' I called to him. He wagged again, not bothering to get off the bed. 'Can you take Stone to the Common, please? And then me?'

Gato yawned and got off the bed. He gave a leisurely stretch and stalked towards Stone. 'Catch his forepaws,' I advised.

Gato touched his nose to Stone's triangles and Stone shimmered visibly before the triangles disappeared. I'd expected it to look a little more impressive when we moved from realm to realm, but no, a Tinkerbell shimmer was all we got.

Gato came to me and we repeated the brief ritual. 'You're probably safer staying here with Gato while you're in the Common,' I suggested to Stone. 'You can watch some TV while I get ready in the bathroom.'

Stone nodded and settled down on the bed. Gato gave him an unfriendly glance; it was *his* bed. Then he jumped up, turned round three times and thumped down on top of Stone. Stone let out an 'oof'. I grinned. 'Aw, best friends already,' I teased.

I grabbed my make-up bag and my dress and went into the bathroom. Being enthralled had made my hair a bit frantic, so I straightened it again. I applied dark eye make-up. I was going for dramatic; Scousers don't do half measures for nights out, and I didn't want to stand out for the wrong reasons. After applying false lashes and dark-red lipstick, I looked suitably gothic for Zanzibar.

I sprayed on Chanel's Chance, my favourite scent, and wriggled into my dress. I surveyed myself in the mirror; I'm not model-beautiful or exotic, but I am pretty, and with the right make-up I can hold my own.

The dress was a one-shoulder number with some ruching across the tummy. It was flattering, though it fell a little higher on my thighs than I'd have liked. But, hell, I was twenty-five and I was entitled to look sexy now and again. It wasn't *all* about the job.

I walked out of the bathroom. Stone had his hands behind his head, muscle-bound arms on display as he lay back against the headboard. 'You look great,' he complimented me. I felt the truth of the statement, which is to say it was true as far as Stone saw it. That was good enough for me.

I smiled confidently. 'Thanks. I clean up okay.'

'I'd better up my game if I'm going out with you. I'll be back in five minutes.' It was ridiculously unfair that was all he needed to get ready, when it had taken me half an hour.

He went through to his room while I put on my boots. I had chosen black suede ankle boots with a sizeable heel, which transformed my usual five feet eight to five feet eleven. They made me feel tall and willowy, but I was still confident I could run or kick ass if I needed to. I also chose a small black bag to hold my phone, cash and bank cards. I squeezed in a powder compact and a lipstick – all the essentials.

I called to Gato to portal me back to the Other. He let out an audible huff as he climbed off the bed again; life was obviously much easier when I was hidden. 'Regretting my presence in the Other already?' I asked him teasingly, and I swear he shook his mighty head.

He gave a couple of full body wags, starting from his tail, then he moved towards me as if to give me a lick. 'Don't you dare! My make-up is perfect.' He gave a doggy grin, his tongue lolling.

'Portal me carefully!' I demanded. He stood carefully on his hind legs, not even offering me his forelegs. I blinked. 'Good trick,' I complimented him. As he walked around on his hind legs, it was like Scooby Doo had come to life. He touched his nose to my forehead. I checked the mirror; sure enough, the mark of the Connection was there.

'Shall we take you out for a pee before I leave?' I asked.

Gato went down onto four legs and walked into the bathroom. He reversed carefully and sat on the toilet. I stared, open mouthed. 'Holy crap,' I whispered. He sent me another doggy grin. When he finished, he pressed the flush handle with a big heavy paw, then strolled back to the bed, climbed up, turned round three times and lay down.

I was shell shocked. Of all the things I'd learned during the last twenty-four hours, the fact that my dog could use the toilet was the most shocking. Another realm, I could take in my stride, but my dog flushing the loo? I was dumbfounded.

Stone knocked on the interconnecting door. 'Come in,' I called, managing to sound normal.

He looked great in ripped jeans, a black shirt that was unbuttoned just the right amount and a black blazer. He scanned the room and, as usual, missed nothing. His eyes narrowed. 'What happened?'

I didn't know how to say it without sounding weird. 'My dog just used the toilet.'

Stone started to smile. 'Elementals with fiery hair and dryads with green skin are solid, but your dog using your toilet blows your mind? Plenty of people in the Common train their dog to do it.'

'Yeah,' I objected, 'but I haven't! He's just used the loo of his own volition!'

Stone crossed to Gato and stroked his head. 'He's a clever boy.' Gato's tail thumped enthusiastically as he gave me a reproachful look. I should have been giving him this praise.

I crossed the distance between us. 'You *are* a good boy,' I agreed. 'The best boy.' He tapped his happiness with his tail. 'Now that you're all loved up, can you send Stone to the Other?' I asked nicely.

'I'll duck down.' Stone lowered his head so that Gato didn't have to move. My dog gave him an enthusiastic lick on the face before touching his forehead. Stone rippled and his marks were back. 'Thanks, man,' he said.

'Full disclosure,' I said. 'I have no weapons on me.'

Stone smiled wryly. 'Full disclosure,' he said. 'I *am* a weapon.' *True.*

'Cool. Well, you're on protect-me-from-vampyrs watch.'

Stone lost his smile. 'I'll protect you from everything I can.' His words rang with truth, and a shiver ran down my spine. That statement was a big deal to me. I've never had anyone to watch my back, not since my parents were killed. It's just me and Gato against the world. Having Stone in my corner meant something.

'Thank you,' I replied honestly. I needed to lighten this conversation; it was too deep for me, too raw. 'So,' I quipped, 'are you ready to rock?'

'Rock and roll,' he replied easily.

Gato barked and I flipped the channels on the TV until he settled down again. I refilled his water bowl, gave him one last stroke, then Stone and I headed out. The chapterhouse wasn't far from the centre of town and Zanzibar was on Seel Street. It was a ten-minute walk, but thankfully my heels were made for walking. I'd once run down a benefits' scammer in these boots.

We took the slightly longer route down Lord Street, the central street in Liverpool. It was about 10:30, and the city was just warming up. Micky D's was already doing a fair trade. As we walked, I looped my arm through Stone's, mostly to fit in but partly because I wanted to.

In a little over twelve hours, I'd become strangely accustomed to the idea of the Other. My whole life I'd thought there must be something more, and now I knew that there was. Its existence answered so many questions – and it raised a hundred more.

As we walked down the street, there were almost more Other than Common. Stone wasn't kidding when he said Liverpool was the London of the Other. A trio of troublesome trolls, a bushel of six dryads, a gang of preening vampyr men, a kindling of elementals … I amused myself by thinking up collective names for them all. I'm easily amused.

Of all the Other things I saw, the ghouls were the worst. A ghastly of ghouls. I imagined they were the ones who'd look like they were homeless if you were in the Common. Stone had promised me that although ghouls enjoy robbing graves, they're largely harmless – but, man, did they smell. They were dirty and grimy, like they hadn't showered for several weeks. They were mostly solitary, with only a few in pairs.

Up ahead was a dragon, an honest-to-goodness fire-breathing dragon. He was smaller than I'd envisaged but still nothing to scoff at; his body was about three metres long, and he had a couple of other metres in his tail. He was a vibrant, ruby red, had lethal-looking black spikes running down his spine, and his golden wings were furled. He was talking to some elves. He eyed Stone with a bright-emerald gaze, tracking his every step.

It took everything I had to walk around him calmly without gaping or shaking. Holy hell. But I clearly stared for too long because the dragon's gaze met mine and he froze. For one long beat he studied me with an intensity that made my heart race. He wasn't looking at me in a predatory way but as if I were a missing piece of a puzzle. The moment almost hummed with intention and then … the dragon winked at me. I stumbled a little, blushing, and he flashed me a toothy grin. I was amusing him. Great. When we were safely past, I leaned in to Stone. 'That was an actual dragon.'

He grinned. I think he was enjoying seeing the Other through my unencumbered eyes. 'Yeah. It was.'

'Talking to freaking elves.' I blew out a breath. 'If I wasn't so damned cool, I'd be screaming right now.'

'You're as cool as ice,' Stone agreed.

We reached the club and joined the queue outside. It was still relatively early and we were let in quickly. The bouncers were looming trolls with long hair and large, pointy noises. They were nearly seven feet tall, and not so much well-muscled as bulky. They were like huge, hulking rugby players with long, shrew-like noses.

Inside the club the lights were low and the music was loud. A young, hopeful band were playing their hearts out on the stage at the front. It was a bit screamy for my liking; I like classic rock, and the guttural throat thing isn't really for me, though I accept that it's damned hard to do. David Draiman's cover of 'The Sound of Silence' is one of my all-time favourite songs.

Stone and I headed to the bar. Without having discussed it, we were posing as a couple – it was the most natural cover. I wanted to talk to the staff and any regulars, so I got the picture of Hes and Nate up on my phone. When it was my turn to be served, I ordered two Coronas with lime. 'Hey,' I shouted across the bar. 'Are my friends here yet? I haven't seen them, but they said they'd be here at ten.'

The barman studied the picture. He had a lip piercing and an ear expander in each lobe. His hair, a bright-red mohawk, rose from his skull by a good seven inches. I dated a guy with a mohawk once, and I know how hard it is to style.

He shook his head. 'No, they're not here tonight, but their friends are sitting over there.' He gestured with his chin to a distant table. 'You might know them.'

'Thanks so much!' I gushed.

I pushed my lime into my beer and took a pull. 'Shall we ask around or go straight to the friends?' I asked Stone.

'Ask around first, in case we blow it with the friends,' he suggested.

As we threaded through the tables, I flagged down a waitress. 'Can you get us two shots of tequila?' She gave me a friendly smile and a nod, then swished off to get our shots. She came back with tequila, salt and lemon. 'Thanks, lovely.' I handed her a fiver. 'Have you seen my friends yet?' I showed her the picture.

She shook her head. 'Sorry, I haven't seen Nate since early this week – Monday, maybe? I think he was with your friend. They were having a boss time.' She gave a wicked grin.

I rolled my eyes. 'That's my Hes, always having a good time. Which drugs were they doing this time?'

The girl shrugged. 'I might have seen Nate doing some coke. They were partying hard, hitting the bevvies. Your friend's a good tipper – I was made up.'

'Hes is like that, she's super-generous. Did they stay here long or bounce off somewhere else? I'm trying to think where I can track her down.'

The waitress shrugged again. 'Sorry, honey, they were here pretty much all night. Nate was doing his usual skydiving bit, getting all the freshers excited about jumping out of planes.' She brightened. 'They said something about doing that soon. Maybe that's where they're at.'

I gave her a 'get real' face. 'No way would Hes jump out of a plane,' I said dubiously.

'Honey, she'd do anything Nate told her to. She's loved up! She was dead excited about it.'

'Christ, all I need is for Hes to suddenly start jumping out of planes.'

'You don't have to do it with her! But skydiving is sound, you know.'

I stared at her. She was blonde, tanned and buxom and she didn't look the type to throw herself out of a plane. 'You've skydived?' I purposefully sounded insultingly incredulous.

'You bet I have, chick. It was boss. Nate took me and a few of the lads from here up one time. We did it for charity. We raised money for our local hospice.'

'Wow, that's so cool.' I was genuinely impressed. 'Did Nate pay for your jumps, or did you have to raise the money yourselves?' It costs around 250 quid for a tandem skydive.

I wondered how often Nate was dragging people to the drop zone. He might just be really passionate about skydiving, but he was a vampyr. Maybe I was being discriminatory, but I couldn't help thinking something else was going on.

'The drop zone paid for our jumps because it was for charity.'

Now alarm bells were definitely ringing. After my parents' death I'd gone crazy for a while – life was too short, etcetera, etcetera. Between the ages of eighteen and twenty-one, I'd spent a good portion of time at drop zones – DZs – and I'd got my skydiving licence. Eventually the risk of breaking a limb when I was self-employed outweighed the thrill of the jumps, so I stopped, but I still miss the rush of it. Not once had I seen a DZ pay for someone's jumps, even for charity. A DZ can't run on empty; it has to cover the cost of the DZ, the plane, the fuel, the pilot and the skydiving instructor. At the end of the day, the DZ is a business, a thrilling one, but a business nonetheless. So why would the DZ pay for their jumps?

I smiled at the waitress. 'That is so cool. Which drop zone did you go to?'

'The one in the Lake District – Cark, I think it was. They were sound.'

I nodded. 'Great. Do you think that's the DZ Nate would take Hes to?'

'Oh totally,' she said. 'It's his home DZ. I think he even has a static caravan there. Hey, it's been fun chatting but I'd best go. My boss is giving me the hawk eye.' She gave a friendly wave, picked up her tip and moseyed off.

I waited until she was out of earshot. 'I used to sky-dive,' I explained to Stone. 'There's no way the DZ paid for their jumps, so I'm thinking Nate must have done. He's rich, right? So why does he care so much about getting people into the sport? It's weird.'

'Some people are just fanatical about their pastimes.' Stone paused. 'You used to skydive?'

I rolled my eyes. 'I used to everything. I had a phase.'

'I bet you were fun back then.'

'I was a liability. Luckily I grew out of it fairly quickly. Skydiving stuck around longer.'

'Why did you give it up?'

'My business was taking off, and I needed to work more weekends. I went to Skydive North West – also known as Cark – a couple of times, but my home DZ was Chiltern Parks Aerodrome, closer to home. Skydive North West has a great reputation, and it's one of the longest established centres in the UK. Skydiving as a sport has a pretty small community, with only 5000 or so active skydivers, so the scene is really friendly. I was in danger of making friends, so I left.'

Something like sympathy shone in Stone's eyes, irritating me. 'Come on.' I said. 'Let's hit up Nate's friends.'

CHAPTER 11

WE APPROACHED THEIR table. Some of them were discreetly passing drugs around while the bouncers were out of sight. As we got nearer, I realised that three of the men were vampyrs. The ditsy-friend routine wasn't going to cut it, not with multiple triangles on our foreheads. If we were in the Common, we'd have had a better chance at playing dumb. I was beginning to see that the Common could have its advantages.

'Your deal,' I said to Stone. He nodded and took point.

'Evening,' he greeted the table calmly.

One of the vampyrs dismissed the Common humans around the table with a tilt of his head; that left only the three vampyrs. The one closest to me was blond, blue eyed and impossibly square jawed. The next was a dark brunette with matching dark eyes and tanned skin. The final vampyr was a redhead with bright-green eyes and a strong jaw. They were all ridiculously good looking. No hint of fangs.

'We're not doing anything wrong,' the redhead said

pugnaciously.

'I didn't say you were,' Stone said mildly. 'Which clan are you?' There was a hard silence. 'Which clan?' he repeated slowly, drawing out the words.

'Volderiss,' the brunette replied. There was a 'well, duh' element to his tone. This was Volderiss clan territory. I wanted to point out the old adage about making an assumption, but calling a vampyr an ass didn't seem like a good move, so I held my tongue.

Stone ignored the tone. 'Good. We're looking for Nathaniel Volderiss. Have you seen him since Monday night?'

The vampyrs exchanged glances and didn't reply. 'You're being rude,' I said. 'The inspector asked you if you've seen Nate since Monday.' I met the brunette's eyes and held them.

'No. Nate was supposed to be going to the Lakes this weekend with his new girl. I figure he's gone up early.' *True.*

I fixed my eyes on redhead. 'And you?' He shook his head, but I needed him to articulate an answer so I could tell if it was true or a lie. I pressed him harder. 'Have you seen Nate since Monday?'

He shook his head again, but I pressed him harder, and he reluctantly started to talk. 'I saw him packing his car on Tuesday, early hours. His new bird was with him. Don't know where he was going.' *True.*

Well, at least Nate and Hes had left voluntarily. Maybe there wasn't something nefarious going on after all, though the trashed room suggested otherwise. 'Where do you think Nate was going?'

'The Lakes,' he said. 'Skydiving. His bird was into it.'

I turned to the blond. 'What about you? Did you see Nate after Monday night?'

He shook his head. 'No.' *True.*

'Why does Nate pay for other people to skydive?' I asked the question but didn't compel the answer.

'We're done here,' said the brunette. All three of them stood up and walked away. Dammit, I should have compelled the answer. My mistake. I looked at Stone but he shook his head. We were done here too.

We spent another hour moving around the bar. A new band was on stage, punk rock, more my scene. Between songs I asked more questions about Hes and showed her picture. Some people remembered seeing her recently, some remembered seeing her with Nate, but no one could place her after Monday night.

Stone and I split up so we could flirt a little to get some answers. Although a few of the people I spoke to recognised Hes, more of them recognised Nate. I was getting the vibe that he was something of a minor celebrity.

One of the guys I questioned, Dave, was already on his way to being stinking drunk. Drunk Dave was effusive in his praise of Nate and his charitable work. Apparently Dave had signed up for a charity skydive, and they'd even had a mobile blood-donation bank on site for a blood drive. Nate had spoken to them all about the importance of giving blood because of hospital shortages and people in dire need. He had been first up for the blood donation and most of them had followed. Dave boasted that he had donated five more times since then. I asked if he'd always donated to a mobile unit, and he confirmed that he had for convenience because no appointment was necessary. His man Nate had sorted him out.

It didn't take a genius to work out that Nate's mobile blood donations didn't make it to the hospitals they were supposedly for. Nate was a vampyr con-artist; he built a bond with his victims based on their love of an exciting sport, got them high on life with a skydive and then got them to donate their blood. Not a bad gig for a vampyr.

I wondered how widespread the con was. Did Daddy Volderiss know about it? Did Daddy sanction it? We would find out tomorrow. But it seemed like a ridiculous rigmarole to go through to get some extra blood. It also seemed like a bad business model. Even if Nate was paying Skydive North West a reduced rate for getting so many people skydiving, it was going to be at least 150 pounds a jump. One hundred and fifty quid for a pint of blood seemed a little steep to me. Surely, the vampyrs could just advertise and get people to donate for 30 pounds?

All I knew for sure was that Hes had climbed into Nate's car and they'd driven who knows where. The Lakes were my best bet, but before we could follow that lead, we had a meeting with Nate's father. The delay was a pain but it was necessary; there was something more going on here than two missing kids.

I gestured to Stone that I was done and we reconvened. 'Anything?' he asked.

'Something,' I confirmed. 'Let's talk when we're back at the hotel.' These walls may not have ears, but they definitely had vampyrs. I didn't want Nate and Hes to know I was on their trail. Where that trail would lead, I had no idea, but I intended to follow it.

It was 1 a.m. and the streets were rowdy with drunken laughter and shouting. Liverpool is a fun city that rarely sleeps, and Thursday night is no exception. It was student night and they were out in force.

The Other contingent appeared to be just as intoxicated. The dragon we'd seen earlier was holding court, but now had a pugnacious air. He was arguing with a troll. Stone assessed the situation and decided to intervene. He sighed. 'Dragons just shouldn't drink. Especially not *that* dragon.' He grimaced as we approached the fracas.

'Here we go! The law's here! The bizzies have come to shut me up!' the dragon snorted in a broad Scouse accent.

I don't know why that surprised me but it did. He continued his yammering. 'And I'll be the one in trouble even though *he* started it, the jobsworth.' He pointed at the troll.

'I haven't started anything yet, you gasbag. You'll know when I start with you,' the troll snarled back.

'Enough,' Stone said commandingly. 'Disperse home. Both of you.'

The troll started giving lip and protesting. Stone levelled a hard stare at him. 'Do you know who he is?' he asked the troll, pointing to the dragon.

The troll shrugged. 'He's a dragon, that's all I need to know. He thinks he's better than me. Well, we're both magical creatures,' he sneered. 'We're both as lowly as each other in the eyes of the almighty Connection.'

'Do you know who I am?' Stone asked evenly.

The troll rolled his eyes. 'Oh, Mr Important Hoity-Toity, I'm sure.'

'Inspector Stone.'

The troll froze. He remained statue still, and he paled behind his forked beard. Stone took his arm and walked him a few steps away to talk privately, leaving me with the dragon.

The dragon eyed me with a curiosity and a wariness that I wanted to tell him wasn't warranted. 'You're awesome,' I blurted out. I blushed as my words caught up with my brain. 'I'm new to the realm,' I explained.

'Dragons … wow.'

He gave a toothy grin. 'A babe in the woods,' he commented, brushing over my fan-girl behaviour. 'Be careful with him.' He gestured at Stone. His accent now was sharp British English; gone was the strident Scouse of a few moments ago. Huh. He stopped swaying and all hints of intoxication disappeared. 'His only concern is for the Connection. He'll do anything for them.'

'We're working together,' I explained.

'Stone works alone,' the dragon stated. 'Watch yourself.'

I nodded, feeling something dark curl in my gut. The dragon believed that everything he'd said to me was true. I trusted Stone, but my gut still felt uneasy – and I believed the dragon. I didn't know how to reconcile those two things. Finally, I told my gut to shut up. I liked Stone, I trusted him and that was the end of it. Besides, he was sexy as hell.

Stone and the troll were almost done talking. The troll's voice carried as he tried to apologise. 'No disrespect was intended, Inspector Stone. I'm going.' He raised his hands in the universal symbol for surrender. 'This isn't the path for me. No need for heads to roll.' He turned and almost ran. Trolls might be massive, but they can really haul ass.

The dragon watched him scarper with barely concealed contempt. 'Stone,' he said flatly. 'I've got information for Ajay.' His accent remained neutral; whatever show he'd been putting on for the troll wasn't necessary for Stone and me.

'You can give the information to me, Emory,' Stone said firmly. There was no hint of warmth in his eyes.

The dragon's eyes narrowed. 'It's Prime to you, Stone.'

Stone gave Emory the barest inclination of his head. 'Prime.' It was clearly a title, but Stone didn't seem to be into bowing and scraping – except to Mrs H, of course. 'Tell me,' he demanded.

Emory shook his massive head. 'I don't think so. Things die around you, and I don't intend to be one of them. Tell Ajay I want to meet.' Before Stone could protest, the dragon gave me a nod, turned and ran a few steps. He unfurled his golden wings and launched himself into the sky. He didn't look back as he flew off with powerful strokes. The gust of wind from the force of his wings took my breath away. Wow. Just wow.

Stone frowned as he watched the dragon fly away. I wondered who Ajay was. Could a dragon be an informant? There was clearly a lot going on here. Emory didn't trust Stone, and Stone didn't seem to have the warm and fuzzies for him either. 'Not best friends?' I enquired.

Stone shook his head. 'Not so much.'

'I would totally want to be best friends with someone called Emory. Do you think he's good at filing nails?'

A smile grew on Stone's lips. 'I dare you to ask him.'

'A bad idea?'

'He's the leader of all the dragons in the UK, probably in Europe. Even I tread carefully around him.'

Great: I'd called the king of the dragons awesome. I groaned internally. 'Why didn't he have the triangle and circle thing on his head?' I asked.

'Dragons aren't part of the Connection. It's their choice. The magical creatures don't have the triangles like we do, and they don't need to go to the Common realm. They exist wholly in the Other.'

I frowned. 'Vampyrs have to go to the Common, but dragons and trolls don't?'

'Anything human-based has to go to the Common to recharge – wizards, seers, elementals, dryads, pipers, vampyrs,' Stone explained, still watching Emory's flight. It seemed to me that gave the non-human creatures a massive advantage. They would never run out of their magic in a fight.

When Emory disappeared, Stone seemed to shake off his mood. As he wrapped a proprietary arm around me and we headed home, I tried not to think about how nice human contact felt. Wizard contact.

I was freezing. Usually when I wear a dress, I take a jacket or coat with me, but that's not the Scouse way. Here it's better to freeze and look good. It had been an unseasonably warm October day, but by 1 a.m. the warmth had long since faded, and I was shivering my ass off. Stone gave me an extra squeeze around the waist before he let go, took off his blazer and wrapped it round me. It was warm and smelled like him. My stomach flip-flopped. 'Thanks.' I muttered.

He gave a small smile. 'You're welcome.' He wrapped his arm around me again and we continued to mosey down Lord Street. We encountered five more trolls, and I saw Stone frown at them; they avoided eye contact and scattered. I had no idea if that was normal or not. On the next street, we saw another four trolls and Stone's frown deepened.

On any other night, I would have gone dancing at Heebies or had cocktails at Alma de Cuba, but Stone and I were here for work not pleasure. Then I suddenly remembered my promise to Lucy. And Stone really needed something to help him ease up – he'd been tense since he'd bumped into Emory. 'Hey,' I said, 'do you fancy going to Alma de Cuba for a drink? Um, not work, just for a drink. I promised Lucy I would.'

'Not work, just pleasure?' Stone asked softly. I blushed a little and nodded. Did this count as asking a guy out? I wasn't sure because I hadn't done it before.

We about-turned and walked back to the bar. It wasn't far; nothing is far in Liverpool, which is one of the reasons I love the city. It was relatively late, and the queue to get into Alma was almost non-existent. I gave Stone his jacket and we walked in. We were instantly assaulted with sound as the Cuban beats poured round the club. Man, I loved this place.

Alma de Cuba is in an eighteenth-century church. The windows are stained glass, and the lighting is supplied by candles in antelope-horn chandeliers. It has an amazing atmosphere, and the Latin music demands to be danced to. The cocktails are great too.

We went across to the busy bar, and Stone effortlessly manoeuvred us to the front. He had a presence that people made way for. As he moved me in front of him, he pressed his body close. 'What do you want?' he asked, his breath teasing the shell of my ear. Wasn't that a loaded question?

I bit my lip. 'Sex on the beach?' I asked flirtatiously.

He smiled. 'You want me to ask the barman for sex on the beach?'

'Not really. I'm more of a pina colada girl, to be honest.'

'Do you like getting caught in the rain?'

I laughed aloud and hummed the first few bars of 'Escape' by Rupert Holmes. 'I do,' I admitted. 'I love a run in the rain.'

'Me too.'

The barman jerked his chin towards us, the universal sign for 'what's your order?'.

'Pina colada and a mojito,' Stone ordered. I watched,

fascinated, as the barman expertly mixed our cocktails, all the while singing to the music and dancing a little. He poured my pina colada into a tall glass and decorated it with pineapple and some flowers. It was a work of art.

Stone paid before I could offer, and we went to a free booth. 'I love the music here,' I confessed. 'Lucy and I came a lot when she was at uni. Have you been before?'

'A time or two.'

'I love it when they throw down the rose petals at midnight.'

'The food's great here too. Have you eaten here?'

I shook my head. 'Too pricey on a student budget.'

'You weren't a student,' Stone pointed out.

'No, but Lucy was, and I didn't want to make things awkward for her. Besides, I'd only just started my business, and it turned out that no one wanted to hire an eighteen-year-old private investigator. I had to pretend that Jessica Sharp was my mum and I was her daughter running errands for her. I was poorer than Lucy, and I didn't want to dip into my inheritance.'

'You've really accomplished a lot. I'm sure your parents would be proud of you.'

Suddenly I had a lump in my throat. Even years later, grief can kick me in the chest with no warning. 'Thanks.' I managed a tight smile as I swallowed a few times to shift the golf ball in my throat. I took a sip of my drink and blinked against the sting in my eyes. The truth is, I have no idea what my parents would think about my life. I don't think growing up to be a PI was a path they envisaged for me. All I know for sure is that they wouldn't be terribly thrilled by the two triangles adorning my forehead. *Stay off the radar.* Dammit. I blew out a harsh breath.

Stone squeezed my hand, gave me a sympathetic smile and changed the topic. I let him distract me; sometimes, with grief, you just have to live in the moment. Sometimes that's all you get.

'Dance?' I asked. Toe-tapping, hip-swinging samba music was playing. The hugely popular dancing girls were on the stage dressed in tiny bikinis with ruffles and tassels and feathered head dresses. Their outfits were covered in gems and sequins, and they glittered as they moved. On closer inspection, I noticed a shimmer around two of them that marked them as sirens. No wonder they were worshipped, though, to be honest, their dance skills alone were enough to inspire infatuation. They had triangles on their heads, so I guessed they were on the human side of the magical realm.

Stone and I joined the crowd on the dance floor and moved to the music. I wished we were properly off duty so we could stay all night; however, regretfully but sensibly, I jerked my head at the door after a few dances. 'We'd better go,' I said. Stone agreed, but I could sense his reluctance. We were having fun, but the job came first.

As we left, Stone wrapped his jacket around me. The walk back was uneventful, though I spotted three more trolls and a ghoul. The streets were clearing as the revellers started to make their way home. We walked in companionable silence; I didn't want to say the wrong thing. I really, really liked Stone. I trusted him and I was having the best time. I didn't know what Stone's silence was about, but I hoped it was for a similar reason.

He used his card to enter Hard Day's Night without going through the Other reception. He was avoiding the siren. I didn't want to examine how happy that made me.

'I'll come in and we can talk about our interviews at Zanzibar,' Stone said, all business.

I nodded and opened my door. Gato was waiting by the doorway when we came in, wagging away. 'Hey, boy!' I greeted him with a cuddle and body rub. 'Are you okay? Has everything been good while we were away?'

He gave another happy wag and licked me, then greeted Stone. My men liked each other. Christ, I was getting ahead of myself, but I'd never felt a connection with anyone like I felt with Stone. Maybe it was the whole introduction thing; it's a pretty big deal to show a girl a whole other realm. Maybe the buzz between us would fade with time, but for now I was enjoying it.

I shrugged out of Stone's jacket and passed it to him. 'Thanks for that.' I filled the hotel kettle with water from the bathroom; I needed a cuppa to warm my fingers. Next, I pulled my PJs from my duffel bag. 'I'm going to change into comfy clothes. Do you want some tea?'

Stone nodded. 'That would be great.'

In the bathroom, I peeled off the black dress, slid off my shoes and pulled on my blue-cotton jammies. I hesitated before I removed all my make-up, but Stone had already seen me bare faced, so it wouldn't be a dramatic revelation. Besides, I'm not a big make-up girl, and if we were going to be hanging out for a while, I was going to be myself.

When I walked out, Stone had made tea for us both. He turned the chair at the dresser to face the bed. We didn't talk for a moment, but the silence was comfortable. Finally, I started to give Stone the run down. 'So Nate is pretty worshipped in Zanzibar. He targets kids like Hes who are desperate to fit in, who want to do something a bit wild. He recruits students to join the university skydiving club, of which he's president, and organises weekly trips to the drop zones. Most university clubs do one trip a month, especially in winter when the weather is bad, but he's sending people to the DZ or the wind tunnel every week.'

'Wind tunnel?' Stone asked.

'It's basically simulated skydiving. You enter a chamber, someone turns on some massive fans and you experience flat fly.'

'Flat fly?'

'I guess what you think of as skydiving – belly to the ground free fall. Free fly is when you skydive upright, but that's something only experienced skydivers do. Some people prefer flat fly and focus on formation skydiving, when a bunch of you jump together, hold on to each other and go through a predetermined set of formations as you fall.'

'There's a lot more to it than I realised,' Stone commented.

'Yeah, there are loads of disciplines. For example, there's accuracy where you try to land on an established target – the best precision jumpers can land on a ten pence piece. There's crew jumping, BASE jumping and wingsuit flying. I never tried wingsuit flying – basically, it lets you stay in freefall a lot longer, and you can track much greater distances.'

'Track?'

It felt nice to be the one in the know rather than the one asking the questions. 'Tracking is when you move away from other skydivers. It makes you go forwards really fast, and it's the closest you get to actually flying. You feel your forward motion more than you feel that you're falling,' I explained.

Stone watched me as he sipped from his mug. 'You really loved it, huh?'

I smiled wryly. 'That obvious? Yeah, I loved it. It was

amazing, but my business had to come first. A lot of PI work, like serving papers and surveillance, has to be done on weekends – and that's when people get up to more mischief. Most DZs only open on weekends so I had no choice but to drop it. But I do miss it. It was a big part of my life for a couple of years, and it helped me focus on something other than my parents' deaths.'

I shrugged. 'Anyway,' I said, bringing us back to topic, 'Nate appears to be as big on skydiving as I am. He fires up people's enthusiasm. After the jumps, there was a mobile blood donation unit at the DZ and Nate used his charisma to get people to donate. Almost certainly the blood is for vampyr consumption rather than for transfusions – but I don't get why skydiving is even in the equation.'

Stone frowned. 'I do,' he muttered darkly. 'Apparently blood tastes better after a thrill. It's why, traditionally, vampyrs always show their fangs to Common humans – to get them scared. Their victim runs, they give chase and the blood tastes better because the human has been scared. Nate is recruiting blood donors, giving them a thrill to make the blood taste better, and then taking it.'

'Is that illegal?' I asked. It seemed like it should be.

'I don't think so. The wording of the Verdict is that vampyrs must consume blood donated willingly, not taken forcibly. What Nate is doing skirts around the law, but I don't think it breaks it. They're encouraging donation under false pretences, but the Other law isn't well developed in that area. The donors are willing, and they're not being scared or intimidated.'

'What if Nate Volderiss is selling the blood?'

Stone shook his head. 'There's nothing to prohibit that. We'll speak to Lord Volderiss about it tomorrow. Then depending on how the meeting goes, I guess we should head up to Skydive North West and see if that's where Nate and Hes have gone. At least it looks like Hes has gone willingly, despite the state of her room.'

I nodded. It was reassuring that she seemed to have gone of her own accord, but I was concerned that she was wrapped up in a vampyr conspiracy she knew nothing about. She was defenceless. 'What about the drugs?' I asked finally. 'Nate was taking them, and the other vampyrs were taking them and sharing them with the humans. Could Nate be dealing too?'

Stone shrugged. 'Maybe. The Other law hasn't really touched on drugs. We let Common law deal with that.'

'Are you telling me that if a vampyr is seen dealing and the human police try to arrest them, the vampyr would just go willingly?'

'In theory. Look, I'm not saying it's a perfect system but the Connection has a lot more to focus on than drugs. Trying to get a multi-creature world to co-exist isn't easy, and the Connection has only been in existence for eighty years or so.' Stone was choosing his words carefully.

'Before the Connection was the Chaos. Vampyrs and dragons were killing each other. Trolls lived in isolated tribes and killed every elf or dragon they could find. Dryads killed anyone who harmed their trees. It was a chaotic and violent realm. You couldn't have walked the streets of Liverpool and seen a troll, a dragon and an elf without blood being shed. Now the Connection exists and the inspectors are feared and respected. Everyone buys into the Symposium and the Unity because we're all represented; every faction, no matter how small, has an equal say. We're ruled by majority vote.'

'I thought the dragons weren't part of the Connection?'

'They're not, but the Connection is strong enough that if a dragon went rogue we would hunt it down. They know that and they toe the line, but they don't want to be part of the government. It's their choice, not ours.'

Stone continued. 'Your friend Lady Seer Harding played a large part in building the British Symposium. She was very young, just out of training, when she foresaw a terrorist attack on the Symposium. She came to St George's Hall with a bunch of inspectors she'd corralled, and stopped the attack before it really got started. Only three Symposium members died. One of them was the Lady Seer at the time. Lady Harding was appointed to the position then and there. Her bravery and quick thinking saved hundreds of lives. She's the speaker of the Symposium now.'

I flashed him a grin. 'Is that why you were so flustered when you met her?'

'I wasn't *flustered*, I was surprised. She's the Speaker Lady Seer. You'd expect her to have a mansion, not a small semi-detached house in Beaconsfield.'

'What's wrong with Beaconsfield?' I said defensively.

He grinned. 'Nothing. The model village is very cute. It's just not where I expected her to live, that's all.'

'She didn't want to move away from me,' I said jokingly.

'I get that.'

I checked the time – 3 a.m. 'I'd better get my beauty sleep. What time is breakfast?'

'It's open until 9:30am so let's meet at 9:00, then we can get ready and head out by 9:45. It's a five-minute walk to Exchange Flags, but I want to arrive early and get a feel for the place.'

'You want to recharge over night?' I asked, gesturing at a sleeping Gato.

Stone thought about it. 'Yeah, I guess that's a good idea. I don't like being without the IR, but we're safe in the chapterhouse. And it would be handy to have a full charge for tomorrow.'

I woke my grumpy dog and he touched us both into the Common. Stone said goodnight; his eyes were warm and friendly, but I deliberately kept my distance. We didn't need an awkward moment as to whether or not we needed a goodnight kiss. I gave him a finger wave instead, which made him grin. He shut the door between our rooms but left it unlocked.

I climbed into bed next to Gato. I contemplated chucking him onto the dog bed but dismissed the idea; he would only wait until I was asleep and climb back on the bed. I cuddled him and he licked me. No matter what else was going on in my life, Gato was my constant.

'Night, pup.' I snuggled down under my covers and cleared my mind. In minutes, I had drifted off.

CHAPTER 12

D ESPITE OUR LATE night, I was up at eight to go for a run with Gato. Five hours sleep wasn't really enough, but a good run blew away the cobwebs. Afterwards I showered and dressed. I couldn't go and interview the lord of the vampyr clan in jeans and a T-shirt, but I decided to change after breakfast so that I wouldn't spill beans down my nice shirt.

There was a soft knock on the door jamb and Stone came in. 'Good morning,' I greeted him.

'Good morning, Jinx, Gato.'

I was already in the Other, so Gato padded over and portalled Stone. We took my dog with us and went downstairs. The breakfast room was largely empty – most detectives and inspectors must start work early. Stone nodded to the few detectives who were there, and they looked a little overawed.

Stone and I talked quietly over our cooked breakfasts while Gato sat beside us. I'd ordered him some sausage and bacon too, and he was a happy hell hound. 'So is Lord Volderiss the vamypr Symposium member?' I asked.

Stone shook his head. 'He used to be, but he was outvoted two years ago. Lord Volderiss heads the clan for Liverpool and the surrounding areas of Wirral and Merseyside. The new Symposium member for the vampyrs is Lord Cathill, who heads up the Manchester clan. You can imagine the rivalry between them. The clan votes were split pretty evenly. There's a clan for every county in the UK, eighty-nine in total, and apparently the vote was forty-four to forty-five. Lord Cathill has another two years to make sure the election goes in his favour again.'

'So someone can get re-elected?'

'The appointment is a four-year term, but there are no limits to how many terms you can serve. Volderiss was the vampyr member for sixteen years, so his dethroning was a big deal in the vampyr community. Liverpool is the heart of the Other community and our government rules out of St George's Hall. For Volderiss to have to tolerate Cathill in his territory is a big ask and tensions have been high. Also, Cathill hasn't been making it easy for Volderiss and he's been openly disrespectful. Inspector Ven has had to do some fast talking to diffuse the situation.'

'So you're warriors *and* diplomats?'

Stone shrugged. 'We are what we need to be to keep the peace. I'm the bogeyman, the poster child. You'd better be good, or Inspector Stone will lop off your head.'

'You don't look old enough to be the bogeyman.'

'Thanks. I'm thirty-eight, but time in the Other slows the ageing process a little. I started young – I joined the Connection at sixteen and became an inspector at twenty-one.'

'I'm guessing that's an achievement for someone so young?'

'Yeah, it's a little unusual,' he said modestly, pouring me a fresh cup of tea.

'Thanks. So, we need to question Volderiss – but no compelling?'

'We're authorised to compel if there is due cause, but at the moment, there isn't. Nate is missing and Hes is missing, but I don't think Volderiss is involved. However, Hes's room was ransacked, and he might know what was being looked for. We have the authority to question him, but no reason to compel him or clear his mind. He is the lord of the Liverpool clan, so we need to tread carefully and persuade him to give us information voluntarily. He will try to test us. In vampyr culture, it's the strong who take precedence.'

'Wonderful,' I said drily. 'This will be a walk in the park.' It made me think of my recent walk in the park near my home where a vampyr had sliced up a human. Being wary was sensible.

'We're up to the task,' Stone said confidently.

I was confident *he* was up to the task, but I wasn't quite so sure what I was bringing to the party.

We finished breakfast and headed back to our rooms, where we changed into black suits and white shirts. Stone told me this was the Connection's uniform, like the FBI's, and it passed muster in both the Other and the Common.

I hooked on Gato's collar and lead; he was coming along for this jaunt. His presence might intrigue Volderiss, and maybe he could be our ice breaker. Besides, I felt better having him watch my back, especially if I was walking into a vampyr stronghold. The obsidian spikes on his back would be an asset in a fight.

The walk to Exchange Flags was short and brisk. Rain was threatening and I hadn't packed an umbrella. I was wearing my sensible flat shoes; I could run down a criminal in these shoes – or run away from a vampyr. My morning run had made me feel limber. I could definitely kick vampyr ass today. And if not, I had my small switchblade. And a hell hound.

As we entered Exchange Flags my jaw dropped slightly and I grabbed Stone. 'What the hell?' I exclaimed, pointing to the massive birds in front of me.

Stone looked at them. 'Oh, that's just Bertie and Bella,' he said calmly.

Gato was equally calm, not phased in the slightest by the huge creatures. The birds were at least fifteen feet tall and looked as if they'd been made out of copper. They had their backs to each other and were trilling and clacking away. They were *Liver Birds*. The Liver Bird is a mythical, cormorant-like bird, which is the symbol of the city of Liverpool. At least, I'd thought it was a symbol; it turns out they freaking exist. I watched, entranced, as ordinary people walked through the square unable to see them. Intriguingly, although Common folk couldn't see them, some other sense directed them around the huge, hulking birds.

'They're Liver Birds!' I exclaimed loudly.

Stone smiled, enjoying my shock. 'They're *the* Liver Birds. They have some children too – a hundred or so by the last count. Their children aren't quite so statuesque.'

'They can't face each other, right?' I said. 'Or Liverpool will cease to exist?'

'That's what people believe.'

'So how…?' I gestured. 'Erm, how do they procreate if they can't face in the same direction.'

'Imaginatively?' Stone suggested.

I blushed. I was still watching the gargantuan birds. I noticed that when anyone in the Other walked past them, they respectfully inclined their heads. 'Wow,' I said, awestruck. 'The Liver Birds are real.'

'You don't bat a lid at someone who is completely purple, but large birds have you breathless.'

'I did bat my eyelids a little at Mrs H. But these are the *Liver Birds*! And they're not large, they're huge! Do they really protect the city?'

Stone's smile faded. 'They do.' He tugged my arm. 'Come on, or we'll be late.' Despite his irreverence, he carefully inclined his head as we walked past Bella and Bertie. I did the same. The birds continued their conversation, but I noticed that Bertie watched us carefully as we moved past.

We entered the reception for GV Law. The reception-ist had a single triangle on her forehead, and she didn't turn a hair when she saw Gato. So much for an ice breaker. 'Inspector Stone and Detective Sharp to see Lord Volderiss,' Stone said calmly.

It was a bit of a thrill to be called Detective Sharp. One fine day a few years ago, I'd dreamed of being a police detective, but I'd been told I was too young and to go away and get some life experience. Instead, I had started my own PI firm and hadn't looked back; it turned out I liked being the boss of me.

The receptionist was stunning. She was Asian, with dark eyes and jet-black hair that tumbled over her shoulders in effortless curls. Vampyr, no doubt. She motioned for us to take a seat, but Stone remained standing and I copied him. He had his back to the wall so he could watch the entrances and exits. He had a lighter in the palm of his right hand, and I guessed he was part warrior wizard and part primer wizard. His weight was on the balls of his feet and he was ready for an attack. It made me a tad nervous.

One of the doors opened and a male vampyr emerged. He made to walk past us but, just as he got near to me, his fangs shot out. He leapt at me with shocking speed.

My blade was in my hand instantly and Gato jumped in front of me, teeth bared, spikes raised, growling fiercely. We reacted quickly, but we had nothing on Stone. He flicked the lighter and suddenly the small flame became a sword of fire. He beheaded the vampyr before Gato managed his second growl.

I kept my reactions hidden. 'Easy,' I said to Gato with a calm I didn't feel. I flipped the blade back and pocketed it. 'Sit,' I instructed, and he sat and fixed his gaze on the nearest door. Presumably, he could hear something we couldn't. His spikes stayed raised and ready.

The vampyr's head was near the coffee table, his neck black and cauterised. There was no blood. I guessed that would make the crime scene a little easier to clear up. His body shimmered for a moment and then, poof! – it was ashes.

Stone opened a window. He blew out a breath, made a gesture and his exhalation grew into a small, controlled tornado that picked up the ashes and funnelled them outside. Then he released the IR and the wind stopped. He shut the window and took up his position again facing the doors. Not a single emotion crossed his face.

I should have been scared, but it happened way too fast for me to register. 'You really should let the vampyrs clean up their own mess,' I chastened. A hint of a smile touched his lips.

Through it all, the receptionist had continued to file her nails. 'Lord Volderiss will see you now,' she said coldly, pointing to the door closest to us.

'Thank you,' Stone said politely and led the way with Gato close behind.

The office was light and airy, with windows on three sides. It was enormous and almost empty, as if to say, 'Here, look how rich I am. I have all this space and no need to fill it.' There was a large rug on the floor and a few plants either side of the desk. In front of the mahogany desk were two chairs.

The man behind the desk was older, but still impossibly handsome. His dark hair was dappled with silver and his eyes were a bright, piercing blue – he was a real silver fox. We were alone, which increased my hopes for a frank conversation – though those hopes were tempered by the assassination attempt. Volderiss didn't bat an eyelid at Gato; perhaps the dead vampyr could be the icebreaker instead.

'Thank you for sorting out that mess, Inspector Stone,' he said calmly. 'He attacked someone in the Common last week. It saves me the expense of a trial.' A chill ran down my spine as I wondered if he was the vampyr who'd attacked the human at my local park, but then I dismissed the idea as too much of a coincidence.

'I live to serve,' Stone said drily. He sat down opposite Volderiss, his body language relaxed as if he questioned lords of vampyr clans all the time.

'Quite.' Volderiss gave a sharp, unfriendly smile. 'What brings you to my door, Inspector?'

As I sat next to Stone, he glanced at me then dismissed me. His returned his gaze to Stone. That was fine with me; I'd just sit here quietly being a human lie detector.

'Your son, Nathaniel.'

Volderiss raised a perfectly plucked eyebrow. 'What has he done this time?'

'He's gone missing.'

The vampyr's smile widened. 'Someone is wasting your time, Inspector. He's not missing.' He believed that to be true.

'He was last seen in the early hours of Tuesday morning packing a car. He left with a Common human, whom I have been instructed to locate.'

'And who is instructing an inspector to find a Common girl?'

'Lord Samuel has an interest in her safe return,' Stone responded. Wilf! He *had* hired Stone – or at least pulled strings to get him on the job.

Volderiss made a moue of distaste. 'That mangy wolf

is sending you on a wild goose chase, I'm afraid. Nathaniel continues his work for the clan. He is not involved with this girl going missing; in fact, I suspect she is not missing at all.' He believed that too.

Stone held Volderiss's gaze. 'Three clan vampyrs confirmed his presence with her. But your son is not the focus of my investigation. The human's room was professionally searched. Do you know what someone would be looking for?'

'No,' said Volderiss. *Lie.*

Damn. Stone and I should have agreed on a signal. Oh well, I was just going to have to call him on it. 'That's a lie.' I said firmly. 'You know what they were searching for.'

Volderiss looked at me with a little more interest. 'Ah, an empath.' He said it as if my presence now made sense. 'It's been a long time since the last truth seeker joined the realms.'

'We know about the mobile blood drives, and we're not interested in them,' I reassured him.

Lord Volderiss smiled tightly. 'And why would you be? I had my lawyers look into them carefully. We're not doing anything wrong by procuring and selling the caviar of blood. The operation is imaginative and wholly legal.' He was proud of it.

'Paying 200 quid for a skydive just to get a pint of blood seems excessive,' I pointed out.

'Not when I can sell that pint for nearly a thousand pounds. As I said, the caviar of blood. Or perhaps the champagne.' He shrugged. 'Vampyrs are happy to pay a premium to have a taste of the old life.'

'Was it Nate's idea?' I asked.

'His project,' Volderiss said proudly, 'and it's been a great success. Every term he finds a new human girl to be his – what do they call it? – his beard. It helps to humanise him that little bit more – the humans perceive him as less threatening when he appears to be mated. I assume your human is his latest.' He shrugged. 'I can't help any more than that.'

'You can tell us about the object that Nate holds that he is being hunted for,' I countered.

Volderiss leaned back in his chair and studied me. 'Who are you, truth seeker?' he asked.

'I'm a detective with the Connection,' I said calmly. 'Answer my question.'

'You look familiar.'

He was a long-living vampyr, and there was every chance he had tangled with one or both of my inspector parents. *Stay off the radar.* 'Answer. My. Question,' I repeated. I didn't compel him, though I wanted to. I really wanted to.

Volderiss's smile widened. He was detached, looking at me like a spider would look at a fly it planned to eat for lunch. When he chose to answer me, I knew he was indulging me. 'My son had an elven dagger in his possession. It is priceless, and he is known to carry it on occasion. I suspect some thieves thought he might have left it at his … girlfriend's home.' All true.

'And who do you suspect are the thieves?'

'Surely you want facts, detective, not supposition.' He was dancing around the question.

I tried flattery. 'Supposition from you is like facts from a lesser man.'

Volderiss laughed. 'Oh, you are fun. Let's play again soon.' He sobered. 'Cathill. I suspect Cathill. He tried to buy the dagger from me and I told him no. I don't know why he wants it, but I told him it's not for sale. He can commission a new one from the elves if it's so important to him, but he's not having mine. It was entrusted to me, and I intend to keep it.' He leaned forwards and pressed a buzzer on his desk. Two muscle-bound vampyrs stepped into the room. 'These gentlemen will escort you out.' The interview was over.

Stone remained seated; it wasn't over until he said it was. 'Are you sure your son is well? Have you managed to speak to him since Tuesday? Perhaps Cathill caught up with him,' he mused.

Volderiss gave a soft sigh. 'I spoke to him on the phone on Wednesday morning. He is skydiving in the Lake District. No doubt you'll find him and his lady friend there. Lord Samuel is seeing conspiracies where there are none. Good day, Inspector. Detective.'

Stone rose and moved closer to Volderiss, ostensibly to look out of the window. 'Your oath of silence on my companion's skill set,' he demanded. His face was hard and unyielding; there was no trace of the fun-loving Stone I'd come to know. The bogeyman was here.

Volderiss arched an elegant eyebrow. 'And why should I agree to that?'

'Because if you don't agree, I'll lop off your head,' Stone said lightly.

The muscle-bound vampyrs tensed and suddenly their fangs were out. The tension in the room ratcheted up several notches, but Stone was closer to Volderiss than the guards were to him. Suddenly Volderiss laughed and waved his hand to the two guards, who subsided. 'You'll have your oath. It means nothing to me.'

He turned to me. 'But I'll find out exactly who you are.' My mouth went dry. His teeth elongated and he bit into his wrist. Blood welled up. 'My oath that I will not reveal to any soul, living or dead, the powers of this woman.' He nodded at me.

'Witnessed,' Stone confirmed, then walked out of the office without a backwards glance.

I looked at Volderiss once more and wished that I hadn't; he was holding a goblet to his wrist as blood poured out. When he met my eyes, he gave me a mocking salute and took a sip. My stomach turned. It was entirely too cannibalistic to me. I followed Stone out with the muscle-bound guards on my heels.

CHAPTER 13

WE LEFT EXCHANGE Flags in silence. Bertie and Bella had taken wing and were nowhere to be seen. I was disappointed; I wanted to see them again. I wanted to touch their copper wings to see what they felt like. I searched the skies, but there was no sign of them. It was probably a good thing; touching the Liver Birds might be a bit intrusive – and their beaks looked deadly.

Still not looking at me, Stone pulled out his phone. He tapped in a number and spoke. 'Do you have time to meet with me? I need a favour.'

The other person must have answered in the affirmative. Stone rang off and turned to me. 'We're meeting Inspector Ven at Moose Café.'

'The inspector that's done some quick talking to prevent a clan war?'

'That's the one.' He paused. 'Do we need to talk about the beheading?'

I blinked. 'Not really. I mean, I should say thank you, shouldn't I? Thanks for saving me.'

'You just keep surprising me, Jinx.'

'I'm the gift that keeps on giving,' I assured him.

He nodded. 'You certainly are.'

'Um … the oath?'

'Like I said before, truth seekers used to be enslaved. You don't want people knowing what you can do. That was pre-the Connection, but it's better to keep your skill set quiet.'

I nodded, still uneasy even though I knew he was protecting me.

It only took five minutes to walk to Moose Café. 'I love their pancakes,' I said enthusiastically. 'Oh, and their milkshakes.'

'You had a full cooked breakfast about an hour ago,' Stone pointed out.

'So? What's your point?'

He shook his head. I told Gato to wait for us outside the café. Inside it was busy: brunch is their big thing. It's an America-Canadian food joint all about good things like pancakes, bagels and waffles.

Stone led us up to the mezzanine floor. The sole occupant was African-Caribbean, around thirty-five and solidly built. He had three triangles. He looked up as we walked in and smiled widely at Stone. 'Zach! Good to see you, man.' He stood and shook Stone's hand.

'Ajay!' Stone greeted him with equal enthusiasm, pulling him in for a man hug instead of accepting his hand. Ajay? That was who Emory had mentioned.

'This is Jinx.' Stone stepped back.

'My honour to meet you,' I said, touching my right hand to my heart and giving a slight bow like Roscoe had shown me yesterday.

'The honour is mine,' Ajay said warmly, bowing back. 'My honour to meet you. Please, join me.'

'We've not long eaten,' Stone excused himself.

I snorted. 'Speak for yourself. I'm one hundred percent having an Oreo milkshake. And maybe Moose apple and home-made salted caramel pancakes. Definitely the pancakes.'

Stone looked bemused. 'You know the menu off by heart?'

'I've had a lot of hangovers in this place,' I said fondly.

Ajay grinned. 'I'm a fan of the Mighty Moose.' He gestured to a waitress who was standing by and put in our orders. Then he said, 'So, what's up? You need a favour?'

'I need an audience with Lord Cathill. Today.'

Ajay blinked. 'Sure – and the moon and stars, while you're at it?'

'It's important. We're tracking a Common girl. She's inadvertently got involved with the Volderiss clan. Someone broke into her flat and rifled through her things. Now she's missing.'

'And Volderiss fingered Cathill,' Ajay said flatly. 'Of course he did. If it rains, it's Cathill's fault.'

'Apparently the girl might be safe and sound in the Lake District with Nathaniel Volderiss, but Lady Seer Harding said the girl was in danger and that she was between realms. Something else is going on. Cathill may know what.'

Ajay raised a sardonic eyebrow. 'And what? You're going to ask nicely if he's involved?'

Stone nodded. 'Yeah. Jinx is a truth seeker.'

'You just said to keep it quiet!' I protested.

Stone shrugged. 'You can trust Ajay.' *True.*

Ajay looked at me with renewed interest. 'That's a rare talent these days.'

'I've always had it.'

He blinked. 'Even in the Common?'

Oops. I flicked my eyes to Stone. 'You can trust Ajay,' he assured me again. 'He's the football baker.'

I grinned. 'How many footballs did you cook?'

Ajay groaned. 'One! I cooked one football and that's all I've heard about for the last twenty years.'

'Stone said you had a late introduction?'

Ajay nodded. 'Yeah. My dad was a wizard, my mum was Common. My dad decided it would be too hard for me to keep it from my mum at a young age, so he didn't introduce me to the realm until I was sixteen.'

I blinked. That wasn't late. Twenty-five was late! 'Did you want to be an inspector right away?'

'From the get-go,' he confirmed. 'Dad was disappointed because he was from the healing sect, and he wanted me to follow in his footsteps. I think he's accepted it a little more now. My mum is a doctor as well, and they expected me to be medical. But I just don't get excited about melding pieces of skin together. Tearing it apart is a lot more fun.'

I laughed. 'Are all inspectors as bloodthirsty as you two?'

Ajay shrugged. 'You can't be backwards about coming forwards. Being an enforcer in the Other is tough. One wrong move and you're a dead man. Act fast, think later.'

I thought of the vampyr who had come at me in Volderiss's offices and nodded. 'Sure.'

Ajay's gaze sharpened. 'So you can truth seek even in the Common?' I nodded. 'Can you compel in the Common?' I nodded again. He let out a low whistle. 'Watch out, Other realm – Jinx is in the house. I can't wait to see what you bring about. I can see why Stone's riding with you. He's normally a lone wolf.'

'I'm thinking about expanding my pack,' Stone said, not looking at me.

I felt a massive smile creep across my face. Just then, the waitress arrived with our food and drinks. I thanked her happily and took a good pull of my milkshake. I passed it to Stone. 'Try this. Honestly, it's great.'

He took a small slurp and grimaced. 'That is pure

sugar.'

'I know! Isn't it fab?'

Stone shook his head. 'You should be obese.'

I stuck my tongue out at him.

Ajay got out his phone and tapped a message before he dug into his Mighty Moose potato hash on granary bread with fried eggs and bacon. Yum. My pancakes were amazing, but I still had food envy. We ate while Stone sipped his black coffee.

Once I'd finished eating, Stone left to use the bathroom and I took advantage of the moment alone with Ajay. 'I know Stone trusts you, but I don't know you. Will you give me your oath that you'll keep my truth-seeking abilities to yourself?'

Ajay nodded. 'I'm Stone's man, if he trusts you, I trust you. I give you my oath. As we will it, so shall it be.' *True.*

I blinked. 'No ripping into your veins and spilling vast amounts of blood?'

Ajay grinned. 'Wizard oaths are a little lower key, but no less binding.'

I nodded and took a slow slurp of my milkshake as Stone returned to the table. No sooner had he sat down than Ajay's phone beeped. He read the message and grimaced. 'We've got to move.' He pulled out his wallet and flung some notes on the table.

As we made a hasty exit, he said, 'Lord Cathill will see

you now. His car will be coming down Dale Street. You have two minutes.'

My instincts were shouting at me and I'd learned to listen. I shrugged out of my black suit jacket, unbuttoned a few of my shirt buttons and released my hair. I pulled some lipstick out of pocket and applied it hastily.

Gato stood as we exited the café and came to greet me. 'Send me to the Common,' I ordered. I bent low and he touched his head to my forehead. Bam. Now I looked like I was Common – or at least Cathill wouldn't see the two triangles and know I was working for the Connection. He wouldn't suspect that I could truth seek from the Common. I hoped he would underestimate me.

Gato was sniffing at Ajay. 'This is Ajay,' I told him.

I handed Ajay my suit jacket and turned to Stone. 'I'm going to claim to be an antiques dealer trying to get a hold of Volderiss's elf dagger. If we only have two minutes, we need to get straight to the heart of the issue. You pretend to be my security.'

Stone nodded easily; he knew how to roll with a plan.

Ajay grinned at me. 'You're bonded to a hell hound.' He nodded at Gato. 'Of course you are.'

'This is Gato,' I introduced him.

'You do look like a big cat,' Ajay commented. Gato let out a low growl. 'Dog!' Ajay said, holding up his hands. 'Massive, manly hound.' Gato wagged.

Ajay shook his head. 'Leave the hound with me. He's

not going to fit in the car.' He thought about it then added, 'Well, he might fit in the car but I'm not sure Cathill would want him to. Here it is – here's the car.'

'Gato, stay with Ajay. I'll be back in a minute.' Ajay walked away before the car pulled in, with Gato at his heels.

A black, brand-new Mercedes Benz Mayback S650 Pullman pulled up. I let out a whistle. 'Oh boy. Look at that beaut.'

Stone opened the back door of the car and climbed in. The man inside was dressed in jeans and a casual shirt; he looked a little like Heath Ledger but with longer surfer-dude hair. He had three triangles on his head and a circle around them. It was hard to imagine this guy as a big scary vampyr – he was seriously hot!

The Mayback had two rows of seats facing each other in the back of the car. I climbed in next to Stone, opposite Cathill, and shut the door. The moment we sat down, the car started to move.

'Hello, beautiful,' Cathill greeted me, ignoring Stone. 'What's your name?'

I wanted to say, 'My name is Fuck Off,' but I corralled my snarky instincts and aimed for friendly instead. 'I'm Jinx,' I said warmly.

He beamed. 'I'm sure you're nothing but good luck.'

I smiled back. 'To my friends,' I agreed. 'But not to my enemies.' Damn, that snark had slipped out.

'I'll make sure to be the former.' *Lie.*

Well, that sucked. We'd only just met and he'd already decided we were enemies? Did that mean he knew who I was? If so, how? And he was so yummy looking, too. Dammit – why were the yummy ones always gay, taken or homicidal vampyrs? All right, the gloves were off. 'I'm looking for two things. One is a friend of mine, Hester Sorrell. Have you heard of her?'

'No, sorry, my love.' *Lie.* Smarm oozed out of Cathill's every pore.

I kept my smile with some effort. 'She's friends with Nathaniel Volderiss – and I'm sure you know him.'

Cathill lost his smile. 'I know him. Insolent little ankle biter.'

'Have you seen him in the last day or two?'

'No,' he said shortly. *Lie.*

Oh Cathill, you are in it to your eyeballs, I thought. If only I knew what *it* was.

'Nate – erm – Nathaniel, I mean,' I was doing my best clueless-blonde routine, 'said he had a priceless dagger to sell me? It's elven, you see, and they're pretty hard to come by. I just need to touch base with him. One of the vampyrs I spoke to said he saw you talking to Nate the other day. He didn't sell you the dagger first, did he?'

'I don't know anything about a dagger,' he reassured me. *Lie.*

I pouted. 'You don't have it? Because I will totally buy

it off you. I have a very interested buyer.'

'No,' he said firmly, 'I don't have the dagger.' It was the first true thing he had said.

'Oh, man. And you don't know where I can find Nate or Hester?'

'No,' he repeated. *Lie.*

Cathill knocked on the roof of the car and it pulled over. 'Sorry,' he said insincerely. 'I have a call to make now.' Well, another truth. He turned to Stone. 'What's your interest in this matter, Inspector Stone?'

'Just providing some security to Ms Jinx.' *Lie.*

Cathill's eyes were still wary. 'Good day, Inspector Stone. Jinx.'

I gave a finger wave. 'Such a pleasure to meet you,' I lied with a smile.

'And you.' *Lie.*

Stone and I climbed out of the car and watched it head towards St George's Hall. We'd been dropped by St John's Gardens. 'Well,' I said to Stone. 'He is a big fat liar.'

CHAPTER 14

S TONE RANG AJAY, who said he'd meet us in the Gardens. Then Stone suggested, 'Let's debrief before he joins us.'

'I thought you said you trusted him,' I said, surprised and a little alarmed.

'I do, with my life, but the fewer people involved in this investigation the better. I don't want to put Ajay in an awkward position. Cathill has got cops and inspectors and politicians in his pocket. Let's keep it all between us for now.'

I shrugged 'Your friend, your call. Cathill was lying when he said he didn't know Hester. He was lying when he said he didn't know where Hes and Nate are and that he hadn't seen them in the last day or two. He was lying when he said he didn't know about the dagger. About the only truth was that he didn't *have* the dagger. But here's the kicker. You know I said whoever searched Hester's room was full of rage? Cathill felt just like that. I only caught the edges of it because it's a lot harder in the Common, but I've never felt rage like it. What's he got to be so angry about? He's head of a vampyr clan and the vampyr member in the Symposium!'

Stone's eyes narrowed. 'He might have meddled in areas he shouldn't have.'

'What do you mean?' I asked.

I could see Stone debating whether to answer me. 'Daemons,' he said. 'He might have summoned a daemon. Once summoned, they share your body until either you cast them out or they cast you out. Until then, you're locked in a battle for your lives.'

'Why would anyone summon a daemon when that's their potential fate?'

'Desperate people do desperate things. Cathill only just won the election, and his win was a surprise. Maybe he had some daemon help. On the day of the election, many people couldn't explain why they voted for him. At Volderiss's request, we investigated tampering, but there were no indications of a compelling or a clearing of anyone's mind. But a daemon can slide in and out without leaving a trace. They're rarely summoned because the price is too high.'

'Your body?'

Stone nodded. 'And your soul.'

I swallowed. 'Is Cathill still in that body?'

Stone shrugged. 'I don't know. If we're right, after two years who knows where the daemon starts and Cathill ends?'

I saw Ajay and Gato coming towards us and gave a friendly wave. Gato leapt towards me, licking me and jumping up. He touched his nose to my head and boom: the sky was lilac and the grass was turquoise. I'd kind of missed it; I guess I was getting used to life in the Other. 'Good cover,' I praised Gato. He leapt down and wagged his tail. 'Thanks, pup.'

Ajay joined us. 'I hope you got what you needed.'

I shrugged. 'Hard to say what we got, but it was helpful. Thanks.'

He waved it away. 'No problem. I'm sorry but I've got to go. There's been a disturbance on Bold Street. I need to do some clearing.'

'Need help?' Stone offered.

'Nah, I know you're on a trail. Get to it before it goes cold.' Ajay smiled at me. 'I'm sure I'll meet you again, Jinx.'

'I hope so,' I said warmly. 'Thanks for watching Gato.'

'I'm pretty sure he was watching me!'

'One of your creatures touched base with me,' Stone said to Ajay, 'The Prime. Said he has news for you.'

Ajay nodded. 'Cheers. I'll reach out.'

Stone nodded, then he hesitated. 'Any rumblings about trolls? I saw at least eleven last night, all on Church Street.' Church Street is one of the main arteries running through the heart of Liverpool. Whatever the deal was with these trolls, they weren't being subtle about it.

Ajay raised an eyebrow. 'That's odd. You normally see one or two off the path, but not that many. I haven't heard anything about the trolls, but I'll do some digging. I'll get Elvira on it.'

Stone's face tightened at the name, but he didn't object. Ajay waved goodbye and broke into a light jog. In a moment he was gone – I mean, blink and he was gone, superman fast. 'Woah!' I said to Stone. 'Where did he go?'

Stone avoided my eyes, but I saw him clench his jaw. He wasn't impressed with Ajay's display, whatever it was. 'Let's head back to the chapterhouse,' he suggested, changing the subject.

Hmm. Okay, so he didn't want to tell me. That was fine. I was a private investigator; sooner or later I'd find out the truth. I appreciated that he hadn't lied to me, though. 'You can just tell me you can't say,' I said uncomfortably.

'I can't say,' he replied softly. 'Sorry.'

I bumped him gently. 'No problem. We all have secrets, and sometimes they're not our own.'

Stone smiled gratefully. 'Yeah, something like that.'

We went back to the chapterhouse and up to my room. 'The way I see it,' I said, 'we have two avenues of investigation left. We can try to speak to the elves to see what's so special about this dagger. That might lead us to who is tracking Nate and Hes. Or we can go to the DZ in the Lakes and try to find Nate and Hes ourselves.'

'I agree. Let's do the latter and follow the people.'

That was my preference too. It was just before twelve. I picked up my phone and rang the DZ. No answer. Most DZs are closed through the week and open on Friday afternoon or evening. It would only take a little under two hours to get to Skydive North West. I brought up their website but it didn't show their Friday opening times. We'd just have to roll the dice. The worst-case scenario was that we'd have to wait a couple of hours to see someone, but missing persons' cases are all about timing. As time moved on, the likelihood of us finding Hester alive decreased.

We packed our bags and left. As we walked towards Stone's car in the garage, a woman dressed in a black suit and white shirt, which looked painted on, stepped out. She was wearing ridiculously high heels. Her skin tone was Mediterranean, her dark hair was swept up, and her eyes were expertly outlined in black kohl. She was beautiful and she had three triangles on her forehead. The Other was really going to give me an inferiority complex if I kept seeing beings who looked like her. Her nose had the tiniest kink in it, so I was fairly sure she wasn't a vampyr. Kink or not, I'd never felt more plain-Jane.

'Zach,' she greeted Stone warmly. She appraised me with a quick flick of her eyes, lips pursed. 'A new partner? I thought you weren't allowed to train anyone anymore?'

'I *chose* not to partner up. Now I choose to do so.'

'With her?' she said disdainfully. 'Is it because she lets you use her hound?'

'No,' Stone said shortly. *True*, thank goodness. I'd had a moment of fear that I was about to find out an ugly truth.

He skirted around her and unlocked his car. He put our bags in the back and opened the boot for Gato. Gato let out a horrific fart. 'Better out than in,' I commented.

'Better out of the car than in,' Stone corrected.

I followed his lead, ignored the Spanish princess and climbed into the passenger seat. Stone started up the engine, and I plugged the DZ address into the GPS. As we drove out of the secret underground parking space, Kohl Eyes watched us leave. 'So,' I said brightly. 'An ex?'

'Something like that,' Stone admitted.

I waited a good five minutes before he slid me a glance and relented. 'My family wanted me to marry Elvira. I said no. That wasn't well received by my family, or Elvira.'

'Like an arranged marriage?'

'Like an arranged marriage.'

'Man, that's not cool. We're in the twenty-first century. Who does that?'

'It's fairly commonplace in the Other. If you want to maximise your chances of your children being Other, you want to breed true. The seers help predict the best matches.'

'What about love?' I knew the question was naïve, even as I asked it. But my parents had loved each other; that had been a constant part of my childhood, and I'd always wanted to find a love like theirs.

'Apparently, I would grow to love her,' Stone said drily.

'It could happen.'

'No, it couldn't.' He reached over and turned on the radio, so I guessed he didn't want to talk any more. I really didn't blame him – and I wondered if he even knew that the last thing he'd said was a lie.

I decided to use the journey to do some chores. I emailed a few clients from my phone. There was a service request that was time sensitive; I declined, explaining I was on a case out of town, but sent them details of another PI firm that I was friendly with.

I turned down the music a little and rang the Sorrells. I wasn't sure how much I could update them without mentioning the Other, but I needn't have worried because Jackson answered the call and told me he would take a message. I explained that Hester had been seen during the early hours of Tuesday morning with a 'friend', and that we were travelling to their last-known destination. I would call later when I knew more. I rang off and cast a sidelong glance at Stone. 'You want to talk about it?' I offered. 'You're stewing.'

He opened his mouth to deny it and closed it again with a snap. I guess hanging out with a truth seeker can be really annoying at times. Then he sighed. 'Elvira is supposed to be working in Scotland, so it was surprising to see her in Liverpool. I'm concerned my father arranged for me to run into her, and that he hasn't given up on the pairing.'

'This isn't what you want to hear, but at least your father is alive and he cares enough to interfere in your love life. Silver linings, and all that.'

'Sorry,' Stone said shortly.

'Don't be sorry. Just because my parents are dead, doesn't mean you can't bitch about yours. I'm merely saying there are worse problems. Just keep saying no. Your dad will get the picture one day.'

'You'd think,' Stone agreed drily.

'How long has it been?'

'Twenty-two years.'

'Twenty-two years?! Holy hell. Okay, that changes things. You need to tell your dad to fuck off.'

Stone barked a laugh. 'I can't wait for you to meet him. He's not going to know what to do with you.'

'Most people go for adoration.'

'You're good with people,' Stone agreed. 'So why such a small pack?'

It was a heavy question. 'I always knew I was different. No one else could tell if people were lying or telling the truth. As soon as I could talk, my parents told me that I needed to keep that piece of myself hidden. I grew up being warned not to trust anyone, and that message was reinforced by the number of times I heard people lie to me, about me and for me. People lie all the time, and it gets wearing after a while. The fewer people you love, the less hurt you experience when they eventually lie to you. Now I know that my parents were inspectors – that they were Other – I realise how carefully they phrased things around me. They didn't lie to me, but they gave the truth a damned fine makeover. I could always tell they were keeping something from me.'

I cleared my throat. I hadn't meant to be so honest. 'Anyway, it's easier having fewer people in your pack. You, Gato and Lucy. That's enough for me.'

Stone reached across, laced his fingers with mine and rested our joined hands on the gear stick. It was only then that I realised I'd told him he was a part of my pack. If my hand had been free, I would have done a facepalm. Way to play it cool, Jinx.

CHAPTER 15

T HE SATNAV TOLD us we were nearly there. We were surrounded by rolling field after rolling field. The mountains stood proudly in the distance, the essence of the Lake District for me. I'd climbed them all with my parents at one time or another.

I had only jumped at Skydive North West once or twice, but the beauty of its location from the air had stuck with me. I had jumped in Portugal and Spain, but the Lakes were still one of the most picturesque places I'd seen.

Stone slowed the car and turned left onto a road that had so many potholes he had to swerve around like he was in slalom. I breathed a sigh of relief as we rounded the corner and saw a row of cars. The DZ was busy. Skydive North West often had its own weather system, different to the surrounding area, but, for once, we were being treated to mild October weather with blue skies and low winds. There wasn't a cloud in the sky – good jumping weather. The old excitement thrummed through me.

Stone parked and released my hand.

'I figure we act like I'm here for a jump, then we can snoop around a bit under the radar?' I suggested, already missing his touch.

Stone grinned. 'Great minds think alike. I had the same idea.'

'Cool.' I beamed – I was going jumping! I hopped out of the car, opened the boot for Gato and let him stretch his legs. Then I grabbed some jeans and a T-shirt from my duffel. I wasn't going skydiving in my suit. 'I'll get changed in the toilet cubicle.'

'I'll meet you in the office.' Stone handed me the car keys.

It didn't take me long to change. The toilet facilities were clean but basic, and I didn't want to linger in them. I dumped my suit back in the car and locked it.

Stone was in the office with a woman I vaguely remembered from last time. She looked up as I walked in. 'You've a familiar face. Have you jumped here before?' She was a salt-and-pepper brunette in her fifties, and she looked warm and friendly. Her face was creased with laughter lines. I felt sure her name began with an S – Susan, maybe?

'Yeah. I'm Jinx. I've been here before, but it's a long while since I've had my knees in the breeze.'

'Is your BCPA licence still current?'

I shook my head. 'Nope, you're going to have to sign

me up.'

She pulled out some papers. 'Sure thing. I'm Sarah and I run the DZ. If you have any questions, you find me. Our CCI is Chris. You'll find him out front with a hat on and some bright trousers. Will you be hiring a rig?'

I nodded. 'I used to jump a 160, but to get back into it, I guess a 180. Plus, I've put weight on, so my wing load has probably changed.'

She eyeballed me. 'You'd be fine on a 160, but 180 would be a good idea considering it's been a while. How long?'

'Four years.'

She shrugged. 'We'll get you a refresher course, but it's like riding a bike – you don't forget.'

'Look! Locate! Peel! Pull! Punch! Recover! No, you don't forget.'

She gave me a thumbs up. 'How many jumps under your belt?'

'Two hundred and twenty-one.'

We completed the paperwork, including purchasing my BCPA license, which came with one million pounds of insurance cover. 'Can I hire a jumpsuit too? Preferably one with booties?' I asked.

'No problem. Just get your name on the manifest, and we'll get you sorted. Speak to Chris for the retrain.'

'I'm here because I bumped into Nate Volderiss at a club in Liverpool. He inspired me to start jumping again.'

She smiled. 'Nate is so passionate. We're so lucky to be linked to such an active university like Liverpool. The skydiving community is really growing. I'm glad Nate touched base with you.'

'Is he here?' I asked. 'He said he would be.'

'I haven't seen him, but it wouldn't surprise me. He's usually here if the weather is good, though sometimes the students come up later on Fridays after lectures. I'm sure you'll see him tomorrow if you're sticking around.' All true. She hadn't seen him. I felt a tendril of worry for him and Hes. If they weren't here, where were they?

'Doesn't he have a caravan here?' Stone asked. 'I'll pop a note under the door.'

Sarah nodded. 'Yes, he does. Someone can show it to you after Jinx's jump if you want to check in with him, though obviously we can't let you inside it.'

We left the office and jotted my name down on the lift manifest chalkboard. The old excitement was buzzing through me. The airplane was on the runway, and the jumpers were walking across the field. I watched enviously as they climbed in the PAC. It was a top-of-the-range specialist skydiving airplane and had been new to the DZ when I'd jumped here last. It went effortlessly up to 15,000 feet.

The plane took off and I watched it circle and climb. It was only a few minutes before I saw the wind drift indicator – the WDI – being thrown out. It was the first lift of the day, so they were checking the uppers before the first lift jumped. Thirty seconds later, the jumpers started to leave the plane. They were in the sky a minute or two before their canopies started opening. Man, it was so cool.

Stone was watching me. 'Better than sex?' he asked curiously.

I felt my cheeks warm. 'Not quite.' I considered his words. 'Close, but not quite.'

Stone laughed. 'Thank goodness.'

I was called over by the CCI – the Club Chief Instructor – Chris. He had a strict, no-nonsense approach, which I appreciated. He ran through the recovery drills, we discussed my exit from the plane and did a few practices out of the mock-up. I was feeling confident and excited, though there were a few nerves thrown into the mix too.

I pulled on my hired jumpsuit and checked the fit of the booties, then grabbed the rig and pulled it on. After I'd secured my leg and chest straps, Chris checked me over. He told me my AAD – Automatic Activation Device – was a cypress that would fire at 1,600 feet. That meant my reserve parachute would fire automatically at 1,600 feet if I was still falling. He told me to pull at 3,500 feet, as it had been a while since I'd jumped. He gave me an altimeter, which I secured and checked; it was set at 0. I put on my goggles and my helmet, and he handed me a hook knife to use if I had a line over. I secured it to my chest strap. Once I was fully geared up, Chris checked me over again. When he patted my back, I knew I was good to go.

As I joined the other skydivers waiting to jump, I made small talk about Hes and Nate. No one knew Hes, but everyone knew Nate; he was everyone's best friend, passionate about skydiving and charitable work, and he liked to combine the two. He often donated blood and encouraged others to do so. Some of them spoke about him like he was the second coming. I wondered what they'd say if they knew what I did about him.

I wondered what kind of man – or vampyr – Nate really was. I'd assumed he was amoral because he was using humans as a food source, but everyone spoke so kindly about him. No one was lying; he was genuinely liked. Maybe there was more going on than appearances suggested. I hoped so, for Hes's sake.

The PAC landed and the chatter stopped as we headed for the runway. I waved to Gato and Stone. Gato had been gambolling around with the DZ dogs, but he started to bark as he watched me walk away. It was his 'something is wrong' bark. I figured he didn't want Mummy jumping out of the plane. I'd bought him after I'd stopped jumping, so this wasn't something he'd seen before. I waved, trying to reassure him, then climbed into the plane and sat down.

The plane had a great sound system and rock music

blared out at us as we started rumbling down the runway. 'Okay?' the jumpmaster asked me. I was at the front, first out.

I beamed. 'Psyched!'

He gave me a fist bump. 'Enjoy it!'

The plane climbed and the small light by the door turned from red to green. As the jumpmaster pulled the door up and open, the cold air at 15,000 feet rushed in. My tummy was churning with excitement and nerves. I sat in the doorway, chin up, legs dangling, and then I did the most counter-intuitive thing – I pushed myself out of a perfectly working plane.

The wind took my breath away as I started to fall. I arched my body, pushing my pelvis forwards and my chin up, and waited to level out. It only took a few seconds – an eternity in free fall – but then I was stable.

I checked my altimeter: 14,500 feet. Okay, time to check the basics. I dropped my right shoulder, slowly turned to the right and checked my altimeter again. After I'd done a complete turn, I dropped my left shoulder and did a left turn and checked my altimeter. Feeling confident, I decided to do some flips. I brought my knees sharply to my chest, did a back flip, arched my body and regained stability. I checked my altimeter yet again. I was at 7000 feet. I decided to do some tracking before pulling, then I'd pull early and enjoy the canopy ride.

I straightened my arms and legs and tracked across

the sky away from the DZ. I'd have time under canopy to fly back because the winds were in my favour. At 4000 feet I waved off in case anyone was around me, then reached behind with my right arm and pulled my parachute. I waited for the usual jerking as the descent suddenly slowed. Nothing happened. I looked up – my main parachute was floating off. The lines had been cut and it wasn't attached to me. *Shit*. Someone had sabotaged my rig.

I couldn't imagine that someone would go to the effort of cutting the main and not screw the reserve parachute, but, nevertheless, I ran through the reserve drill. Look, locate, peel, punch, pull. Recover.

I pulled the handle that opened my reserve canopy. Nothing. No parachute. I wasn't sure what was wrong. My AAD *might* fire at 1,600 feet, but I couldn't rely on it; the saboteur had done a good job so far. If they'd turned off the AAD, I was on my own.

I checked the altimeter – 3,000 feet. I had time. It was a coastal DZ, so I turned and tracked towards the sea.

I tracked and tracked, not checking my altimeter because every second might count. The world was coming up fast; I was having ground rush. Every nerve screamed at me to pull my reserve parachute again, but I kept tracking. I must be at 1,000 feet now and my AAD hadn't fired.

I kept going. I was over the water, twelve feet in depth

or more, so I might survive. But I had a trick up my sleeves. Now I had two elements to work with: air and water. I prayed I had an affinity with one or the other, or I was going to slam into the sea as if it were concrete. I was falling at 118 mph, terminal velocity.

I gathered my intention. I wanted the air to thicken and solidify. I blew out a breath. 'Thicken!' I ordered sharply.

The air around me obeyed. My descent was too fast for it to stop me completely, but it slowed me dramatically. By the time I struck the water it was like I was moving at the speed of jumping into a swimming pool. I had a moment's relief that I was alive.

My next challenge was the weight of the rig on my back as I started to swim towards the shore. It was becoming saturated, getting heavier and heavier, and I'd have to take it off. I took a deep breath and dropped under the water's surface. I fumbled with the leg straps; my fingers were cold, and the water had made the straps slippery.

The knife! I grabbed my hook knife and cut the chest and leg straps. Released from the rig, I swam to the surface. I gasped a few relieved breaths and gave myself another moment to be grateful that I was still alive. A moment was all I allowed myself – I wasn't out of the woods yet. I started swimming to shore again. I needed to keep moving or I'd freeze up. A black Range Rover was roaring down the beach towards me.

Something bobbed up next to me. I turned to look. It was a merman. Of course it was.

If I'd had any energy left to be shocked I would have been, but I was all out of shock. His skin was so pale it was almost translucent, and his hair was nearly as long as mine but a dark, vibrant green. He had bright-blue scales from the waist down that matched his eyes. His shoulders were broad, his hips narrow, and his muscles had muscles. 'Hey,' I greeted him causally.

The merman smiled. 'Hey. Are you okay? That was a dramatic landing.'

'I'm all about making an entrance,' I joked.

The adrenaline was leaving me and I was starting to experience shock. 'Can you help me to the shore? I'm getting tired.' I had no idea if mermen were friend or foe, but I could really use a hand – or a tail.

'Sure,' he said. 'I'm Jack Fairglass.'

'My honour to meet you, Jack. I'm Jinx.'

'My honour to meet you, Jinx. Lie on your back.'

I flipped over and he carefully put an arm around my head and started towing me in a classic lifeguard move. I relaxed as we moved through the waves quickly and easily. After a long minute, he slowed. 'You should be able to stand now, Jinx.'

Sure enough, I reached down and felt sand under my feet. I'd never been happier. 'So,' I said, 'what brings you to the Irish Sea?'

He grinned. 'You're pretty unflappable, you know that?'

'It was my most exciting skydive so far, but I was hoping I'd be able to use air or water to save me.'

He gave me an incredulous look. 'You didn't know if you could prime air or water?'

'No, but it seemed like a good time to find out. I'm new to the Other.'

'How new?' Jack asked.

I considered. 'About thirty hours, I guess.'

He threw back his head and laughed. 'Sweetheart, you're something else. Well, just so you know, mermen don't officially exist.' He was tracking Stone's progress down the beach. 'I'd better go. The cavalry's here. Nice to meet you, Jinx.'

'Thanks for saving me, Jack – even if you don't officially exist.'

He waved off my thanks. 'You'd already saved yourself. I just gave you a ride. My honour to meet you, Jinx. You take care.'

'You too,' I called as he moved away. He gave me another friendly wave before he dived into the sea and disappeared.

I started wading on to land. The Range Rover came to a stop close to me and Stone leapt out. Gato charged out too. 'Hey, guys,' I called out. 'I'm a bit wet.'

There was relief on Stone's face. 'If you fancied going for a swim, you should have said.'

'You want to join me? The water's not too bad.' I wasn't lying; the sea was pretty warm, although the air was biting. It was mild for October, but it was still too cold to be soaking wet.

Gato ran into the water to greet me and barked at me reproachfully. 'Next time I'll listen when you tell me something's wrong,' I promised, stroking him. He huffed but gave me a lick – I guess he'd forgiven me. We walked out of the water together. Stone had grabbed a towel from his sports bag and he wrapped it round me, hugging me close. His warmth soaked through to me. 'That was a bit scary,' I offered.

'I'm going to have nightmares for a week.'

I stayed in his arms enjoying the feeling of safety. 'You give good hugs,' I murmured into the crook of his neck.

His arms tightened around me. 'It's listed as part of my skill set on my CV.' That buzzed as a lie, which made me smile. Imagine if it were actually in his skill set!

I was still smiling into his neck when I remembered abruptly that everyone at the drop zone had seen my skydive. Chris, the CCI, would have been watching my progress through binoculars. I grimaced. 'You're going to have to do some mind clearing. We'll say my main had a line over so I cut away, then got fixated on the sea under my reserve canopy. It happens.'

Stone nodded. He was rubbing my back, trying to warm me. 'I'm okay,' I reassured him.

He didn't stop hugging me. 'Someone tried to kill you,' he pointed out levelly.

'Yeah. We must be doing something right.'

CHAPTER 16

I DUG OUT some fresh clothes from my duffel and used the car door as a changing-room shield while Stone pointedly faced in the other direction. 'All done,' I called.

I didn't mention Jack to Stone. Jack had said merman didn't officially exist and I didn't want to sound crazy; also, Jack had helped me, and I wasn't going to betray his trust if they wanted to remain hidden. I trusted Stone completely, but I understand about keeping secrets. Stone definitely had some, and I've spent my whole life protecting mine.

'Can you do a group mind clearing, or will it have to be one by one?' I asked.

'I can do a mass one. It's a good thing we recharged last night.'

After I'd rubbed Gato down, we climbed into Stone's car and returned to the DZ. As we got out, everyone rushed towards me. As Stone grabbed me with one hand and held up the other, they all froze, statue-still. I felt power whip around me, but it didn't touch me.

'Clear,' Stone intoned. Only one person didn't freeze:

a man. He saw that I'd noticed and started running. There was a flare of light, everyone was released and Stone took off after the guy. I decided it would be best if I stayed and faced the music.

'Are you all right?' Chris asked, rubbing his eyes and looking a little dazed.

I nodded. 'I got a line over, so I cut away the main. Then I guess I got fixated on the sea. I flew right into it.'

'It happens,' Sarah reassured me. 'How are you feeling?'

'Fine – but I lost the rig. I'm so sorry.'

She shrugged. 'That's what insurance is for.' She gave me a one-armed hug. 'Was it your first cut away?'

I nodded. 'Yup.'

'You know what that means, right?'

I smiled ruefully. 'A beer fine.' A crate should do it, but maybe two would help the investigation get underway a little more easily. Alcohol lowers inhibitions, which is always handy when interrogating – sorry, *interviewing* people.

'You want to do a hop 'n' pop?'

'Yeah. I need to get back on the horse.'

The crowd cheered. While Stone was still chasing the suspect, I geared up for another jump. Various skydivers agreed to jump again so another lift could be put together for me, and I realised how much I'd missed the community feeling of the sport. The sun was dipping and the light was fading. Time for the sunset lift.

I watched my rig being packed. Gato was by my side and he seemed happy for me to jump again. No sabotage this time. Stone appeared. 'You're jumping again?' he said incredulously. 'You nearly died!'

'I watched this rig being packed and I know it's safe. Gato's happy for me to go. I'm only doing a hop 'n' pop.'

Stone rubbed a hand over his eyes. I could tell he thought I was nuts. 'A hop 'n' pop?

'I jump at 5000 feet instead of 15,000 feet, then pull high and have a canopy ride. It's just to get my knees in the breeze again so the last jump I have isn't a nightmare.'

He shook his head. 'I don't think I can watch.'

I followed the others and we climbed in the plane with the same jumpmaster as last time. 'You okay?' he asked.

'I'm not as psyched this time round but I'm steady.'

He nodded. 'Don't fly into the sea this time.'

'Thanks,' I said drily. 'I'll bear that in mind.'

The jumpmaster gave me a cocky grin and shut the door. The plane's engine roared. When it stabilised at 5000 feet, the jumpmaster opened the door. He gave me a fist bump. 'Smash it,' he instructed.

I felt more confident this time and dived out head first. I enjoyed the fall, did a flip, then I banged out an arch and stabilised. I checked my altimeter: 4000 feet. I gave it another few seconds then waved off and pulled.

This time the canopy opened above me, big, rectangular and beautiful. I checked it. All the cells were open, the slider was down, there were no line overs. I was good to go. I pulled down the toggles and started to steer. The view was stunning even in the waning light.

I flew towards the DZ and started to pull on my right toggle, causing me to spiral down. I normally enjoyed a canopy ride, but Stone was feeling anxious about me so I spiralled down, losing height fast. I flared my canopy and landed easily on my feet. I turned and pulled in the parachute, gathering it and tossing it over my shoulder. I walked into the hangar to raucous applause. That jump had been textbook from start to finish.

After I'd removed my rig, suit and helmet, I found Stone leaning against the hangar. 'Okay?' I asked.

'You're nuts,' he said.

'Takes one to know one,' I countered, sticking my tongue out at him.

He shook his head and slung an arm around my shoulders. As we left the others behind, I asked quietly, 'What happened with the runner?'

'The good news is I found your saboteur. The bad news is he was killed before I could get any real information out of him.'

I blinked. 'Jesus, that's a bit extreme.'

'Not by me,' Stone hastened to explain. 'He confessed to sabotaging your rig, but he said that his mistress meant it as a test. She never expected you to die. Before I could ask more, his face turned red and he stopped breathing. He clawed at his throat, but something was blocking his airway.' Stone's jaw clenched with frustration. 'I couldn't work out how to release the binding in time. He died.'

'Not your fault,' I reassured him. 'That one's not on you.'

Stone rubbed his hand through his dark hair. 'I should have drawn a rune on him, but it was all over too quickly. I thought it was a band of air round his throat that I could move.'

'You're not a god. You can't save everyone.'

'Yeah,' he agreed, but I could tell he hadn't let it go.

'What did you do with the body?'

'Nothing. When he died his body shimmered and disappeared.'

I blinked. 'And turned into ash? Like the vampyrs?'

Stone shook his head. 'No ash. He just disappeared.'

'Was he definitely dead?'

'Yeah.'

'Is that normal?'

'It's a new one on me,' he admitted, 'But this realm is something else.'

'You got that right,' I agreed. 'Well, there's no point in crying over spilt milk. We need to buy some beer. The Liverpool students should be arriving soon. When everyone's drunk, we'll break into Nate's caravan.'

We grabbed Gato and drove to a local shop. It was only small but it was well stocked with alcohol; they understood the skydivers' needs. In the packing shed there was a motto on the wall: *My drinking club has a skydiving problem.*

We bought sandwiches and crisps for dinner. The DZ had a café but it was closed on Fridays, so we were fending for ourselves. We hadn't planned where to sleep – we could use the bunk house, which was free, but in my experience bunk houses were small and dank with row after row of bunkbeds, often with amorous students sharing the tiny single mattresses.

There was a Premier Inn with twenty-four-hour reception about fifteen minutes away, which got my vote, and there was always Stone's car. We had options, so we decided to see what the night brought us.

Normally a beer fine was one crate of beer but I bought two. The DZ was busy and I wanted people to start drinking so they'd start talking. To help things along I also bought a crate of white wine. It was all being charged to Lady Sorrell, so I could afford to splash the cash.

As Stone and I ate in the car, we discussed tactics. We'd split up again, lie, flirt –whatever was needed to get us some answers. If Nate wasn't here, I wanted to know where he might be. And had any of these students met Hes? I also planned to dig into the drugs a little more.

Hes and Nate had both been using – was that connected to their disappearance? And was Nate dealing, either to the students or to the vampyrs? Had a deal gone wrong? I didn't feel like the drugs were key, but we needed to explore all avenues.

Stone and I drove back to the DZ and carried our alcohol offerings into the packing shed to loud cheers. The students had arrived. 'Beer fine!' someone hollered and the freeloaders descended. I was the lady of the hour. Everyone had heard about my little incident. As the evening wore on, I grew sick of recounting the sanitised version of the jump. I got a fair amount of friendly ribbing for fixating on the sea. My pride demanded that I tell them what had really happened, but I couldn't. Instead I took the teasing with as much good grace as I could muster, which was none at all.

Everyone was getting drunk. The students were play-ing drinking games, the regulars were sitting off and chatting. The staff and their spouses were mixing with the students. I learned that a few people had met Hes, but none of them appeared to be close friends with her. A lot of the university girls were jealous of her and Nate, but nothing buzzed that the jealousy had gone too far.

There were a few smokers, and a few of them were on the wacky-backy. I targeted them for some answers. I flirted, smiled, giggled and even compelled the odd answer. Nate had been expected on the university minibus but after an hour of waiting they'd decided he was a no-show and left without him. There was no resentment about that; Nate was an easy-going dude – he must have just got lost in the moment. If I'd been stood up like that I'd have been furious, but there was a lot of love for Nate.

Many of the crowd were second- or third-year students and Nate had been on the scene since the beginning. He was a second-year student, but he was doing his *third* degree. I guessed he needed an excuse to stay at the university, and multiple degrees was the answer.

Nate smoked weed but didn't deal. One of the students was a small-time dealer and he sold a bit to Nate and his friends. He was small fry, just a student making an extra buck.

I met Stone's eyes across the room and gestured for us to move out. Sarah had given me directions to Nate's caravan; it was time to see what it held. I was hoping it was a love shack for Nate and Hes and they were in there, lost in each other, but I knew the chances of that were slim. I'd got a vibe from Cathill. I thought I knew where Hes and Nate were, I just wasn't sure if they were still amongst the living.

Stone followed me out, and Gato joined us silently. I'd come prepared. Once again, I was wearing my trusty bum bag complete with lock-picking tools. I needn't have bothered – the caravan was unlocked. Uh-oh. I took out some disposable latex gloves and handed a pair to Stone. Stone took point and opened the door. Gato let out a low growl…

It was a crime scene. The caravan was trashed: it hadn't been meticulously searched, it had been maliciously vandalized. And the worst thing was, I could feel the echo of pure joy reverberating around the place. Whatever – whoever – the searchers had been looking for, they'd found.

CHAPTER 17

N OT ONLY WAS the caravan smashed up but Gato found blood. Reluctantly Stone put in a call and it wasn't long before we were joined by a police officer. He had two triangles on his head; he was part of the cross-over, and worked in the Common police to help smooth things over between the two realms. 'Detective Daniels.' He had a broad Lancashire accent.

'Inspector Stone, Detective Sharp. We're tracking down a missing Common girl and a vampyr. There's blood here. I need to know if it's the girl's or just some lunch.'

I grimaced a little at that. Stone had explained that many vampyrs drank cow or pig blood. If the blood in the caravan was human, the police could work out if it was fresh because donated blood tended to be older. If it was human and fresh, things would look a lot worse for Hes.

Daniels dipped a swab into the bloody residue and put it in a small test tube which held clear liquid. When the swab touched the liquid, it glowed bright white.

Magic. Daniels grimaced. 'Fresh human blood, less than two days old. Because it's so fresh, it's not likely to be donor. Donor blood can be stored and used for up to forty-two days.'

'I need you to secure the scene discreetly,' Stone said. 'We're going to move on this.'

The officer nodded and waved us away. He was calling it in as we left.

Stone rubbed his eyes. 'It's half-past midnight. We can drive back to the chapterhouse or try the Premier Inn.'

'Either way, we need to sleep and recharge,' I said. 'We've both used a lot of energy today. I vote Premier Inn. We can set an early alarm and get moving. I'm too tired to drive far, and I think you are too.'

'I could keep going with some energy drink but, yeah, clearing the group's minds took it out of me. Let's get some sleep. We're already two days behind Nate and Hes, so a few hours' sleep won't make too much difference and we'll be sharper in the morning.'

We went back to the packing shed to say our goodbyes. We didn't want to slink off in the night when tomorrow they would awaken to a crime scene on their DZ. We didn't want to be linked to that.

When we arrived at the hotel, there was a slight hiccup: there was only one room. 'It doesn't matter,' I said wearily. 'I'm shattered. Let's take it.'

At least it was a double bed, but the room was pokey and there was barely enough room for Gato. Still, it was better than the bunkhouse.

We changed and brushed our teeth. Gato portalled us to Common and we tumbled into bed. Gato looked up at us with longing. 'No,' I said firmly. 'You're a floor dog tonight.' He huffed but settled down, looking at me reproachfully to make it clear that he considered his bed barely adequate. I patted his head. 'Sleep well, pup.'

If I hadn't been so tired, it would have been awkward but thankfully I was exhausted. I hadn't had much sleep the previous night, and the adrenaline of my near-death experience, as well as using the IR, had taken it out of me. I closed my eyes. 'Good night, Stone,' I whispered.

'You know, when I'm in bed with a woman she can call me Zach.'

I laughed. 'Good night, Stone.' I repeated.

He let out a breath that might have been a sigh. 'Good night, Jinx. Sleep well.'

I always meditate before sleep, so I cleared my mind and envisaged a beautiful sandy beach stretching out ahead of me. The sound of the ocean washed over me as the waves lapped at the shore. Then I was out like a light.

WHEN MY ALARM woke us, we were wrapped in each

other's arms like pretzels. There was a moment of embarrassment on both sides, then we disentangled and tacitly agreed not to mention it. I tried not to think about the feel of his warm arms around me or his wonderful smell.

We dressed and were in the Other and on the road by 7 a.m. Stone had tapped out a text to Ajay, who had arranged a 9:30am appointment for us with Volderiss. It was easier to make an appointment with a former Symposium member than the current one.

Ajay texted back that he'd touched base with the dragon, Emory, who'd said there was a worrying surge in troll numbers in the city, about a hundred of them. Dragons and trolls don't get on, and it was making Emory edgy. Stone hoped that the dragon was exaggerating; twelve trolls was unusual; hundreds was unheard of.

We grabbed a drive-through Micky D's breakfast and parked at the chapterhouse. I was secretly pleased not to see Elvira or the siren again. As we walked to Exchange Flags, Bertie the Liver Bird was there, looking over the city. Bella was nowhere to be seen. Stone and I inclined our heads to the giant bird, who clacked in response. We walked on towards GV Law.

'I hope you don't have to decapitate more vampyrs today,' I said lightly.

'Probably not. Ajay said Volderiss accepted the appointment very quickly – he's probably realised that Nate really is missing. Vampyrs are a strange society, but they value their "children". As a result of the Verdict, they're only allowed to turn a new vampyr when one of them dies – it's a form of population control. The newly turned vampyr is assigned to a clan and given a family unit. Unusually, Nate is Volderiss's genetic son, born to him when they were both human. They were attacked and turned together in pre-Verdict times. There's nothing Gabriel Volderiss won't do to secure Nate's safe return.'

I filed that piece of vampyr knowledge away in my 'Other' Rolodex, along with 'mermen are real but are pretending not to be', and 'dragons don't like trolls'. 'How are we going to do this?' I asked.

'Carefully. We don't want to start a clan war between Cathill and Volderiss because that would end badly for everyone. When a war breaks out, there's always huge collateral damage. We need Volderiss to accept that we're going to handle it.'

I bit my lip. 'That seems a tall order.'

Stone sighed. 'Yeah.'

'You know, normal missing persons' cases are a lot easier than this. Usually I find them and they don't want their family to know. I report back that they're alive and well, but choosing to cut the family ties. Or I find a dead body. I've never actually had a full-on kidnapping situation before.'

'Something new for you,' said Stone flatly. 'Lucky

you.'

'I can add dealing with kidnappers to my CV,' I said lightly.

'Silver linings.' His tone was dry.

'Should we agree a signal so I can tell you if someone is lying?'

Stone shook his head. 'Vampyrs have heightened senses. Even if we chose even a small signal, it's likely they would notice it. I'll start the questioning and you take over if there's an avenue you want to explore. We'll discuss it afterwards. Volderiss knows about your skills, so pay attention to how you phrase your questions and how he replies. He's had centuries of practice in giving the truth a makeover.'

We entered the headquarters of GV Law. The same exotic receptionist was there. She was biting a nail as we walked in, but she stopped and straightened when she saw us. 'Go right in,' she instructed. She wasn't so cool this time.

We weren't alone with Volderiss; he was sitting behind his mahogany desk with a vampyr on either side of him. One was the brunette we'd seen in Zanzibar, the other was Lord Cathill. The atmosphere was tense. The brunette was folded in on himself, almost rocking back and forth. Every line of his body said he was in pain.

When I'd last met Cathill I was in Common, and I realised now how much it had protected me from him.

I'd felt his anger before, but now I could sense the malice rolling off him in thick, choking waves. I had to remind myself to breathe.

Volderiss glared. 'You requested this meeting. Get it started.'

'Lord Volderiss, we went to your son's caravan in the Lake District,' Stone said. 'It was empty, ransacked like Miss Sorrell's flat. Blood was present at the scene. I believe your son and his girlfriend have been taken captive against their will.'

Volderiss looked at me. 'As I told you last time, I know nothing about that.' *Lie.*

He knew what I was. He wanted us to know he was lying, otherwise he would have been more careful with his response. He was trying to help us. We needed to ask the right questions.

'Has Nate contacted you since you spoke on Wednesday?' Stone asked.

'Yes. We spoke yesterday.' *True.* Well, that was positive; if Nate was alive, I hoped Hes was too.

'Did he mention his girlfriend, Hester Sorrell?'

'Yes,' Volderiss confirmed. 'He said they were together.' *True.*

'You don't believe he is being held against his will?' Stone asked.

'No,' said Volderiss impatiently. *Lie.* He was an accomplished actor; if I hadn't had my internal lie detector

I would have believed him.

Cathill was lounging on the front of the desk, smirking, confident. I felt malevolence pouring from him, giving such a thick stench I could hardly stand being in the same room. His very being was filled with rage and malice. I knew without a doubt that he was blackmailing Volderiss. It was simple: Volderiss was to send us away empty handed or he would kill Nate. But Volderiss knew my skills and was banking on Stone and me being able to do something while he outwardly complied with Cathill's orders.

'I'm glad Nate's okay,' I said. 'But I'm more concerned about his dagger. It wasn't recovered at the scene. Do you have it?'

'Yes,' said Volderiss. 'It's back in our possession.' *True.*

'Can I buy it from you?' I asked.

'No,' he said firmly. *True.*

'Can I see it?' I asked hopefully.

Volderiss smile was flat and unfriendly. 'No,' he repeated. 'It's in our armoury for now.'

'How long will it be there?' I asked. 'Perhaps I can get an offer from my employer that you can't refuse.'

'It will remain there until tomorrow.' *Lie.* 'After that, who knows? No price you can offer will be accepted. It is worth more to me than any amount of money.' *True.*

'Then I want to commission my own dagger. Where

did you get yours from?' I saw a hint of approval in Volderiss's eyes. I was asking the right questions.

'I can't be expected to recall the history of every piece I come across. I believe it was made by Harfen. They called it "Glimmer" or something like that.' *True.* 'It's not an important dagger. I don't know why you're so focused on it.' *Lie.*

I shrugged. 'Stone is hired to find the girl, I've been hired to find the dagger.' I met Cathill's eyes. 'I expect we have the same employer.'

'I don't have an employer,' Cathill spat out, straightening.

'Well, benefactor then – whatever you want to call her,' I replied, gambling.

'Bitch is what I want to call her,' Cathill muttered.

I suppressed a surge of satisfaction. Whoever had sabotaged my parachute was pulling Cathill's strings too. A small, petty part of me hoped it was Elvira.

'If that's all,' said Volderiss, 'I'm a busy man. Cathill and I have much to discuss.' *True.* Damn, we needed to hear this discussion.

I looked at the brunette, Nate's friend. He was clenching and unclenching his hands; his jaw was locked, teeth gritted as if to stop him from crying out in pain. 'What's up with him?' I asked, pointing to him.

'Punishment,' said Volderiss blandly.

I walked up to the mahogany desk and leaned down

next to Volderiss, ostensibly to examine the brunette. In clear view of Volderiss but not of Cathill, I pressed a small round bug to the underside of the desk. 'What did he do?' I asked with relish. 'Did he slice a human?'

'He betrayed his clan,' Volderiss said in hard voice.

'Why isn't he ash?' I asked flippantly.

'Death is quick, this is not. Besides, I may have use for him.'

I nodded, like the casual torture of your troops was totally fine. It wasn't, but the brunette was collateral damage right now. I needed to find Hes and the urgency was zinging through me. I moved back to Stone. 'If you change your mind about selling Glimmer to me, you know where I am.'

Gabriel Volderiss looked at me. 'Indeed I do, Jinx. Indeed I do.' *True.*

Uh-oh.

CHAPTER 18

I HURRIED OUT, pulling Stone with me. Cathill gave us a mocking finger wave as we left. I hauled out my phone and headphones and turned on the app that let me listen to the bug. We ran round the corner and leaned against a building to share the headphones.

'Get out,' Volderiss snarled. We heard the door open and close. Was it the brunette or Cathill who had left? I hoped the former.

'Well,' said Volderiss, 'fun as that was, I fail to see why you had us meet with them.'

'They would have been suspicious if you hadn't met with them,' Cathill replied. 'You must be seen to be co-operating with the Connection. Soon it will be destroyed, but for now it poses a threat that we must be mindful of.'

'I thought your mistress was all-powerful.'

Cathill snorted. 'She is not my mistress!' *Lie.* 'We are a team.' *Lie.* 'Tonight is only the first step of our plan. Together we will bring down the Connection and the Unity, and freedom will be returned to the Other.'

'The Verdict has worked in our favour,' Volderiss

pointed out. 'We have never been wealthier. We can walk about, embrace what we are with no need to hide in the shadows for fear of vampyr hunters.'

'Wealth?' Cathill spat. 'What is wealth when we cannot turn new vampyrs at will? When we cannot drink from the source? Drinking donated blood is an insult to everything we once held true.'

There was a pause. 'You didn't used to believe that,' Volderiss said. 'You were the most vocal supporter of the Verdict. You were sick of the Chaos. We were in danger of agreeing,' he said drily.

'Things change.'

There was a moment of silence. Volderiss broke it. 'I get to choose the location for the handover.'

'You are not in a position to demand anything, Gabriel. Tonight, midnight. St Luke's – the bombed-out church. Bring Glimmer, and we'll give you your son back still undead.' *Lie.*

'The Church will be crawling with inspectors. You know what it holds,' Volderiss hissed.

Cathill laughed. 'We'll deal with the inspectors. You bring Glimmer.'

'What will happen to the Common girl?'

'That is none of your concern. Bring the dagger by midnight or your son will be ashes.'

We heard the door open and close again then Volderiss said, 'I hope that helped you, Jinx. The handover is tonight. You may stand by to try to apprehend Cathill after I have my son back safely. If you interfere, I will kill anyone in my way.' *True.* There was a pause, then there was a high-pitched whine. My app flashed. Volderiss had destroyed the bug.

I gestured for Stone to pass me his phone, googled GV Law and rang the number. I asked to be patched through to Lord Volderiss immediately. 'We have nothing further to discuss.' His strident voice rang out firmly.

'They intend to kill your son. Cathill was lying when he said he would hand him back still undead.'

There was a pause. 'You can use your skills over electronic devices?' Volderiss asked.

'Yes,' I said impatiently. 'What are you going to do about your son?'

'I'm going to rescue him. Good day, Jinx.' He rang off. We were done.

Movement down the street caught my eye and for a moment I thought I saw myself before I realised it was my reflection in the glass of the bus shelter. Man, I was feeling jumpy.

'We need to go to the chapterhouse,' Stone said urgently. I nodded and we started briskly walking back towards the Hard Day's Night. Stone was silent, frowning, gathering his thoughts.

'You okay?' I asked.

He nodded and made an effort to smile at me. 'You can use your empath skills over the phone?' he asked, obviously impressed.

'I can't in the Common, but I guess I can in the Other. That's handy, isn't it?'

'So you can interview people remotely. If we'd known that, we wouldn't have had to go all the way to the Lakes.'

'We needed to look at Nate's caravan and we needed to get people chatting. If we'd cold-called, we'd have been stonewalled. Anyway, we have to go and see this Harfen. Volderiss is throwing us some breadcrumbs.'

'He wants us on board,' Stone noted, 'but not in the way. Leo Harfen is an elf. Giving us his name might be a red herring to send us gallivanting off rather than preparing for the take-down tonight.'

'Maybe, but I don't think so. Volderiss was trying hard to act casual. It's important.'

Stone studied me. 'Well, go with your instincts. I'll call Ajay and update him, and I'm summoning all the inspectors and detectives within a three-hour radius. We're going to need more bodies tonight. Volderiss might think he's running the show, but it's ours now. I'm going to have to report this up the food chain.'

I could see that Stone was struggling with not telling me something. Sometimes being an empath sucks. 'Be careful,' I said urgently. 'We don't know who is involved, or how high it goes. Be careful who you trust.'

He nodded. 'I'll have to report it to the Symposium. There's a lot of people in that, but it can't be avoided. I need the Symposium to authorise full and deadly force to end this threat.'

I shook my head. 'Stone, Cathill is part of the Symposium. It's possible that other members are part of this plot.' My instincts were shouting at me. 'You need to contain this.'

Stone nodded reluctantly; I guess he didn't like the thought that the Symposium couldn't be trusted. 'I'll report to the wizard member. We'll need a quorum of five members to authorise an operation like this, and to agree to keep it from the Symposium. I don't like it, but you're right – we can't assume Cathill is the only one compromised. Jinx, we're going to have to split up. You take my car. Visit Leo Harfen then meet me back at the chapterhouse.' He wrote down the Elves' address. I was off to Caldy – they were rich Wirral squirrels.

Stone chucked me his keys and his leather-covered inspector's ID. 'Use this on the toll booth, it's like a fast pass. Make sure you drive in a fast-pass lane.' As Gato and I set off towards the underground garage, he called 'Jinx!' I turned to look back him. He hesitated. 'Be careful.'

'You too,' I replied, smiling reassuringly. Stone disappeared, with only one more hesitant glance backwards. I knew how he felt. We'd been stuck together like glue for the past two days, and I felt wary about splitting up, too. But Stone had more responsibilities than just Nate and Hes.

I unlocked Stone's Range Rover and went to open the boot for Gato. He let out a low rumbling growl of warning. I turned around. Elvira. 'Do you always hang out in garages?' I asked facetiously.

She ignored that as she studied me. 'Why is Stone working with you?' she demanded.

'Ask him yourself,' I suggested.

Elvira's hair was down today, cascading over her shoulders. I studied her. 'Are those eyelashes real?' I asked.

She smiled, looking smug. 'Yes. Everything about my body is real.' *True.* Damn. She had a fine figure; she was skinnier than me, with bigger boobs. And she didn't even have fake eyelashes. She was beautiful and she knew it.

'Where does the skin tone come from?' I asked curiously.

'I'm of Italian descent,' she said proudly.

'You're very beautiful.'

She blinked then smiled wryly. 'You're making it very hard for me to hate you.'

'You don't need to hate me,' I assured her. 'Stone and I are just working a case together.'

She shook her head. 'You're a private investigator, so how can you be so blind? Everyone's talking about how the mighty Stone has fallen for some two-bit PI.' Charming.

'We're friends.' I said calmly. *Lie.* I hated that the truth seeking worked even on myself. Still, she didn't need to know that.

'Stone is supposed to be *my* eligible bachelor. We're betrothed.' *True.*

I felt a sharp sting of jealousy. 'I don't know anything about that. We haven't so much as kissed. He is his own man.'

She laughed. 'He's a Stone, he will never be his own man. He will always be his father's man. One day Stone will accept what he's been running from his whole life, and I'll be ready. I've been ready my whole life. I even joined the Connection and became an inspector for him. We're meant to be together. The Seers have cast on it.'

'Oh, honey,' I said with genuine sympathy, 'you don't choose your life's path for a man, you choose it for you.'

I finished putting Gato into the boot, pulled myself up into the driver's seat and plugged the address in the GPS. I adjusted the seat and the wing mirror. 'I've got to go,' I said. 'You take care.' I meant it. I got lots of vibes from her, but most of them were desperation. She wanted Stone; I don't know if she loved him, but she definitely loved his status. I'd hoped that she'd turn out to the mastermind behind this case, but my ever-reliable gut said no.

I started the engine and drove out of the underground garage. Elvira watched me leave. I wasn't her favourite person, and I couldn't blame her – she wasn't mine either.

Stone and I had an undeniable connection. There'd been a spark between us ever since we'd first met – literally – and the chemistry between us set my heart racing. We'd only known each other a few days but I trusted him and I liked him. And you'd have to be dead not to find him sexy. There had been a moment when we were dancing together at Alma de Cuba when I was certain Stone was going to kiss me, then someone bumped into us and it passed. It was probably a good thing; we didn't need to be distracted right now.

I was feeling mixed up. I pulled over and put on my phone's Bluetooth, then pulled back onto the road and rang Lucy.

'Hey, Jess!' she trilled. 'How are you?'

'I'm okay. You know I'm on a missing person's case in Liverpool?'

'Yeah.'

'So I'm working it with another detective. A guy detective.'

'Is he hot?' Lucy asked.

'So hot. He's older, like thirty-five or something. He's got this air about him – he's so confident, you know.'

'Jess has got a crush,' Lucy said in a sing-song voice.

'I really like him, Luce.'

'So what's the problem? Does he like you?'

I thought about the almost kiss. 'I think so.'

'I repeat, what's the problem? Go for it! You haven't dated in forever – like ever.'

I rolled my eyes. 'I know my own dating history, Lucy.'

'What history?' she demanded. 'You've had five one-night stands.'

'One guy lasted a whole weekend,' I said defensively. 'But I really like this one. Maybe we should just be friends.'

'I never thought I'd say this,' Lucy muttered, 'but you've got enough friends.'

I laughed. 'I can't believe you just said that!'

'Whatever. You don't want to be friend-zoned, Jess. I know you're a little messed up about your parents dying and leaving you, but you can't be alone your whole life. They wouldn't want that for you.'

It was hard to say what my parents would want for me. They had hidden the Other realm from me, and here I was hip deep in it. And it was always on my mind. I was always wondering if they'd wanted me to stay in the Common for a reason. The sensible part of me thought I should cut all Other ties, go back to the Common and not look back. But the bigger part of me wanted to dive in. This was my world: I could make a ball spin by thinking about it, I could save myself from plummeting to my death, I could date Stone.

'Thanks Luce. This has helped.'

'Has it?' She sighed. 'Are you going to ask the guy out?'

I kind of already had. 'Nope. But I won't say no if he asks me.'

She clapped her hands. 'I'll take that. I've got to go. Take care, beautiful.'

'Bye, Luce, Love you.'

'Love you, Jess.'

As we rang off, I drove out of the Kingsway Tunnel and onto a fast-pass lane. I hoped this would work. I waved Stone's ID at the barrier and it beeped and rose up. I was good to go.

I had ten minutes for another call, so I dialled Wilf's number. I wouldn't say that he and I were friends – although he would – but we had someone in common: Hes. I was invested in her safe return – I wouldn't return a corpse to Lady Sorrell if I could help it.

'Hello?'

'Wilf?'

'Jinx! How wonderful to hear your voice. Have you found our Hester?'

'Nearly, but it's messier than I would have liked. I know you hired Stone. I'm Other too, Wilf.'

There was a pause. 'I took you to Rosie's…'

'I was hidden then, so I didn't know. I'm a wizard.'

'I knew it!' He exclaimed. *True.*

I laughed a little at his enthusiasm. 'Sometimes my gut instincts shout at me, and I've learned to listen. Hester's in trouble. Stone is rounding up the inspectors, but I think more firepower might be needed. There's a conspiracy to end the Verdict, destroy the Unity, the Connection, all of it, and they plan to use Hester to do it. She won't come out of this alive if they do. Stone's focus is stopping them. Hes has been hanging out with Nathaniel Volderiss. His father is coming to save him, but no one is coming for Hes.'

'I'll come for Hes.' Wilf's voice was surer, stronger; he sounded like the Wilf I'd seen talking to his son, not the flirtatious drunk he usually played with me.

'She deserves to be saved,' I said softly. 'She's no less because she's Common.'

'We're on our way,' Wilf said firmly.

'We?' I asked.

'My pack.'

'Midnight, tonight. Liverpool, at the bombed-out church. And bring Roscoe if you can.' The fire elemental might be an asset.

'I'll ask him,' Wilf confirmed, 'but he doesn't owe me any favours.'

'Tell him I asked him to come. He said he would answer my call. I don't know if this counts, but it's worth a try. Take care, Wilf.' I rang off, certain I'd done the right thing.

CHAPTER 19

I DROVE TO the address Stone had given me, a stunning Edwardian manor house, rendered cream with a soft slate-grey roof. It must have had at least six or seven bedrooms, and it had sprawling outhouses, which I suspected held a pool or a gym. It was set in several acres of woodland.

When I grew up, I wanted a house just like this one. I parked up on the wide gravel drive and let Gato out of the boot. There were some forlorn-looking bushes in the centre of the circular driveway. Gato looked at me, then peed on them like they were his own territory. 'Gato!' I chastened him. I hoped there weren't other hounds around to take offence. He looked at me, big tongue lolling. He wasn't sorry.

I waited until he was done and back at my side before I knocked firmly on the white front door. A moment later it was opened by a female elf wearing a summery blue dress despite the winter cold. Her golden hair tumbled around her shoulders and her pointed ears poked out. I flashed Stone's ID. 'Can I come in? I have some questions.'

The Elf studied the ID. 'Come in, Inspector…?'

I sidestepped. 'Call me Jinx,' I offered.

She nodded and let me in. Gato barked at her in greeting, and she smiled warmly at him. 'Hello, boy.' She gave him an overly affectionate stroke. Weird.

I cleared my throat. 'I need to speak to someone about daggers, one in particular. Glimmer.'

She faltered and looked at me, wide eyed. 'You'll have to speak to my father, Leo,' she said. 'This way.' She led me through the sprawling mansion to her father's study. It had a roaring fire, a large oak desk and two cream sofas facing each other.

The elf behind the desk looked old. He had long grey hair – from which poked two pointed ears. I thought that elves were immortal like vampyrs, but apparently not. Gato bounded over to him and got a faint smile and a stroke in response. Maybe elves and hell hounds just get on really well?

He met my gaze with sharp eyes; he might be old, but he wasn't senile. 'What brings you to my door Jessica Sharp?'

Well, that was freaky. I swallowed. 'How do you know my name?'

'We've met before, in this time or another.'

Okay, so maybe he was a little senile. 'I've never met you before,' I said firmly.

'Then it was in another time.' He rose from the desk. 'Erin, bring us some tea, please.' He settled down on one of the sofas and gestured for me to do the same. 'You come with dire warnings,' he went on serenely.

'Are you a seer?' I asked.

Leo shook his head. 'No, not in the classic sense. But your parents always came with warnings, and I see the same tension in you.'

'You knew my parents?' I knew I shouldn't be derailed, but I needed to know about them and their Other experiences.

'Until their disappearance. Since then, I haven't seen them.'

'They're dead,' I said levelly and watched for his response.

No emotions crossed his face. 'They're not in this time,' he agreed.

Erin came in and wordlessly laid tea on the table, complete with biscuits. We might be Other, but we're British, and a cuppa and a biscuit are a must. I poured a cup of tea for myself and doctored it with milk, then poured one for Leo and passed him the milk. 'You have a fixation with time,' I said as I took a sip of my tea.

'Don't we all?' he quipped. 'It marches on and we age and fade and die. Time is all we have, and it is never enough. Unless you have access to the Third.'

'The Third?'

'The Third Realm. The Common, the Other and the Third.'

I was glad I was sitting down. Stone had three triangles; all the inspectors did. They had been marked by the Third Realm. I should have realised. I felt a surge of irrational anger at Stone for keeping this from me. 'The Third Realm is time?' I asked.

'Yes and no. The Third Realm allows us to *access* time, to mould it, to borrow it.'

Stone had told me he was thirty-eight but he only looked thirty, and he'd said it was time in the realms that allowed that. I'd assumed it was the Other realm he was referring to, but it was the Third Realm. The little shit. He'd deceived me; cunningly he didn't lie, but he'd misled me. I felt a sharp sting of betrayal.

'We are forbidden to speak of the Third Realm to those who are not authorised to know of it,' Leo explained.

'Can you read my mind?' I demanded.

Leo smiled. 'I have lived many centuries and studied all walks of life. You are young and impetuous. I can read your thoughts on your face as if they were painted there.'

Charming. Here I was thinking I was some bad-ass PI, and he was telling me I was a young child whose every thought crossed her face. I frowned. 'Why are you telling me about the Third? Aren't you breaking the Verdict?'

Leo waved that away. 'We have spoken of the Third

Realm before, you and I. You came to me knowing of it, so I am breaking nothing. The Verdict stands.'

I had no recollection of that conversation, so it looked like I had time travel in my future – or was it my past?

Leo continued, 'The inspectors use the Third Realm to move supernaturally fast. They reach out and, with the lightest touch, time slows around them. That enables them to move with speeds unmatched even by vampyrs or werewolves. It is their very own super power.'

I let that sink in. I remembered seeing Stone and Ajay moving faster than I could follow. I'd assumed it was some other kind of magic, and in a way I was right. They were accessing another realm. 'How do I access the Third?' I asked.

'You do not delve into the Third rashly. You can unravel your very existence if you're not careful.' He gave me a hard gaze.

I nodded to show that I understood his warning. It's not like I was raring to hop back to the eighteenth century or anything.

'A portal is needed to gain access to the Third, as with the other two realms. Unless you have a bonded hell hound handy, of course. Inspectors access the Third Realm with their own artefact, but by using the portal through an artefact, the access to the Third is limited. They can temporarily slow time, but that is all. They can't travel through the portal to the Third. Only a unanimous vote by the Symposium can authorise the use of the portal. Only one portal to the Third Realm exists in the UK, in St Luke's, the bombed-out Church in Liverpool.'

Shit. No wonder Stone had reacted the way he had, wanting to call in the cavalry. This was definitely about more than just Nate and Hes. I grimaced and rubbed a hand over my eyes. 'What would happen if the portal in the bombed-out church was destroyed?'

Leo took a sip of his tea. 'Destroying the portal could end our access to the Third Realm forever.' He said it calmly, like we were discussing the weather.

This was getting too big for me. I was just a PI. I brought the conversation back to Hes and Nate. 'Tell me about the dagger, Glimmer.'

'Ah.' He sighed. 'My biggest regret. In my youth, I was rash. I saw the Other and thought it good. I felt sorry for those in the Common to never know the touch of magic, to exist in a world where the grass was green, and the sky was blue. I wanted to find a way to give everyone access to the Other. First, I tried to create mini-portals that could take those from the Common into the Other. That failed and I perceived that blood was the issue. Common blood and Other blood are fundamentally different. The vampyrs had told me so. The blood of a wizard is addictive to them, like heroin to a Common. It makes them animalistic, bestial. It tastes far better than common blood, but it temporarily robs them of their higher cognitive reasoning and it creates a harsh dependency. It is also a great healer for their deadliest wounds. However, weaning them off wizards' blood and onto Common blood is a hard task. It is a harsh punishment amongst vampyrs to be given wizards' blood and then to suffer withdrawal. As immortal creatures, they live on through great pain.'

I thought of the brunette vampyr in Volderiss's office; I suspected that this had been done to him. I made a mental note not to piss off Volderiss.

'I created Glimmer as an experiment, no more. Theoretically, it took blood into its blade from one of the Other while sustaining their life despite the wound. If you then pushed the dagger, and the magic it was now imbued with, into the heart of a Common it would push Other blood through them. It would end their Common life and start their Other existence. It was heretical even to think of such a thing, let alone to create the blade, but as I said, I was young and foolish. I wanted to prove that it could be done.

'I made the blade, imbued it and hid it in my safe, where it stayed for five hundred years until it was stolen from me. A wizard, Gregory Faltease, took it and used it. He found that one in three Other donors, and one in ten Commons, died in the process. We were killing Other to make Common folk become Other, and that made no sense to me.

'Faltease was fanatical. He wanted to make the whole world Other, regardless of the loss of Other life. He wanted to copy the weapon and send it to the corners of the Earth. He was stopped before too many died but it was a harrowing experience for those who were converted. He targeted young teens. Many joined the Connection when they were of an age to do so to ensure that such actions wouldn't occur again, to stop life choices being taken from other Common folk.'

He sighed. 'I regret my involvement in the whole tawdry affair. The Symposium recovered the dagger but, try as we might, it could not be destroyed. They gave it to the vampyrs for safe keeping. The vampyrs were uniquely suited to resisting its … charms.'

I stared at him levelly. 'They're handing it over tonight. Volderiss is being blackmailed – they have his son.'

Leo shook his head gravely. 'That cannot happen. You cannot allow Glimmer's use, Jessica Sharp, no matter the cost.' He said my name with great emphasis.

I blew out a breath. Sure: stop an unknown evil from killing Others and converting unwilling Common people into Others. Piece of cake. I missed the days when my greatest concern was cheating spouses.

I said goodbye to Leo and went outside. As I shut the door behind me, I checked the time: 11 a.m. I debated with myself for a moment but, in truth, I'd already decided. Leo said we'd had a conversation about the Third already, so I needed to go back in time and have that chat with him. 'There's no time like the present,' I said to Gato. 'Except maybe the past and the future. I need to go into the past to meet Leo for the first time and to tell him I know about the Third Realm. Do you know how to do that?'

Maybe I was a bit crazy to let a dog dictate where I time travelled, but Gato was a hell hound, a magical creature. I trusted his instincts rather than mine on this.

He barked and jumped up, touching my forehead with his nose. I checked the time on my watch. 11:01. Huh. So it hadn't worked. Then I looked around…

The forlorn-looking shrubbery was green, vibrant with bright flowers. The sun was beating down on us. I took off my jacket. I had no idea what time we were in, but it was definitely summer. 'Thanks, pup,' I said to Gato, glad to see he was still with me. He wagged his tail.

I reached into my pocket for Stone's ID but it was gone. At least I still had my clothes. I knocked on the white door again and Erin opened it. I smiled. 'Hi, I'm here to see Leo Harfen. He's not expecting me. Well, not this time anyway.'

Erin sighed. 'Come on in. You can join the others.'

Others? I'd hoped for a quick, quiet conversation with Leo, in and out. 'Maybe now isn't the best time,' I started as she opened the door to Leo's office. I stopped.

Stopped talking, stopped moving, just stopped. Leo looked significantly younger, and in the room with him were a very young-looking Mary and George Sharp. My parents.

My heart stopped and I couldn't breathe. My eyes welled up. My dad looked at me with sympathy. 'First time in the Third?' he asked and gestured to the third triangle which I was sure was appearing on my forehead.

I nodded dumbly and made myself walk into the room. Gato pressed reassuringly against me. Erin excused herself and shut the door behind her.

'Would you like a drink?' Mum poured me a glass of water.

I nodded mutely as my eyes filled with tears again. To hear her voice, after seven long years … it was heaven and hell. I took the glass from her and sipped, trying desperately to swallow the rock in my throat.

My parents looked young – my age young. I sat down on the couch and glared at Leo. 'You could have warned me!'

He looked at me with equanimity. 'I'm sorry. I don't know you.'

I clenched my jaw. 'Well, you do in the future, and you sent me to the past. And here I am, having a drink with my parents.'

George grinned at me. 'I knew you looked familiar.' He turned to Mary. 'I told you I'd keep asking until you said yes.'

She was smiling at him with undisguised affection. 'Ask me one more time.'

'Will you marry me?' George asked, confident in his answer.

Mum laughed. 'Not yet, George, not yet.'

He groaned. 'You're killing me.'

Mum looked at me pointedly. 'There's a time for everything.'

'Apparently so,' I said grumpily. 'Not that I'd know about that since you didn't tell me a damned thing about the Other or the Third Realm. Why would you do that?'

George shrugged. 'Mostly because you just told us not to.' The reason they'd said nothing my whole life was because of me. It was a self-fulfilling prophecy and I'd started it by messing with the Third Realm.

'Oh fuck,' I swore, dropping my head in my hands.

Mum sat down next to me and put her arm around me. 'It'll be okay. It'll work out as it should. The Third has its own rules, and it won't let itself be abused.'

I pulled myself back to the mission; I needed to, for my own sanity. This was too much. I was here for Leo. I turned to him, unable to stop myself glaring. 'Leo, my name is Jessica Sharp, also known as Jinx. I'm the daughter of George and Mary Sharp. I'm an empath and a wizard. You sent me here so I could tell you that I know about the Third Realm.'

'Evidently.' He smiled, gesturing to my presence next to my mum.

I ignored him and continued. 'Someone intends to use Glimmer. The vampyrs are going to hand it over to some unknown party.'

My mum straightened next to me. 'You can't let that damned dagger be used, honey. You must stop it, at all costs.'

I grumped, 'That's what *he* said last time.' I pointed at Leo. 'So here I am, delving into the Third Realm and talking to you.' I couldn't hide the wistfulness in that last statement.

Mum ran a hand through my hair. 'We're dead, huh?' she asked calmly. 'How old were you?'

My eyes filled with tears again and I swallowed hard. 'Eighteen. A week after my eighteenth birthday. I never thought I'd see you again to have one last hug, one last word of advice…' I broke off. Man this was hard. Even harder because I had to go back, leave them of my own volition. 'I don't want to go back,' I whispered brokenly. 'Let me stay with you.'

Mum pulled me into her arms and Dad hugged us both. 'You can do anything you put your mind to,' my mum said softly, as she had said to me so many times in our life together. 'But not this. You aren't born yet. You can't stay in this time.'

I nodded against her shoulder. I knew it was true, but

for now I stayed there, relishing the forgotten feeling of her arms around me. 'I don't want to say goodbye,' I said softly.

Mum squeezed me. 'It's never goodbye, darling. We'll be with you always.'

Dad nodded. 'We love you always.'

'You haven't even given birth to me yet!' I pointed out.

'That's something to look forward to.' Dad grinned. 'I'm already proud of you and I've only known you for five minutes.'

I rubbed my eyes angrily. Dammit, I didn't want my parents to think I was a wet drip. 'Hey, Gato,' I called. 'Come and meet my parents.' Gato frolicked forwards enthusiastically and started licking Dad.

'Hello, Isaac!' he greeted Gato warmly. He paused and looked closely at him. 'Hello indeed. Who's a good dog? Have you been looking after our Jess?' Gato wagged.

'Good pup,' Mum said, petting him.

'What?' I said dumbfounded. 'You know Gato?'

My mum sighed. 'Damn. I guess you didn't know him when you were growing up.'

'We must have sent him away while she was growing up. Great Danes are only supposed to live nine years or so. I guess his life span would have been hard to explain in the Common,' Dad extrapolated.

I gave Gato a rub. 'I'm sorry, boy, I didn't mean to

make you go away.' He kept wagging; I guess he didn't hold a grudge.

'I'll take him in the interim,' Leo offered. 'It's always handy having a friendly hell hound around. When Jinx is ready, I'll send Gato back.'

I sighed. 'Yup. That makes sense. You and Gato were weirdly familiar with each other when I met you in real time. I've had him nearly two years now. I got him December third.'

Leo nodded. 'Wonderful. I do love a good plan.' This Leo seemed a little more grounded than the future Leo. Time and old age had not been kind to him.

'So what's the plan for the dagger?' I asked.

'Just don't let it be used,' Dad said. 'It can't awaken.'

I looked at him levelly. 'Dad, that's an awful plan.'

He laughed. 'Keep It Simple, Stupid.'

Mum cuffed him round the head. 'Don't call our daughter stupid, she's clearly very clever.'

I grinned. 'Thanks, Mum.'

Gato barked; it was his urgent bark. 'Time to go?' I asked. He barked again.

'It's never wise to stay long in the Third,' Dad said.

'But it's barely been a minute,' I complained. 'I lost you forever, I've dreamed of this moment and now I have to go?' I shook my head. 'It's not fair.'

Dad smiled ruefully. 'Life is rarely fair, I'm afraid.'

'All the things I wanted to say to you if I could see

you just one time … but you don't even know me.' I scrubbed my eyes again. They didn't know me and they didn't know who their killer had been. This wasn't like communing with ghosts because they were alive, just a decade or two before I was.

Gato barked again. 'Yeah, okay,' I said irritably. 'This is hard for me.' I hugged my parents one last time. 'I love you both so much,' I said, my voice muffled against my mum's shoulder. 'Thank you both for everything. I'll never forget you.'

Mum wiped a tear from my cheek. 'I'm sorry we left you, honey.' *True.*

Gato barked insistently. It was time to go. Apparently the Third Realm had its own rules, and Gato knew them. I nodded through the tears. 'Me too. I love you both.'

Gato touched his nose to my forehead and boom – my parents disappeared.

I took a deep shuddering breath and checked my watch through watery eyes 11:01. I'd fall apart later, I promised myself. I looked around. I was still in Leo's study and Leo was old again. 'Back again so soon?' he asked.

'I just left,' I said, my voice thick with unshed tears.

'Ah,' he said with some sympathy, 'I miss them too, my dear. But remember, they are only a realm away.'

CHAPTER 20

I STUDIED LEO. He seemed knowledgeable, if a little lost in time, so I decided to pick his brains. Thinking of Cathill I asked, 'What do you know about daemons?'

An elegant eyebrow rose. 'As much as most people, I suppose. They are creatures of the Other, created from acts of great malice and hate. They exist like a shade, roaming the world as they steadily gain sentience. As they are born of the Other, they have exceptional skills in manipulating the realm's magic when they have corporal form. They roam, seeking out the angry and twisted and trying to do a binding deal with them to give them great powers in exchange for being the daemon's host. In reality, the daemon and the host body are locked in a contest of wills until one eventually gives up and is cast out of the body again. Of late, they have often been agents of chaos. They seek to break the Verdict and bring back the age of Chaos that went before. Things went better for them when the Connection didn't exist, and they yearn for that time to come again.'

That was about as much as I knew about daemons

too. 'Cathill has a daemon in him,' I said confidently. 'I can feel him. The hatred roaring off him almost made me choke. Can I help Cathill cast it out?'

Leo shook his head. 'It may be possible, but I have never heard of it. Besides, Cathill may not want the daemon to go. As a vampyr, he has great strength, speed and almost immortal restorative powers – but he does not have the IR. He is not an elemental. Vampyrs are both strong and weak. They have speed and strength, but little magic of their own. If Cathill is bound with the daemon, he will have powerful, destructive magic. Be wary.'

I couldn't get much warier. 'Is there anything else you should tell me about my parents, my dog, the dagger?'

Leo tilted his head in thought. 'I don't think so,' he said. 'But I may be missing something vital.'

'That's not reassuring,' I said flatly.

'No, I imagine not.'

'Cheers for that, Leo. I'll see myself out.'

'Goodbye, Jinx, I'll see you again soon.' He said it with certainty, but I didn't reply. Try as I might, I felt downright grumpy with him. He was playing God with my life, and I didn't appreciate being moved about like a chess piece.

I shut the study door. Erin was waiting outside. 'Did he help you?' she asked. 'Some days he's more … present … than others.' She gestured to the third triangle on my head. 'He's dabbled too much in the Third Realm, and now he struggles to know which time he's in. Let that be a warning to you,' she said sharply. 'And to you,' she said to Gato. 'Don't let her go there too much. The past can be addictive, but it's confusing for those in their present. Leo visited my mother often and it was hard for her to have two of him so often. There is a timeline for a reason.'

I swallowed hard and nodded. Time was not a toy to be trifled with at will.

'The same will be true for your parents,' Erin said firmly. 'They'll be busy trying to be good parents to you as an infant. It's too much to ask them to raise you as an adult at the same time.'

I nodded again. I got it, I really did, but it didn't mean I didn't want to go back. But only if there was a real, dire need, I swore to myself. I didn't want to become like Leo, however tempting it was – and God knows, it was.

Now that I'd had a moment to think, I was annoyed with myself for not asking more about my parents' time in the Other, about being inspectors, about all the things I didn't know about them. The moment was gone, but maybe there would be other moments.

Gato and I hauled ass to the car. I switched on Bluetooth and rang Stone as I drove.

'Stone,' he answered and something in me settled when I heard his voice. The world was topsy turvy, but he had been my guide, and he would guide me through this too. I was still feeling the sting of his omission about the Third Realm, but we all have secrets, and some of them are not our own. I still trusted him.

'Hey, it's me. I've got some information.'

'Are you okay?' There was real concern in his voice that was surprising and a bit touching. I'm not sure why he was so worried; I could manage a trip to the elves by myself. Of course, I'd also gone to the Third Realm, but he didn't know that.

'I'm fine. I spoke to Leo Harfen. He was a bit lost in time.'

There was a heavy pause. 'What do you mean?'

'He's dabbled too much in the Third Realm,' I said bluntly.

'I knew you'd work out what the three triangles meant.' There was admiration in Stone's voice. 'Though I thought it would take longer than two days.'

'I'm awesome,' I agreed. 'Though I'm a little bummed you didn't tell me.'

'I'm sworn not to, Jinx.'

'Yeah, yeah, but don't I mean more to you than a little oath?' I teased.

'Yes,' he said softly. *True.*

I bit my lip. A subject change was in order. 'The dagger is bad news. It takes Other blood, pumps it into a Common's heart and changes the Common into an

Other. Sometimes it doesn't work and the Other dies; sometimes it doesn't work and the Common dies. A fanatic tried it on a bunch of people, and he killed a lot of them, but he did convert some Common to Other. The dagger was given to the vampyrs for safe keeping. And I'm certain that a daemon is in Cathill.'

'Faltease,' Stone said, like something had clicked. 'He's a legendary bad guy – I learnt about him in the academy. He killed hundreds, all by stabbing them. I knew he was fanatical about making the world Other, but I didn't know what the dagger did – or that it was Glimmer. It was before my time. The Symposium will have supressed the knowledge, to stop it giving some fools bad ideas.'

'It looks like someone else is thinking the same. They've got Hes, who's a Common, and they've got Nate, who's an Other. By midnight, they'll have the dagger. It doesn't take a genius to work out what they want to do. But I don't understand who'd want to turn Hes so badly, or why.'

'Archie?' Stone suggested. 'He might want his pro-spective future bride to be Other.'

'Maybe,' I said, 'but I didn't get a vibe from him. He wasn't worried about her – he genuinely thought she was off partying. And, besides, whoever is behind this is a woman.'

'I don't know.' Stone sounded frustrated.

'We'll find out soon enough,' I said. 'Just make sure the portal to the Third Realm is guarded like the Queen.'

'It's *more* guarded than the Queen,' Stone affirmed.

'Someone is confident they'll get through it. Don't get cocky. Don't forget there's a daemon inside Cathill.'

'We have containment charms for daemons. I'll get the wizards to rune up a few spares too,' he reassured me.

My instincts were telling me this wasn't going to be as easy as Stone seemed to think, but I knew he'd be prepared for the worst-case scenario. Like me, he always had a plan.

I was on the motorway when a huge Nissan truck overtook the vehicle behind me. It was driving erratically. I'd seen it in my rear-view mirror for the last mile. 'I'm being tailed,' I said to Stone levelly.

His tone changed instantly. 'Where are you?'

'M53.' I moved into the slow lane. 'Near Bidston Golf Club. It's a black Nissan Navara.' The truck manoeuvred behind me again. The road was relatively quiet and I sped up; the Range Rover roared in response but the Navara followed. That was a bad sign; I had a feeling I was about to get rammed.

The truck stopped trying to be discreet. 'Gato, get up next to me.' I didn't want him in the boot. He obligingly jumped over the back seats and sat next to me. I reached over him and buckled him in. 'Don't get captured with me,' I told him and he barked once in acknowledgement.

'Help is en route,' Stone said reassuringly. 'Just keep driving, Jinx.'

I was about ten minutes from the chapterhouse; help wasn't going to make it in time. The Navara slammed into us hard and my car spun. I hit my head on the steering wheel – and it was lights out, Jinx.

I AWOKE, GROGGY and in pain. My head was pounding. I was on a wooden floor in an empty room with my hands tied in front of me and my feet secured. And I wasn't alone: Hes and Nate were huddled together against the opposite wall. Nate looked gaunt and hungry. Hes looked weary.

I sat up. 'Well, it's good to see you two,' I said cheerfully. 'I've been looking for you.'

'Lucky you,' said Nate flatly. 'You found us.'

'The cavalry are coming,' I reassured them.

The door opened and in walked Mrs H. She was dressed in one of her favourite outfits, a pale-lilac number that really let the purple of her skin pop. She wore lilac court shoes and her nails were shellacked to match. As always, her hair was perfectly coiffured in a neat bob. She had no handcuffs, no restraints and no inspectors behind her. The penny dropped: she was behind this. Son of a bitch.

'The cavalry are annoying,' she said stridently. 'Inspector Stone is tearing up the place looking for you, my dear. You're going to ring him and tell him you've had enough of all of this nonsense and you're going home.'

Mrs H was supposed to be my kindly neighbour, not the head of a nefarious plot against the Connection. I stared at her, trying to keep my cool, but her betrayal was slicing through me. Dammit, I'd always had a warning about her in my gut but she'd never given me reason to trust it. Over the years I'd marked her as the exception that proved the rule – but she'd never made it into my pack. It turned out that my instincts were spot on. Again.

'It was you all along,' I snarled.

She rolled her eyes. 'Yes, yes. Do keep up, Jinx. I'm the genius behind all of this. I've been pulling your strings since day one. It's been great fun watching you and Stone dance to my tune.'

A thought occurred to me. 'Did you kill my parents?'

She waved her hand dismissively. 'Why would I do that? I had them right where I wanted them, in hiding and trusting me absolutely. As long as they trusted me, they were safe from me. No dear, it wasn't me. I don't know what killed them.' *True.* 'I was quite affronted, to be honest. Someone destroyed my secret asset without my say so. I was put out.'

I lost my entire family and she was put out. What a stone-cold bitch.

She read my fury. 'All right,' she conceded, 'I cared for them, a great deal as it happens. As I care for you. But my daughter has to take priority. I'm sorry, Jinx, I really am, but I'd do anything for Jane.'

Mrs H continued. 'Hiring you seemed sensible because it was better to have you involved than some unknown third party. Besides, at the time you were still hidden. I didn't expect Stone to introduce you – I thought you'd just bumble around the Common realm. I couldn't have anticipated that you'd get this far.'

'You didn't have anything to do with me being hired,' I argued.

Mrs H laughed. 'Who do you think suggested to Wilf that he should recommend you to Lady Sorrell?' She frowned. 'But then that insolent pup brought in Inspector Stone too. Well, better the devil I knew – I could team you two up, monitor your every move and still run circles round you. It wasn't supposed to get this far.' She brightened. 'Did you enjoy your special skydive? I knew Stone would save you and that would bring you closer together. He's an excellent primer wizard, I'll give him that, but he's like any man: flash him a fine piece of ass and he'll get distracted.'

I was pleased on some level that she'd called me a fine piece of ass. It was interesting that she thought Stone had saved me and didn't know I'd saved myself. She didn't know about my powers; she still thought I was just an empath.

I glared at her. 'And would you have even felt any remorse if he hadn't saved me? You virtually raised me.'

She gave me a patronising smile. 'Of course I'd have felt something, dear. Who do you think dealt with that vampyr who wanted to snack on you?'

I stared at her blankly before I remembered a night, not so long ago now, when Gato had freaked out at absolutely nothing. That night in the park, a vampyr had been stalking me for a midnight snack.

Mrs H continued, 'I even put a protection rune on your home. I care for you – but Jane comes first. And recently you've tipped into the liability column. I'm sorry for it, truly I am, but here we are.' She shook her head. 'Enough chit-chat. Ring Stone, tell him you're fine, and then he can concentrate on tonight's excitement.'

'You *want* the inspectors here,' I said, dread curling in my tummy.

'Of course I do. I need to destroy that little army of enforcers before I can take over properly.'

'You want to bring back the age of Chaos that existed before the Connection,' I accused.

She snorted. 'I don't care about the Connection or the Chaos, I just want control and I don't care how it comes about. For a long time I was content with getting into the Symposium. Wasn't that a piece of genius? I started my own little terrorist plot then cunningly foiled it while making sure that the member Seer got killed in the process. I got her position on the Symposium. Truly inspired. But the Symposium is so tedious. Vote on this, vote on that, majority rule, it gets terribly dull. I decided that I wanted to rule, like our dear Queen does. And for that, I need a dynasty.' Mrs H was smiling but her eyes were feverish; she was unhinged.

A lightbulb went on. 'Jane. You want to make her Other.'

She smiled at me like a teacher would to a small child. 'That's right, dear. Only Jane is dead. She died six months ago. Didn't you notice she'd stopped visiting me?' She shook her head. 'So self-involved. You haven't got the corner on grief, you know. So first I'll test Glimmer on Nate and Hes here. If it works, I'll go through to the Third Realm and save Jane's life. Then I'll make her Other, as she should always have been, and we'll rule the UK together. The Chaos or the Unity can have the rest of the world. I just want my little island.'

'I'm sorry Jane died, and I'm sorry I didn't notice she'd stopped coming.' I spoke honestly. I did regret it; I should have noticed something like that.

'It doesn't matter. She'll be back before you know it,' Mrs H said dismissively. She was in denial – stage one of the grieving process.

'You can't bring back the dead,' I said softly. 'That's one of the rules.'

She waved it away. 'I'm not trying to bring her back to life from being dead, I'm going to prevent her death from happening. I petitioned the Symposium several times for access to the Third Realm, but they turned me down, so I decided I'd have to get there by force. I helped the daemon subsume Cathill, and he told me the truth about the dagger and that Volderiss had it. I was surprised when he said Gabriel Volderiss had given the blade to little Nate here, who carried it around with him like it was a trophy. It came as a bonus that he came with a Common girl attached, because that made them the perfect set to test Glimmer. It was unfortunate that Nate had stashed the blade and told his dear father where he'd hidden it, but I got to him before Daddy could rescue him, and here we are.

She smiled unpleasantly. 'Now, call Stone and tell him you're fine. I need him to focus on me. And if you try anything, I'll kill Hester and find another Common girl.' *True.*

Hester looked at me, her eyes wide with fear.

Mrs H didn't know that I was on the phone to Stone when I was taken. I needed to find some way to warn him that she wouldn't detect.

My phone had survived the wreckage with only minimal screen damage. Mrs H used it to call Stone. When he replied, his tone was guarded. He was expecting my kidnappers. 'Hey, Rocky,' I greeted him lightly.

'Jess?' he asked, immediately understanding that this conversation was in code. He'd never called me Jess, always Jinx. 'Where have you been? I've been tearing up the city looking for you.'

'I'm sorry to have worried you. I just needed some space to work out what I wanted, you know? I'm calling to let you know I'm leaving town. All this vampyr, daemon and seer stuff is too much for me. I'm just a PI. I'm taking Gato and going home. Maybe I'll pick up something funny for Mrs H on the way back. I wanted to say ciao. I'm sorry to bail, but you understand. I've only been in Other for forty-eight hours, and it's all got a bit much.'

'Sure,' Stone said levelly. 'I understand. Maybe we can catch up another time when things have settled down. I'm glad you're okay.'

'I'm fine. Sorry to have worried you. Bye, Rocky. I'll be seeing you.'

'Bye, Jess. Take care.' He rang off.

Short of jumping up and down and saying I'd been kidnapped by Mrs H, that was the best I could do. I was pretty confident he'd got the message, though, and I hoped he was forewarned.

I just wished his goodbye hadn't felt so final.

CHAPTER 21

MRS H WAS studying me closely and her eyes had narrowed when I had said her name, but nothing I'd said had sent up a red flag. 'You think he believed you?' she asked.

'Sure. Why wouldn't he? This realm is crazy. Anyone sane would get out. What time is it?'

She smiled. 'Nearly 11 p.m. Not long now. I still haven't decided what to do with you, Jinx. I've looked after you all these years, and I don't really want to kill you.' I could tell she wasn't exactly cut up about the thought of killing me, either.

'How about a mind wipe?' I suggested optimistically. 'Let me see all the drama and then, when you've won, you can wipe my memories. I'll go on being your friendly neighbour PI, and I'll be none the wiser.'

She considered that. 'It has merit. I'll think about it.' She looked at the three of us. 'Relax, dears, this will all be over very soon.' She left, closing the door behind her. There was the heavy clank of a bolt sliding home.

'Lady Seer Harding is nuts,' Nate commented. He was

curled up with Hes, who had not yet spoken.

'You think?' I retorted. 'Hester? Are you ok?'

She lifted her head. 'I've been kidnapped, it turns out my boyfriend is a vampyr and a crazy lady wants to make me magical. And now I'm between realms, apparently. I'm neither Common nor Other. Sure, I'm fine. Just peachy.'

While she was on information overload, she might as well have it all. 'Wilf and Archie are werewolves.'

Hes sighed. 'Of course they are. Fan-bloody-tastic. Is anyone in my life normal?'

'Your grandmother is, and Jackson. Your parents are, as well. Sybil is.' I shrugged. 'Common people are still – well, far more common. Liverpool is like the London of the Other realm. Others gravitate here so, yes, you're going to find you know some Other people.'

'This was a lot more exciting in fiction.' She rubbed her tired eyes.

'Sure.' I paused. 'Here's the thing, though. Nate is a vampyr. If he feeds from you, it will increase his strength and he might be able to break through the bindings. I'd volunteer to be his snack but I'm a wizard. If he feasts on me, apparently he'll go animalistic so he might try to kill us by accident.'

Hes stared at me. 'To be absolutely clear, you're suggesting that we let my boyfriend eat my blood?' she asked incredulously.

'Well, drink your blood,' I corrected. 'But yes. That's the idea.'

Nate had gone completely still. I guessed he was hungry but hadn't wanted to prey on his girlfriend, but now I'd put the idea out there ... he was hungry.

Hes looked at him. 'Will it hurt?' she asked softly.

Nate shook his head. 'I'd never hurt you, Hes. We can enchant our ... donors ... so they don't feel pain. I won't take a lot, I promise.'

'I trust you,' she said finally. 'Go ahead. If it might get us out of here, do it.'

He faced her. 'Look into my eyes, love,' he crooned.

She met his gaze and instantly her body slackened. He held her gaze as his canines lengthened, then he moved with preternatural speed and bit into her neck over the jugular. There was silence but for the sounds of his drinking and Hes's soft moans, which made me think she was enjoying the experience. I felt vaguely uncomfortable being in the same room. Eventually, Nate pulled back and licked the place where he'd bitten her. The marks sealed and faded until not even a bruise was left.

'Hang on,' I said. 'Vampires can enchant and heal? Because I was told you guys can't do much magic at all.'

'It's not something we make public,' Nate admitted reluctantly. 'It's clan business, and we keep it to ourselves.'

I leaned a little on him; some things were 'need to

know', and I needed to know.

He continued falteringly, 'We have three magics. The first is like a hypnosis, to get our donors to come to us willingly. The second is healing. It's not exactly magic, it's just that there's something in our saliva that heals flesh. It's not a spell or using the IR, it's bacterial or something.' He shrugged. 'We're a private people. The world doesn't need to know.'

I held up my hand. 'I can keep a secret, but it's useful to know. And the third magic?'

Nate shrugged. 'Sorry, I'm not allowed to talk about our powers to non-vampyres unless you've witnessed them. Once you've seen it, we can discuss it. Suffice to say, our captor has cast runes against it here. I tried when we first arrived, but I couldn't do it.'

I'm inherently nosey and I wanted to know more, but if it wasn't going to help then it wasn't any of my business. Anyway, now wasn't the best time to have a treatise on vampyr magic. I turned to Hes. She looked wan – and a little high. 'Hes, are you all right?'

She smiled at me lopsidedly. 'I'm fan-bloody-tastic.'

'It's a little like being drunk,' Nate explained. 'She'll be fine in an hour or two.'

'Let's see if you can get out of the restraints now,' I suggested.

Nate strained his hands until the restraints started to bite into them. Blood dripped down to his elbows.

'Enough.' I said firmly. 'Brute strength isn't working here. We'll go to Plan B.'

'What's Plan B?' asked Hester dreamily.

'Magic.' I turned to Nate. 'I'm going to try to use the IR. I don't know what I'm doing, so knock me unconscious if I get enthralled. You can do that?'

He nodded. 'No problem. I can still punch you with my hands bound like this if you're close enough.'

'Lucky me,' I muttered.

The restraints looked like simple cable ties but obviously they were something more than that; they were imbued with extra strength. Mrs H thought I was an empath; she didn't know I had IR. Everyone believed vampyrs didn't have magic, and Hes was Common. Perhaps we'd be lucky and she hadn't used any charms or runes to make these ties magic resistant. What was the point against a ragtag bunch like us?

I needed these bindings to snap apart. I wanted to watch them break. I wanted them in pieces. I believed it would work. 'Snap,' I ordered the binding around my wrist, and it fell away. I felt the IR leave me once it had done its job. Well, that was a helluva lot easier than spinning a football.

I concentrated on the bindings around my foot. I wanted them to snap apart. I needed them to break. 'Snap.' I ordered. They fell away, and I felt a surge of triumph. One set of restraints down, two to go.

I made quick work of Hes's and Nate's restraints. They rubbed their wrists to get the blood flow back. Nate's injuries from his earlier exertions had already healed. Immortal healing is a real asset.

The next thing was the door. I was confident Nate could kick it down or I could use IR to blow it down, but I was worried about the noise. God knows what was on the other side, and we had no weapons other than Nate's fangs and my burgeoning magic skills that I didn't really know how to use. I was still debating what to do when I heard the bolt being slid back carefully.

I gestured to Hes and Nate, and we lay back down, hands and feet together as if we were still bound. The door was pushed open by a familiar snout, and relief surged through me. 'Hey, boy,' I greeted Gato, climbing to my feet and giving him a grateful hug. 'How did you open the door?'

He jumped up on two leg and stuck his muzzle forwards carefully. 'You opened it with your teeth?' He dropped back onto all fours and gave me an open-mouthed grin. 'Clever boy,' I praised. 'Thank you. I was wondering if you'd been taken.' He shook his big head. 'Thank you for coming to rescue me,' I said, kissing him. 'Though I've got a bone to pick with you. You never warned me about Mrs H!'

'He's a hell hound,' Nate snorted, 'not an empath. He can read body language and pheromones but he can't tell truth from lies. If Lady Seer Harding never acted anything other than nice, he wouldn't have reason to distrust her. She's fooled a lot of people. Hell hounds are extremely clever dogs – but they're still dogs.'

Gato huffed; he didn't like being lumped in with his canine brethren.

Hes was staring dreamily at Gato. 'Is he like … a shapeshifter, or what?'

'He's a hell hound,' Nate explained slowly, like he would to a small child. 'He's a very clever dog that can help send you to either the Common or the Other.' Nate only had one triangle, so I guessed he didn't know about the Third.

Then I had a eureka moment and I had a cunning plan. 'Enough chat,' I said quietly. 'We need to move now, before she finds out we're free. Let's go.'

We were in an underground cellar. We moved quietly towards some steps and I climbed them slowly. At the top I peeked out – and then quickly pulled my head back down again. Jesus.

I crept back down to the others. 'We're in a basement in St Luke's – the bombed-out church.' I shook my head. 'And the whole place is filled with trolls, a few elementals and some eight-foot tall creatures with tusks.'

'Ogres,' Nate supplied helpfully.

'We're talking two or three hundred enemies out there here.' The nave of the church had sparkled and shimmered as the trolls hammered away at it. I suspected it was a kind of defensive shield for the portal. If they broke through, Mrs H would be able to control time.

I turned to Gato. 'Can you take Nat and Hes to the Third with us?'

He shook his big head mournfully. He looked at Hes and me, and then he looked at Nate and me. He could take me and only one other. That would leave one behind, alone and afraid, and it wasn't an option. It would be better to leave the two of them together and come back for them later.

I blew out a sharp breath. 'I'm sorry,' I said to Hes and Nate. 'I'm going to have to leave you for a while. I'll be back with the cavalry soon, but they need to know what they're riding into or a handful of inspectors will get massacred.'

'Where are you going?' Hes asked.

'Not *where*,' I said softly. '*When*. I'll be back.' I turned to Gato. 'Day One,' I said to him and he gave a soft noise of agreement. He touched his nose to my forehead and Nate and Hes disappeared. If Gato had done things right, I was now in Liverpool on Friday night.

I peered cautiously into the body of the church again. Nothing. Mrs H hadn't yet amassed her hordes. Thank goodness for small mercies.

Gato and I crept cautiously out of St Luke's. If it was Friday and all was well, Stone and other me were still at the DZ. At least I wasn't going to run into myself. Once we were out of St Luke's, I paused near the main road. I didn't know which way to go, and I didn't know who to trust.

In the end, I only had one option. I didn't trust easily, but I trusted Stone, and only Stone. I would have to wait to put things in motion until he and the other me returned. For now, I needed to rest. I headed to the chapterhouse.

CHAPTER 22

E SME THE SIREN let me in. She bought my story about losing my key card and gave me another one. I was too tired to shower, but I forced myself. There was some dried blood on me from my future kidnapping. I couldn't wrap my head around these time shifts.

Clean and weary, I climbed into bed. Gato climbed on next to me. I didn't object; I needed his solid presence and I felt safer with him by my side. I set the alarm on my phone for 7 a.m., closed my gritty eyes and pulled the covers around me. I imagined the beach and the ocean and let Morpheus take me as the seagulls screeched.

I WAS UP, showered and dressed by 7:30. I had an early appointment, even if the people I was meeting didn't know it yet.

With hindsight, there had been something too knowing in Volderiss's eyes during our second meeting. Now I was confident that I knew why.

I made my way to GV Law. Bella the Liver Bird was in the courtyard. I nodded to her and she trilled to me as she watched my progress with a sharp eye. I don't know why, but I couldn't help feeling that she knew that I was out of my own time. A shiver ran down my spine.

I left Gato outside the building with instructions not to be seen and entered GV Law at 7:45 a.m. The receptionist was already there. I hoped she was paid well. 'Call Volderiss,' I said firmly. 'Tell him he has an 8 a.m. meeting before Cathill gets here.'

She raised an elegant eyebrow but picked up the phone and dialled. 'Detective Sharp is here to see you again. She says she has an 8 a.m., before your meeting with Lord Member Cathill.' She nodded and hung up. 'He'll see you now.'

When I opened the door, Volderiss was alone and pacing his office. He turned to me with a question on his lips, but I held up a hand to forestall them. 'Lord Volderiss, there isn't time. What do you know of the Third Realm?' He had three triangles on his forehead so I was grateful I wasn't running foul of the Verdict.

He stopped pacing and met my gaze. 'I know of its existence,' he said. 'I know of its use.'

'You know the portal's location?'

He raised an eyebrow. 'Yes – though that is highly classified information.' *True.*

'It's in St Luke's. Tonight, Lady Seer Harding is going

to try to force her way through the portal. She intends to use Glimmer on your son, to make Hester Sorrell Other. If that works, she will use Glimmer on her Common daughter to turn her Other.'

He grimaced. 'I can't accuse Lady Seer Harding. She's the Mother Teresa of the Symposium. No one would believe me.'

'I don't want you to accuse her, I want you to go along with her wishes. But I need you to liaise with Inspector Stone to ensure that she doesn't succeed. I don't know how high the corruption goes. It might just be her and Cathill, but there could be others. You know Cathill has been subsumed by a daemon?'

'I suspected,' he admitted grimly.

I nodded. 'I'm in the Third Realm now. In your meeting with me at 9:30, you need to reference the dagger Glimmer and Harfen.'

He raised an eyebrow. 'Cathill is going to object to that.'

'Just answer my questions and remind Cathill that you need to be seen to be co-operating with the Connection. You can't rock the boat now.' I paused. 'When I last saw Nate, he'd been feeding from his girlfriend. He was strong and well.'

Volderiss simply nodded but I read the relief in his eyes.

'Can you enchant trolls?' I asked.

He stiffened, then nodded reluctantly. 'Not that you'd want to,' he muttered. 'They taste revolting.'

'How close do you have to be?'

'Close enough for eye contact.'

'How many vampyrs do you have that can fight?'

'At the moment? Fifty-five or so.'

Dammit, that wasn't enough. 'How many more can you get?'

'Quietly? Another ten, maybe twenty. If I pull in too many, Cathill will notice their movements.'

'There were between two and three hundred trolls and ogres.'

He shook his head. 'We can't enchant that many because it has to be one-on-one. It takes time and we're vulnerable while we're doing it because all our attention is locked on our victim. We could enchant the trolls and send them away, then try to enchant the next lot, but the rest of them would be on us by then.'

'You won't be alone,' I reassured him.

I rang Wilf's number again. He answered with a groggy hello. 'Hey, Wilf, it's Jinx. Quick question. How many pack members do you have that can fight?'

There was a heavy pause. Now I was back in time, he didn't know I was Other. 'I'm Other, you're a werewolf. Answer the question, Wilf.'

There was a long pause. 'Eighty at a push. Why?'

'I'll ring you again later. And Wilf? We're going to

repeat the conversation about me being Other. Act surprised.' I rang off and turned back to Volderiss. 'Wilf's got eighty, you've got sixty or seventy and we have the inspectors too. We can do this.' It would be carnage, but at least we had a fighting chance.

Lord Volderiss looked at me evenly. 'Get to a troll elder who can command the trolls. The elders don't usually enter the city so the trolls in town do as they like – it's like freshers' week for them. They come to the city to let their hair down. But the elders won't like them answering to someone else. If you can get an elder to come with you, they can order the trolls to leave.'

That would be a huge help. 'Okay,' I said immediately. 'Where do I find an elder?'

'I don't know,' he admitted.

Dammit. Just when I thought things were getting better. Saving the realms wasn't easy work. I needed more pay for this.

I left Lord Volderiss to have his meeting with my other self, but I loitered around to make sure it played out as I remembered. Abruptly, I remembered thinking I'd seen myself. Damn, I *had* seen myself. After this, I was never touching the Third Realm again.

I had a lengthy brunch in Moose as I waited for myself to leave and visit Harfen. When I was sure I was gone, I headed back to the chapterhouse. At reception, I smiled at Esme. 'Is Stone still around?'

'He's in Conference Room A,' she told me a little petulantly.

I thanked her and followed the signs to the conference room. I knocked on the door and walked in. Ajay was there with Elvira, Stone and another man who looked an awful lot like Stone, but older. I guessed he was the obstinate father that Stone had talked about. The other occupant of the room was Emory, the dragon I'd seen on our night out. He took up half the space; his presence was a little overwhelming.

'Jinx?' Stone said, confused. He stood up. 'Are you okay?' As I opened my mouth to explain, his phone rang. He looked at the screen. 'It's you.' He frowned. I nodded. He answered the phone and the conversation played out exactly as I remembered it. Stone kept his eyes locked on mine the whole time.

There was a loud bang as the Navara slammed into the other me and the other me screamed. The phone line went dead. That was strange, I didn't remember screaming.

Stone closed the distance between us and pulled me into his arms. He's an excellent hugger and I hugged him back. 'I'm fine,' I reassured him. 'Just one hell of a headache – concussion, I expect. And obviously, I was captured by Mrs H.'

He froze and pulled back so he could see my face. 'Mrs H? Lady Seer Harding? Are you serious?'

'Positive. Her daughter Jane died six months ago. She wants to use the portal to the Third Realm to prevent Jane's death, then she's going to use the dagger to turn her Other.'

Stone gestured to Ajay, who pulled up a laptop and started tapping away.

'Harding,' Emory mused, nodding like it made sense. He'd obviously had his reservations about her.

'What proof do you have of this?' Stone Senior demanded, ignoring his son. He had three triangles on his head, surrounded by a circle. I guessed Stone's daddy was the wizard member of the Symposium.

'You didn't want to mention that your dad is the wizard Member?' I asked Stone.

He shrugged. 'Didn't seem important.' He didn't want to be judged by his father's success. Elvira's comments about Stone's father made a little more sense now.

I stared at Stone Senior. He looked like he wasn't used to being kept waiting for answers. 'I have my memories,' I said. 'That's it.'

He considered me. 'I will check your memories.'

'You will not,' I countered flatly. 'But your son can. I trust him – I don't know you from Adam.'

Stone Senior frowned at me but nodded. Emory watched our interaction with interest, but he remained silent.

'What's your name?' I asked Stone Senior.

He was taken aback; I guessed he was used to everyone knowing his name. 'Lord Gilligan Stone.'

'Lord?' I poked Stone in the chest. 'You're some sort of lord thing?'

'Some sort,' he agreed. 'Focus on me, Jinx. I need eye contact.' He hesitated. 'When I'm in your memory, I'll feel what you're feeling. Just so you know.'

Great. I'd had a moment when I moaned about being captured without Stone, and now he was going to know all about it. Swell. I sighed a little but held eye contact.

'Memory,' Stone said softly. He looked into my eyes for a full minute without blinking before he pulled away. 'She's telling the truth,' he confirmed to his father. 'It's Lady Seer Harding. We need a moment.' He drew me into the corridor, closed the door behind us then pulled me into his arms. 'I'm sorry,' he said softly.

'What for?'

'I'm supposed to be your partner and I promised to keep you safe. I failed you. You were scared and I wasn't there. I'm sorry.'

I shrugged. 'You're here now. Let's nail this crazy bitch.'

'You're pretty unflappable, you know that?'

'Someone's mentioned it a time or two.'

His arms were around me, and he smelled like heaven. He pulled back just a little, enough to look into my

258

eyes, and the tension between us hummed. He leaned down slowly, giving me time to pull away.

The door to the conference room opened. 'You've had your moment,' said Lord Stone. Stone glared at his father but stepped away from me. I huffed. The moment was lost. We walked back into the room.

'I've got Jane Harding's death certificate,' Ajay confirmed.

'Now that you believe me about Lady Seer Harding, let me tell you what happens,' I said. 'She successfully penetrates St Luke's – that's where I'm being held – with Nate Volderiss and Hester Sorrell. The whole church is full of trolls, ogres and a few fire elementals. I'm talking two or three hundred trolls, a small army.'

Lord Stone sat down heavily.

'Interesting,' Emory commented. 'For someone who has been so anti-creature in all her votes, she's allied herself with trolls and ogres.'

Lord Stone ignored him. 'How many inspectors do we have locally?' he asked Stone.

'I've pulled in everyone from a three-hour radius, so about forty. We've got double that number of detectives, but obviously they're not as combat ready.' Stone turned to Emory. 'The dragons could turn this. Even ten or fifteen of you would make a huge difference.'

Lord Stone snorted derisively; I got the feeling he wasn't a fan of dragons. Emory glared at him and held his gaze until he looked away. The dragon turned back to Stone and shook his head. 'This is not our fight. We guarded the portal once, and the Connection tore it away from us. I will not risk my people in a fight that is no longer ours. But I will attend myself.'

Stone gritted his teeth. 'Not willing to get your wings dirty?'

Emory's emerald gaze turned hard and cold. 'Careful, Stone,' he said softly. I swallowed hard. I had a feeling Emory was at his most dangerous. His huge body was poised, tensed and ready. One misspoken word from Stone and this was going to devolve fast.

'It's not all doom and gloom,' I interjected. 'I've been a busy girl this morning. Lord Volderiss is going to send sixty to seventy of his vampyrs, and Lord Samuel is sending eighty of his pack.'

Emory's mouth twisted in distaste. 'Vampyrs,' he spat. 'They'll bite you as soon as your back is turned.' Getting the species to actually work together might be trickier than I'd anticipated.

Lord Stone rubbed his eyes but didn't acknowledge that Emory or I had spoken. 'Pull in anyone in a five-hour radius. How many will that give us?'

'Sixty-two,' Stone confirmed.

Gilligan grimaced. 'Twenty-two additional tired inspectors. It's not ideal.'

'With Jinx's ... additions ... that brings us to two

hundred, more if we're using the detectives,' Stone said. 'If Jinx's figures are on the low side, we'll be all right.'

Gilligan shook his head. 'Vampyrs are fairly evenly matched against trolls. Even with equal numbers, the losses on both sides will be catastrophic. The bad feeling it will cause will shatter the Symposium. It could even threaten the Verdict.'

'That brings me to my final point,' I said. 'Anyone know where I can find a troll elder?'

CHAPTER 23

I T TURNS OUT Lord Gilligan Stone knew where the troll Symposium member could be found. As he didn't trust me to persuade the troll elder to come, we were going on a road trip together. Yay. At least I had Gato with me.

Stone, Elvira and Ajay were co-ordinating the incoming inspectors and the local police. They arranged for road closures around St Luke's from 10 p.m until 6 a.m. The police were told that filming involving loud stunts was taking place in St Luke's. Hopefully that meant no drunk Saturday-night partygoers would get drawn into the fray.

I told Stone that he needed to tear the town apart looking for me. Mrs H was concerned about him losing focus on her. He promised he'd tear the whole world apart looking for me. He says the most romantic things.

Lord Stone and I headed out in Ajay's black Range Rover to find the troll elder. I whistled to Gato and gestured to my forehead. 'Send me to Common for a recharge,' I said. He barked and touched his nose to my forehead, then jumped into the boot, turned three times and settled. He closed his eyes; he was a tired boy.

Lord Stone slid behind the driver's wheel and I didn't object; he knew where we were going. I turned on the radio. He turned it off. Like father, like son. 'Where are we going?' I asked.

'Wales,' he answered laconically.

'That's a pretty big place. Narrow it down for me. Cardiff or Bangor?'

'Bala.'

I nodded. 'I'm taking a nap. Wake me when we're there.' I wasn't that tired, but I didn't want to make small talk for a two-hour journey and neither did he. Besides, a big battle was coming up, and I needed my wits about me.

I'd never been in a proper battle. I'd had a few fist fights but not an actual-to-goodness trying-to-kill-each-other battle. But Leo and my parents had been adamant: Glimmer was not to be used at any cost. It couldn't be awakened, whatever that meant. So it looked like I'd be fighting. I was trying hard not to think about it.

I leaned my head against the headrest, closed my eyes and focused on my breathing. I imagined the ocean's soothing waves rolling in and out. In less than five minutes I was asleep.

Gato barked me awake. Lord Stone was half out of the car, glaring at him. He hadn't intended to wake me. Son of a bitch. 'Sneaking off without me Gilligan?' I asked archly. 'Who's a naughty boy?'

'It's Lord Stone to you,' he said firmly. 'Your entanglement with my son won't last. No need to get overly familiar.' *True.*

I smiled tightly. 'Rest assured, *Lord Stone,* I don't want to get familiar with you. Stone has already told me quite enough about you.'

That hit home. His mouth tightened and he sent me a glare. 'Whatever you think you know about my son, I assure you you're wrong. You mean nothing to him.' His words rang with truth, but that only meant that he *believed* they were true. Nevertheless, they weighed heavily on me. He continued a little awkwardly, 'I'm not being harsh, I just want to be clear. You're not his future.' He pointed to the path ahead. 'Now, follow me and stay quiet,' he ordered.

I don't do terribly well with orders. 'You know, the days where women were seen and not heard are long gone,' I pointed out.

He ignored me. I indicated for Gato to send me to the Other. He did so, and the world around me was transformed: the sky became lilac and the grass turquoise; tree bark became darker, almost black, and their canopy was almost blue.

We were walking round Bala Lake towards a grove of trees. As we approached, I saw a sprawling log cabin –

well, more of a log mansion than a cabin. Log stronghold. It was a huge two-storey structure with defensive spikes. It looked unfriendly.

I had only seen a few trolls in Liverpool, and they'd been trying to fit in with any Common floating around so they were dressed normally. Outside this compound, a number of troll guards were dressed in forest-green tunics. Their hair was long, and their noses protruded like a shrew's. I doubted they would have appreciated the comparison.

Lord Hoity-Toity Stone gave a shallow inclination of his head. 'We are here to see Elder Farlow.'

The head guard nodded, lifted a bone horn from his hip and gave a single blast that echoed around the woods. The guards took up position again. Apparently, that was it; it was hurry up and wait time. Lord Stone sat down on a boulder. 'Bloody trolls,' he muttered.

I checked the time. It was nearly 3 p.m. At this moment, the other me was unconscious in a cellar with Hes and Nate. We had time, though it didn't feel like it, and I felt the urgent need to do something. The trolls might be glacial in their actions but that didn't mean I had to be.

I figured I may as well practise the IR. If I was going to use it in battle, I needed to feel more comfortable with it than I did at the moment – which was to say, not at all. I spoke to Gato. 'I'm going to go for a walk. Bark for me when it's time to go in.' He sat, facing the entrance to the

HEATHER G. HARRIS

stronghold, and barked once in acknowledgement.

I didn't say goodbye to his lordship; I didn't owe him any explanations and I wasn't feeling charitable. I walked until I was far enough away to still see the compound but they couldn't watch me.

I was a little self-conscious. I picked up a small, smooth rock, no bigger than my thumb. I wanted it to float. 'Up,' I ordered it. The rock flew up quickly and floated in front of my eyes. I wanted it to fly into a tree. 'Go,' I said. It flew gently into the tree then thudded down.

Hmm. 'Up,' I called once more, and the stone rose and flew to me. Now that was interesting. I had intended for it to fly to me, but my order hadn't reflected that. I remembered Stone saying that the actual word didn't matter if I focused my intention.

This time, I wanted the stone to fly forcefully into the tree. 'Go,' I ordered again. The rock obediently flew into the tree but with such force that it buried itself in the bark. If I did that to a human neck, I'd do real damage. I wasn't so sure about a troll neck; their skin looked like rawhide and I suspected it would take more effort to harm them. What a grim thought.

I didn't revel in violence but I was on team 'Get the Job Done'. I'd had to defend myself a few times from attack, and I'd had no compunction about wounding my attacker. I did, however, feel a little bad about the

266

innocent birch tree.

I dug out the stone and told the tree to heal. It did. Despite using so much magic, I didn't feel tired. The IR was coming as easily as breathing. I'd been a fairly resolute child who had grown into an assertive adult. My parents had imbued in me a certainty about my own capabilities – Mum often told me I could do anything I wanted. It transpired that I really could.

I needed all of my energy for the upcoming battle but I also needed the skill set, so I practised and practised for the next half hour. What else could I do while I was waiting, not very patiently, for the Elder Troll to see us?

'You're getting good at that,' a light voice said. I whirled round but there was no one there. 'Thanks for fixing the tree,' the young voice continued from above me.

I looked up as a dryad boy dropped down from the canopy and landed on the ground beside me. He was no more than eight or nine years old, his skin was green and his hair was sandy brown. He looked like he was dressed in leaves. He rubbed the tree gently where my stone had hit it. 'Good job. She feels all better now.'

Now I felt even worse about hitting the tree. 'She can feel?' I asked incredulously.

'Sure. She's a living thing, just like us. Not sentient, but present.' He said the phrase by rote, like it was a dryad catchphrase.

'Sorry,' I apologised to the tree.

He giggled. 'She's not angry with you. She just Is.'

I had a feeling I was already out of my depth when it came to metaphysical philosophy. 'So what are you doing here kid?'

'My mum's in there with the trolls and the mermen. She's trying to mediate a dispute about Bala's water. The mermen say the trolls have been dumping waste into the lake, and the trolls say they haven't. Something's going on, though, because fish keep dying.'

I blinked. 'I thought mermen didn't exist.'

The boy looked a little chastened. 'Oh, they don't. Not officially.'

'Is it like a secret everyone knows?'

He thought about it. 'Trolls, dryads, dragons and ogres know about them. When the human wizards and witches found their way to our realm, the mermen didn't want to interact with them so they stayed hidden. I shouldn't have told you. I'll ask Mum to clear your memory.'

'That's okay,' I said hastily. 'I've already met a merman so I knew they existed.'

The boy looked relieved. 'That's all right, then. They're allowed to reveal themselves. Now that there is the Verdict, some mermen want to come forward – but they're still in the minority.'

I took all that on board. I needed to ask the most

pressing question first. 'How long will they be conducting the mediation?'

'Mum left me with breakfast, lunch and dinner, so it will go on for a while. But she didn't leave me with tomorrow's breakfast.'

'What about your bed?' He looked at me blankly. 'Where will you sleep?' I elaborated.

He laughed. 'In a tree of course!' He stepped closer to a large oak and slowly walked *into* it. My mouth dropped open as he disappeared. A moment later he slowly emerged. He had travelled into the very fabric of the tree; it had not displaced itself or moved around him, he had become part of the tree. Man, this realm was odd. 'Is that comfortable?' I asked curiously.

'Sure, it's like a warm hug. The tree's energy helps sustain and recharge us. We're grateful to the trees that home us.'

I guessed it was the dryad equivalent of popping to the Common for a recharge. I wanted to ask what would happen if a tree was cut down while he was in residence, but that seemed like a brutal question to ask a kid.

I checked the time again: 6 p.m. I could feel the pressure like a physical force. I needed to *do* something, but my deck was empty and I had no cards left to play so I just had to wait. It would take Lord Stone and me two hours to get back to Liverpool, plus we needed time to persuade Elder Farlow. My patience was wearing thin.

I pocketed the stone I'd been practising with and sat down next to the boy. We might as well get to know each other a little more; besides, he seemed like a fount of information and I was mercenary enough to use it.

His name was David. He talked incessantly but I didn't mind because it was informative. As he chattered on about dryads and mermen and trolls, I soaked it in and added it to knowledge of the Other world.

David shared his dinner with me – his mum had packed enough food for a small army. I thought about sharing it with Lord Stone but dismissed it. I did, however, pocket a big pork pie for Gato. Finally, my patience gave way and I called Stone.

'Hey, Jinx.' He sounded calm and it instantly reassured me.

'We're still cooling our heels to see the troll elder,' I huffed, my frustration obvious.

'Trolls are glacial,' Stone informed me. 'I'm sure you'll get to him eventually.' *True.* His confidence in me was nice, but not necessarily warranted. I wasn't at all sure.

'How are things your end?' I asked.

'Good. We've taken over the Common half of Hard Day's Night as well as the chapterhouse. I've got the wolves and Emory on the Common side and the vampyrs on the Other side.'

'They don't get on?'

'Like oil and water. Or maybe wood and fire. Wolves and vampyrs are an explosive mix.'

'Good for us, bad for Mrs H.'

'Let's hope so,' Stone agreed.

'How many inspectors have you got?'

'Only fifty-one, but more are due in.' He paused. 'We need you to get the troll elder, Jinx.'

'I know.' I checked the time again. It was 8 p.m. Dammit. We didn't have time for this. 'I better go. Time to kick down some doors.'

I felt Stone's wince over the phone. 'This isn't the time to start wars,' he pleaded.

'Only a little one,' I replied. 'Stay safe, Stone.'

'Stay safe, Jinx. See you on the other side.' He rang off.

Should I have said something touchy-feely? Maybe this wasn't the time, but maybe there never would be a time if I didn't get this damned troll elder on board.

David was still talking. I'd tuned him out a little but suddenly he caught my attention. 'What was that you just said?'

'I was just saying that today's delegation was from the Fairglass School and the Orion School.'

I blinked. 'Do you know if Jack Fairglass was amongst the delegation?'

'Of course. He's one of the leaders of the faction that wants to come out to the world. He doesn't want the mermen to hide anymore.'

Given that Jack had popped up beside me in the sea, his political leanings didn't come as a surprise but I *was* surprised that he was here. These days I wasn't sure what game the universe was playing with me, though I was certain that someone or something was pulling my strings. There were too many coincidences. I frowned into the darkness. Maybe Jack could help me. 'I'd better go, kid. It's getting late and I need the elders' help.'

'They do everything slowly,' David advised.

'We've been waiting for an audience for more than five hours!'

'Grass grows quicker than a troll's haste,' he intoned. 'They don't like being rushed.'

No shit. 'It's an emergency,' I pointed out.

'It's all a matter of perspective,' David explained. 'Nothing's an emergency when you live for two thousand years.' He was unlike any child I had ever met.

'This is,' I said firmly. Though I supposed that to the trolls the Connection was new. Eighty years, when you lived so long, was a drop in the ocean. It was a sobering thought.

I made sure David was safely tucked into a tree and went back to the compound. Gato stood and gave me a wag when he saw me. He wolfed down the pork pie gratefully. Lord Stone was pacing. It looked like his patience was wearing thin, too.

'I need to see Jack Fairglass,' I said to the guard. 'Tell him Jinx is here and she can help.' The guard looked at me for a moment then nodded slowly. He turned and ambled down the tunnel into the structure, where he disappeared into the darkness.

Lord Stone looked at me curiously. 'Why do you think Fairglass is here, and how do you know him?'

'A little birdy told me,' I said flatly. I had no idea how Lord Stone knew Fairglass; did he know about mermen? Lord Stone glared but didn't repeat himself.

Less than five minutes later, the guard returned with Jack in tow. Unlike the last time we'd seen each other, Jack was dressed. His green hair was darker, less vibrant, and it was tied at the nape of his neck. More importantly he had legs, and I tried hard not to stare at them. I guess I wasn't too successful because a faint smile crossed his lips. I pulled my gaze up to his bright-blue eyes. 'Hey,' I said casually.

'Hey. Are you okay?'

I nodded. 'I'm trying to make a less dramatic entrance this time. I need to see Elder Farlow, but the guards aren't letting us in.'

Jack studied me. 'Is it important?'

I nodded. 'Life and death. Lots of lives and lots of deaths.'

Jack turned to the trolls. 'She's my guest for these negotiations.' Then he put an arm around me and tugged me into the darkness.

'Just a minute!' Lord Stone objected. We all ignored him.

Gato whined. 'Can my hell hound come?' I asked.

'Sure. The more the merrier at this point,' Jack said. The trolls didn't dare contradict him and Gato joined us. We were in.

CHAPTER 24

JACK LED ME down the darkened corridors. The floors were covered by massive uneven slabs, and the halls were lit by torches in sconces. The whole place had a very medieval feel. I guess if you live for hundreds of years, you're not in a hurry to redecorate.

We entered a large chamber where there was a group of six trolls, five mermen and one dryad. Jack and I joined them. In the centre of the room a circular table was laden with every food type you could think of – meat, fish, bread, fruit – and the smells made my mouth water. Thank goodness I'd already eaten with David, or I'd have been tempted to dive right in.

I gave a welcoming nod. 'My honour to meet you. My name in Jinx.' I bowed my head and touched my heart. Might as well follow the formalities.

It was easy to work out who Farlow was – his grey hair was nearly to the floor and his wrinkles had wrinkles. This dude was *old*. But when he stood there was no stoop, no frailty, and his eyes were clear and sharp. 'Be welcome in our halls, Jinx,' he said.

I smiled. 'Thank you, Elder Farlow.' If he was surprised that I knew who he was, he didn't show it. 'I come
to seek assistance and to offer it in kind. I am an empath,
a truth seeker. I understand there is a dispute as to who is
responsible for polluting the lake. Let me question you all
and I will tell you the truth of it.'

Elder Farlow nodded slowly. 'And the assistance you
seek in return?'

'Firstly, your oath of silence about my abilities. Sec-
ondly – and more importantly –there is a disturbance in
Liverpool. A large group of trolls has gathered, intending
violence to the inspectors and the Connection. I would
ask that you come with me, Elder Farlow, and command
the violence to stop.'

He frowned. 'I see no reason why the inspectors can't
handle a few brawls, child.' It grated to be called child,
but I tried not to take umbrage. Everyone was a child to
him.

'Three hundred trolls, Elder Farlow,' I explained. 'It
won't be a brawl, it will be a massacre.'

His frown lines deepened. As the silence stretched out
I opened my mouth, but Jack shook his head. I shut it
with a clack. After a good twenty minutes, Farlow
nodded. 'I accept your proposals Jinx. It is agreed. Done
and done. Ask your questions.'

I turned to Jack. 'First, let me prove my skills. Tell me
two truths and a lie.'

Jack thought a moment. 'My favourite colour is blue. I like rock music. I love apples.'

'Lie, truth, truth.'

Jack looked impressed. He held out a hand to shake and I took it. 'What is my favourite colour?' he asked.

I opened my mouth to explain that was not how it works, but instead I found myself picturing a rich, emerald green. 'Green.'

Jack released my hand. 'She's correct on all counts,' he confirmed. 'She's a real truth seeker.' There was a rumbling in the crowd.

I cleared my throat and turned to a troll. I thought carefully about how to phrase my question. 'Do you know anything about what is polluting the lake?'

'No,' he answered. *True.*

Jack surreptitiously fed Gato a sausage from the table.

I repeated the question to all the trolls, then all the mermen. Everyone answered no, and everyone was telling the truth. I looked at the dryad and asked her the same question. She hesitated. 'The trees whisper of a darkness that comes. I don't know more than that.' *True.*

'You're all telling the truth,' I said. 'No one here knows why the pollution is occurring. You need to look further afield. No blame should be laid here.'

Jack nodded slowly. 'I suppose there's no point in divining any further if we're all telling the truth. Interesting.'

'You were all telling the truth,' I confirmed. I turned to the dryad. 'David ate his dinner and was sleeping in his tree when I left.'

She smiled gratefully. 'Did he chew your ears off?'

I grinned. 'Yes, but he was very helpful. I learnt a lot. He's a very clever little boy.'

'He is,' she agreed proudly.

I gave her a little bow and turned to Elder Farlow. 'Please can we leave now? The matter is urgent.'

He smiled faintly. 'Everything is urgent for you humans.'

'We don't live for very long, so we must fit in as much as we can.'

He considered that before he nodded. 'You are wise, Jinx.'

I blinked. No one had called me wise before. 'Erm … thank you?'

Jack laughed gently at me.

Farlow pushed himself off the seat. 'I will be ready in a moment. First, the oath.' He reached out to a gnarled and twisted staff and tapped it twice on the floor. 'None shall speak of Jinx Wiseword's skills.' A flare of blue light surged out from the staff and swept over the whole room, except for me. He turned to me. 'It is a compulsion. None may speak of it. If they try to do so, they will lose their tongues.'

I swallowed down the bile in my throat and tried to

give a grateful smile as Farlow strode out of the room. I hoped I would be as strong as him when I was seventy. Trolls might think slowly, but they move fast.

The mermen were gathered together and the trolls had dispersed. I turned to Jack and caught him feeding Gato a wedge of pie. 'So,' I said, 'it turns out you have legs too?'

Jack grinned. 'You've been dying to ask about my legs.'

'This whole time,' I agreed honestly.

'In water our legs fuse together to form our tails. Out of water we are – anatomically correct.'

'Sex on land?' I asked nosily.

'Sex on land,' he agreed with a smirk.

I shrugged. 'Water sex isn't that great. You're not missing out.'

'Thanks. That's good to know.'

I decided a change of topic was in order. 'Lord Stone is out there. He seemed surprised you were here.'

Jack grimaced. 'I pose as a mid-level wizard. Mermen have the IR too. Stone has tried to recruit me on occasion, but I don't want to be part of the Connection – not as a wizard, anyway. But I do want to take advantage of the Connection's resources. It's hard to explain my presence here.'

'Why don't you say you're here as an independent mediator between the trolls and the dryads?' I suggested.

He tilted his head, considering. 'That might work. How bad is the situation in Liverpool?'

I bit my lip. 'If the trolls listen to Farlow, it'll be pretty bad. If they don't, it'll be a bloodbath.'

'Then the mermen will come and fight alongside you, Jinx Wisewords.'

I grimaced at the new title. 'I hope that doesn't catch on,' I muttered.

Jack laughed again; he was a happy soul. My gut liked him, not enough to trust him but enough to give him a chance to earn my trust.

Farlow returned eventually. Gato was extremely happy because Jack had fed him some more food. I felt a little bad for Lord Stone; he was bound to be hungry. 'Can we take a little of that out to Lord Grumpy?' I asked.

Jack snorted. 'Wisewords, indeed. Yes, Jinx, let's take Lord Grumpy a doggy bag.'

'I dare you to call it a doggy bag to his face,' I said mischievously.

We all trooped outside, including Elder Farlow. I checked the time: 10 p.m. We were cutting it fine. I tossed Lord Stone his doggy bag. 'Chuck me the keys,' I commanded. 'You can eat while I drive.'

He weighed his options, then tossed me the keys. Farlow climbed into the back of the Range Rover, and I opened the boot for Gato, who leapt up and settled down. He knew there was no time to mess about turning around three times.

'Enjoy your doggy bag,' Jack called to Lord Gilligan Stone.

I had to bite my lip to stop the laughter. I met Jack's eyes and raised an appreciative eyebrow. 'Let's rock and roll.'

Jack nodded. 'We'll follow in our cars. See you at the battle.'

'St Luke's,' I reminded him. I hauled myself into the driver's seat, cranked the radio and started the car. It was time to hit the road.

Farlow was content to travel in silence, Lord Stone was eating and Gato was sleeping. I drove as fast as I dared, watching the miles tumble beneath our wheels. I kept an anxious eye on both the time and the speedometer.

Just after 11 p.m., I felt a shiver down my spine. In that moment, I knew there was only one of me in the world. I felt both reassured and surprisingly vulnerable. For the last day there had been two of me running around, and now there was just little old me flying solo. God, I hoped we weren't too late.

I felt awful about leaving Hes and Nate with Mrs Harding. Logically I knew that there was no other option, but emotionally I felt like a lousy human for leaving them in captivity. Mrs H wouldn't have been impressed at my escape. I hoped they were both all right; I couldn't live with myself if they weren't.

The roads got busier as we approached Liverpool. Didn't the other drivers know I had to be somewhere? I was trying to save the realms! It was 11:45 and the fight was going to start any minute, with or without us. I kept on driving; there was no other choice. I didn't want to call Stone and divert his attention. We just had to keep going.

At 12:05 we were finally in Liverpool city centre. We made it to Rodney Street before a road block stopped us and I had to pull over and park. Lord Stone flashed an important looking police badge to the boys in blue and we were let through the barrier. Then I was running, with Gato flowing effortlessly next to me. Reluctantly Elder Farlow loped into a run as well. We could hear noise from the bombed-out church. We ran up the steps and paused.

The scene was chaotic. Stone had obviously worked out a plan with Volderiss. Vampyrs were enchanting trolls, while inspectors were cutting the trolls' heads off with swords or flames. Ogres were throwing great hulking rocks, and fire elementals were throwing flames around like they were going out of fashion. The primer wizards were trying to contain it, but I could see charred remains on the ground. The thick, acrid smell of smoke made me gag.

The werewolves were in wolf form and they were huge. I caught a flash of a bloody maw and swallowed hard. Shit, they were scary; I was glad they were on our side. They were working in small packs, attacking the ogres, reaching in and rending their flesh with their teeth before dropping back for another wolf to attack from another angle. At least four or five wolves in any one team were attacking each ogre, but the good guys were massively outnumbered. I couldn't see Hes, Nate or Mrs H.

To his credit, Lord Stone pushed past me and waded in instantly. Catching fire and re-directing it at an ogre – he held it there while the ogre burnt. The stench was horrific.

Jack and his fellow mermen arrived just behind us, and they too dived into the fight.

I turned to Elder Farlow. 'Stop this. Please.'

Farlow's brow furrowed. 'This is not the path,' he grumbled. 'Make it so they all can hear me.'

I gathered my intention. Everyone inside St Luke's needed to hear Farlow. 'Hear,' I commanded. I hoped it would do the job.

Farlow reached to his hip and pulled out a bone horn. He raised it to his lips and blew. The bellow sounded out and echoed for all to hear. 'This is not the path,' he repeated firmly. 'Your wandering is revoked. Report to your home stronghold for remedial directions.'

I gestured sharply and the IR was ended.

The effect was instantaneous, and the trolls started

marching out of the church. Their former allies took umbrage, and a few skirmishes broke out between the trolls and the ogres. When the trolls disentangled from the fray, we were left with a field of vampyrs, wolves, ogres and elementals. The battle was not won yet, but it had tipped in our favour. And with the field clearing, I could now see Mrs H.

She looked manic. Her perfect hair was in disarray, and she was covered in blood. I had a heart-stopping moment while I frantically searched for Nate and Hes. When I found them, I saw that they weren't the source of the blood, thank God. They weren't in a good situation, though: they were tied down on stone tables with rope and surrounded by some sort of protective field. It was also protecting Mrs H. She had Glimmer in her hand and was approaching Nate purposefully.

I turned to Gato. 'Keep safe. Let's go.' He barked once in agreement and loped by my side. His obsidian spikes stood ready on his back, and three new spikes protruded from his head. As we ran, my hell hound grew until he was the size of small horse. He let out a growl which reverberated around the walls and his eyes turned red. I stared. I had a flashback to my childhood, watching *He-man and the Masters of the Universe*. Battle Cat! Not that I would dare call Gato a cat except in another language, of course.

An ogre started towards us. Gato lowered his spiked

head and charged into him. The spike bit into the ogre's flesh and he let out a roar of pain. He tried to push Gato back and, in doing so, stabbed his hand on the spikes on Gato's back. Gato thrashed his head from side to side, rending a great hole in the ogre's belly. The ogre stared dumbly at the blood before sitting down on the grass. Gato pulled back then, with a glance at me, he started forwards once more.

I needed to get to Mrs H before she used Glimmer and I followed him closely. As we started towards her, a huge tower of fire came towards me. Roscoe stepped up next to me, caught the flames easily and threw them back. 'I'll keep you safe from fire,' he promised. 'Keep going.'

I nodded and ran towards the other end of the church. Another ogre swung towards me but Gato leapt up and effortlessly ripped out his throat. I was trying to battle my shock; I'd never seen Gato hurt so much as a mouse before. But I didn't have time to be shocked – I needed to keep moving.

Don't let Mrs H use the dagger.

An ogre leapt towards me. I needed him to go away. 'Go,' I ordered. He winked out of existence. I wondered where the heck I'd sent him, but that was a worry for another day.

A fire elemental was in my way, its heat almost crackling my skin, but Roscoe was two steps behind me watching my back. There was no trace of the jovial shopkeeper I'd met; he was all business. I was grateful that he'd been in charge of my introduction, and I was grateful he had come when I called. I'd owe him after this – if we all survived.

I danced around the elemental and left him locked in battle with Roscoe. A vampyr leapt towards me and I was too slow to react. I'd forgotten that some of the vampyrs were Cathills, and not on our side. A sword of fire arced out of nowhere and sliced off his head before I could be bitten. Stone: he was just the other side of me, picking up bricks and firing them at an ogre. If he kept going it wouldn't be the bombed-out church, it would be the rubble church.

Behind Stone, Ajay and Elvira were fighting together to try to contain Cathill. There was no doubt now that Cathill was subsumed by a daemon. Lightning danced from his fingertips and he rained it down on everyone without discrimination. He was laughing as ogres and inspectors alike perished at his hands. I couldn't lose focus. The others would have to deal with him. I needed to get to Mrs H.

An eerie scream sounded through the building, and three winged creatures hovered over St Luke's. Two of them were Bertie and Bella, the Liver Birds, and the third was Emory.

The red dragon plunged in, picked up an ogre, flew high and then dropped it. Bertie and Bella seemed to agree with that as a plan of action and they waded in, backs to each other. Bella opened her beak, let out another screech, and instantly more Liver Birds appeared. These were much smaller, only about eight feet tall, and it took two of them to haul up and drop an ogre.

Cathill struck one of the birds with lightning and Bella let out an unearthly scream of horror. She gathered her wings and flew towards him with a speed I'd never seen from a bird. She thrust her beak directly through his heart with such force that she drove his body into one of the walls, which fell away. Vampyrs are generally immortal but it was hard to imagine anything surviving that. I was glad the Liver Birds were on our side.

I tore my eyes from the spectacle and moved forwards, but once again my path was blocked by an ogre. Using the IR, I struck him with a nearby plinth and he fell to the ground. Another ogre immediately took his place. Dammit, this was fruitless. I couldn't move forwards for new enemies rising in my path.

I needed to be invisible. Stone had told me I couldn't make myself invisible because I couldn't use the IR on myself, but perhaps I could use it another way? I concentrated. I needed everyone's eyes not to see me, to pass over me as if I wasn't there. 'Hidden.' I shouted. Nothing discernible happened but, as I kept on moving, the enemy didn't react to my presence. Unfortunately, neither did the good guys; I learnt that the hard way when I nearly got flamed because Roscoe couldn't see me to save me.

Out of the corner of my eye, I saw Stone battling with Cathill. Cathill was an old vampyr and his injury from Bella was already healing. I felt sick with worry as I ducked and dived, weaving through the chaos but I told myself that Stone knew what he was doing.

I reached the shield around Mrs H and her prisoners, and gestured for my invisibility to end. I needed all my power to get through it. I touched it, but nothing happened. 'Open,' I ordered. Nothing. I wanted it to drop. 'Down,' I ordered. Nothing.

Emory flew over and hovered in the air above me. 'Break through when I strike it,' he shouted. 'It won't be prepared for two attacks at once. Signal when you're ready.' He flew above the shield, watching for me to indicate when he should attack.

Hes's mouth was open in a scream but I couldn't hear her voice because the shield stopped all sound. Hmm: it stopped all sound but not all light. I couldn't get rid of it, but maybe I could change it, make it permeable, make it like the trees were to the dryads. I didn't need the shield to drop or break, I needed to be able to move through it. I gathered my intention and nodded firmly to the dragon. Now.

'Change,' I ordered the shield, just as the dragon struck it above with his talons. He screamed as he poured his magic and divided the shield's power. It was enough of a diversion to allow me to pass through and I came through it in a roar of sound.

I looked around. Nate was in a bad way – Mrs H had sliced him from neck to navel. His vampiric power was trying to heal him, but the wounds were too great without some blood to help him heal.

'Help him!' Hes shouted at me hysterically. 'Help him!' She was sobbing uncontrollably but, bound as she was, she could do nothing to help him. Her wrists were bloody from trying to pull her hands free of her bindings.

I wanted to help Nate, but Mrs H was turning her attentions to Hes now. She raised the dagger. I wanted it to come to me and shouted, 'Come!'

Mrs H smiled at me. 'Nice try, but Glimmer is impervious to the IR.' She struck Hes in the heart.

I screamed. Hes screamed. Nate screamed. Gato, stuck on the other side of the shield, howled. Glimmer came to life. As it poured its Otherness into Hes, it made her Other.

Glimmer called to me, and I called to it. 'COME!' I yelled. It flew into my waiting hands. As I touched it, I became aware that Glimmer itself was conscious. It had awakened and I felt its triumph as it was reunited with one of its children.

My blood ran cold. My empathy was a double-edged sword because it left me open to being subsumed by the dagger. It forced knowledge into me. Suddenly I knew that both had my parents had once been Common, but they had been made Other by Faltease. That's why my surname was Sharp – it was a reminder of what they had been through, what had made them what they were. Because they had been converted, they were not constrained by the rules of Other, and neither was I. I was something else, something *more*.

Glimmer told me it was family. It had made my parents; it was my grandfather. It crooned to me, telling me to use it again, to make more like me, to make a dynasty.

I was locked, dazed, stuck in a fog I couldn't see through, when Mrs H hurtled towards me. 'Give it back! I need it for Jane!' she screamed as we wrestled for the dagger. I couldn't let her have it, and the dagger agreed. Glimmer moved without my control, plunging into Mrs H, sucking out her Otherness.

Groggy and confused, I shook my head to clear it. Mrs H lay before me, her mouth wide and screaming, her eyes unseeing. She was dead.

Bile rose in my throat. I had killed her unwittingly, but she was dead just the same. The dagger had taken more than the Other from her, it had taken her life. I grabbed a fistful of her flowing skirt and cut it from her. I wrapped Glimmer in the fabric, and I felt it howl as I shut it away.

Suddenly everything snapped into hard focus and I

could think again. I shoved the wrapped dagger into the back of my jeans. Hes was sobbing, but her chest bore no marks; she had healed. I used the IR to cut through her restraints, then we both turned to Nate. He was barely breathing. I would not – could not – let him die. I'd left him with Mrs H and I'd been hunting for him and Hes for days.

I gathered my intention. 'Heal,' I barked and I watched as his flesh tried to obey me, striving to knit together.

Volderiss was banging soundlessly on the other side of the shield. I couldn't hear him any more than he could hear me, but I could read his eyes. He was begging me to help his son. He grew his fangs and bit into his own wrist, letting blood bubble and flow, then he mimed drinking. Nate needed blood to heal. I nodded to Volderiss, turned back to Nate and offered him my wrist. 'Drink.'

His eyes were wide and unseeing – he was too far gone to bite me, almost unconscious. But I wasn't going to let him die. As I reached behind me and unwrapped the dagger, I felt its triumphant roar. If I'd been thinking clearly, that would have been warning enough, but I was desperate, tired and confused. I used the dagger to cut into my own wrist – and more than the blade sliced through me.

I battled to hold onto my consciousness as seer magic slammed into me, becoming part of me. It combined with my empathy and swept through my body and my mind. It found something parasitic within: a compulsion. Without conscious direction from me, the magic roared forth and destroyed the compulsion that had been laid on me. The compulsion of trust.

As the compulsion shattered, the moment of its inception played in my mind's eye.

Stone reached out and grabbed my hand. He motioned for me to sit. 'I'm from the Connection,' Stone explained, a little more loudly. He said 'the Connection' as if it should mean something to me. There was no buzz of a lie, but I didn't understand what the truth was.

'Like a Wi-Fi provider?' I asked finally. The café owner guffawed. Clearly no one had taught him that eavesdropping was rude.

That cracked Stone a little and he grinned. 'No, Jinx, not like a Wi-Fi provider. It's easier to show you. Do you trust me?' The question seemed important to him, and he laid emphasis on the last two words.

I opened my mouth to tell him 'hell no, my trust is hard won', but I felt weird and hazy. 'Yes.' My reply bubbled out of my mouth. That wasn't what I had intended to say, but it was true: I did trust him. My 'yes' rang with truth.

Stone had admitted that he had compelled me, but he hadn't compelled me to tell the truth but rather to *trust* him. He hadn't lied, but he had misled me beautifully.

Fuck. I felt sick, betrayed. My gut instinct had kept me alive my whole life; it defined who I was. To have it tampered with – *overwritten* – and by Stone? It was too much to bear.

I couldn't deal with it now. I pulled myself back to the present. Box it up; I would deal with it later. I couldn't let myself be distracted now. My wrist was pulsing with pain and that pulled me back. I was bleeding heavily, and the blood was being wasted. I held my wrist over Nate's mouth and my blood poured down his throat. He swallowed my wizard blood. Shit. My wizard blood was going to turn him animalistic, and we were stuck in a shield with him. 'Get back,' I ordered Hes hastily. 'Get away from him!'

Nat's body started to close the brutal wound on his chest. His eyes flared open, red and unseeing.

I stumbled back, holding the dagger as my only protection as I ran towards Hes to protect her from the monster I'd made. He was faster, and in moments he was on her. 'No, Nate! Don't hurt me!' she screamed. He ignored her pleas and bit savagely into her neck.

I needed him to get his mind back and regain control. I gathered the IR. 'Control!' I ordered. Nate froze. He dropped Hes, and she slid to the floor, sobbing and bleeding.

I needed him to regain conscious thought. I didn't say a release word but Nate's eyes slowly returned to normal.

'Hes?' he said softly, questioningly.

'Get away from me!' she screamed, holding her hands to her bloody, torn neck.

I couldn't blame her for her reaction. 'Come here, Nate.' I ordered.

He obeyed before the last word was out of my mouth. 'Mistress,' he greeted me.

I blinked. 'It's Jinx, Nate, it's just Jinx.'

'I am yours,' he said simply.

I stared at him for a long minute. I just didn't have the headspace to deal with this now. I'd made a mess of everything. 'We can talk about that later. Right now, we need to get out from behind this shield.'

With Nate now sane, I carefully bundled the dagger up again. It was content because it had been used. Twice. I'd failed. Spectacularly.

I walked up to the shield and it recognised me, recognised Mrs H's magic inside of me. 'Down,' I ordered. The shield dropped.

A ragged cheer went up from the inspectors, and the wolves joined in with their howling. We had won the day, but at what cost? What had I become? And what had I done to Nate?

I took a step forwards. Suddenly my skin was hot and itchy. I screamed – and then I was knocked unconscious as I was forcibly ejected from the Other.

CHAPTER 25

I WOKE UP in my own bed, in my own home in Buckinghamshire. I had a moment of total confusion before everything came flooding back. I sat up and Gato whined softly. He licked me, then touched his nose to my head. Suddenly, Gato had spikes. 'Not a dream, then?' I asked ruefully. He shook his great head.

I blew out a breath. 'Well, did we at least get paid?' He wagged enthusiastically. 'That's something.' I gave him some fuss and catalogued the damage to my body. No headaches, no bruises – it was a miracle considering all I'd been through. The damage to my heart, however … that was significant. I was battered and bruised, and my ego was dented too.

What an idiot I'd been to believe that Stone and I could have something so strong, so real, in only a handful of days. I'd justified it by telling myself that we'd gone through a crucible of fire together, that all these feelings made sense. But they didn't, not for me. I was a loner. My pack was small, my trust hard won.

I felt a flare of fury as I remembered telling Stone he

was in my pack. Well, he wasn't – he was excommunicated, effective immediately. How dare he *force* my trust? Trust was earned. I turned to Gato. 'We don't like Stone any more,' I said firmly. 'He compelled me to trust him.' Gato laid his ears low on his head. 'Exactly,' I agreed. 'What a dick move.'

I stroked his head. 'You know, you're a great hell hound but a terrible judge of character. You liked Mrs H and Stone.' He looked at me reproachfully. I sighed. 'I know. I liked them too. We're both idiots.' That didn't sit well with me. I prided myself on my bullshitometer; being a walking lie detector helped a lot in that department, but this whole saga had me doubting everything. Doubting myself.

I rubbed a hand across my face and gave myself a stern talking to. I wasn't letting one tricky, handsome man destroy my confidence. I was stronger than that. He didn't get to affect my happiness to that degree; only I could do that.

I heaved back the covers and paused as I caught sight of a bundle of fabric on my bedside table. I knew instantly what it was: Glimmer. Somehow I still had it. I picked it up and, covered as it was, it crooned to me. I opened my bedside drawer, put the dagger inside and slammed it shut. The crooning stopped.

I let out a long breath and dragged my ass to the shower. It was going to be a boil-the-skin-off-you kind of a shower. I turned the temperature up and let the heat and steam swirl around me as I tried to wash away the last few days.

I dressed by rote. It was a holey-jeans kind of a day. I looked out of my bedroom window and sighed. Mrs H's house was next door, as well tended as ever. I knew one thing: I couldn't stay here any longer. My house held too much history. Every time I looked across to Mrs H's, I would think about being responsible for her death. No matter what she had become, I had still cared for her, and she for me. I'd played in her garden as a child, and she had taught me how to plait my hair. I sighed again and deliberately tied my hair into a ponytail.

I could feel that I wasn't alone in my house. There was another presence – and he was unhappy. I was pretty sure I knew who it was, but I went downstairs to find out for sure.

Nate was in the kitchen with Lucy. Lucy didn't know I was there. She was toying with her blonde hair while she talked to him. Her pale skin was brushed lightly with make-up and, as always, she looked perfect. Something settled in me to see her, my best friend. Whatever else was happening in my crazy world, she had my back.

'Hey, guys,' I greeted them casually.

'Jess!' Lucy shrieked then threw herself at me. 'Don't you ever scare me like that again! I called to talk to you, and Zach explained that you'd worked yourself so hard you passed out! I demanded he bring you home so I could look after you. Zach said you didn't rest the whole time you were in Liverpool!' She ranted as she hugged me. 'Don't you ever do that to me again. You're human, Jess, you need to rest.'

I'm not sure what I am, but I'm definitely not human.

I smiled at my best friend. 'Zach?' I looked round but I couldn't see Stone.

Lucy misread my scrutiny. 'Sorry, honey, he had to go. He got called out on an urgent case. You just missed him, but he didn't want to wake you. He said you needed to recharge your batteries and that he'd be in touch soon.'

I gave a one-shouldered shrug. 'Did Stone tell you that I kicked ass, took names and found the missing girl?'

'The missing girl told her that herself,' said Hes from behind me. She smiled as she came into the kitchen. She had a triangle on her forehead; now she was Other too. 'I told Lucy how you and Stone rescued me from my kidnappers, guns firing, no less. You two are my heroes.'

As Hes entered, Nate tried to become less obtrusive but, despite his efforts, she flinched from him. The emotions that flashed across Nate's face were too fast to read, but I felt them. I could feel him like he was one of my own limbs. What had I done? I met his eyes across the room, and he gave a barely perceptible bow.

'Just doing my job,' I said lightly to Hes.

Lucy let me go. 'Shooting people is not your job.

You're a PI. You're supposed to catch cheating spouses and stuff. Remember the guy you caught with the fox?'

'Fox plushie,' I corrected. 'Not an actual fox, thank goodness.'

'Whatever, that's your gig,' Lucy said firmly.

'I've been thinking of rebranding,' I said, looking a Nate. 'Sharp Investigations and Other Services. What do you think?'

Nate nodded. 'I like it.'

Hes snorted. 'She doesn't care what you think.'

Lucy gave me a wide-eyed look and eyebrow raise, which I took to mean *what's their problem?* I shrugged. *Tell you later.*

'Anyway,' Hes grinned, 'you clearly rock at this. But I bet you could use some more resources. Do you want a very rich, very unable assistant?'

I considered; I could use a hand, and maybe she needed some direction after all she'd been through. 'What about your degree?' I asked.

'I could study remotely, part time.'

'Actually, I was thinking that my business should relocate to Liverpool.' I'd made my mind up as I walked down the stairs. I couldn't live in Beaconsfield, not now, not next to the house Mrs H had lived in to spy on my family. Liverpool was the obvious choice.

Hes squealed. 'Yes! Liverpool would be lucky to have you!'

'Do you think so?'

She nodded and behind her Nate also nodded assent. I was pleased; I wasn't sure if he'd want me in his home town. Not with this … whatever it was between us.

Lucy was shaking her head. 'No, you can't move to Liverpool. That's too far away.'

I smiled at my best friend. 'You can visit whenever you like, and we can go to Heebies and Lagos and Alma…'

That pulled a reluctant smile from her. 'This seems a little sudden,' she said, still not convinced.

'I need to move on from here,' I said softly.

Her eyes filled with tears, but she nodded. She'd been telling me for years that staying in my parents' home might not be the best thing for me. 'Fine. But you need to get a place with a spare room. I get squatter's rights.'

'Deal. You'll be welcome whenever, Luce.'

She hugged me again. 'I'll let you hang out with your new friends,' she said loudly. She continued in a whisper, 'You were right. Zach is so yummy and totally into you. Do NOT screw this up. Call him!'

I managed a weak smile. He had already screwed this up. If there ever could have been a thing between us, there couldn't be now. Stone had fucked with my head and my heart. He had *compelled* me. Perhaps being compelled wouldn't be a big deal to someone else, but it was to me. To take away my free will, to take away my judgment…

When my parents had died, I'd built a business on the back of my judgment. Some days it was all I had. And the worst part of it was that if Stone hadn't compelled me, I would probably have grown to trust him over those intense few days we'd shared together. He'd saved my life, had said nice things about me and *meant* them. We could have had something real. I didn't know why he'd compelled me, but that didn't really matter; it was an action I couldn't forgive, no matter what his motivation.

Lucy gave a friendly wave to Nate and Hes. 'So nice to meet you both. I'm sure I'll see you again very soon.' She let herself out.

I turned to Nate. 'Are you okay?' I asked as casually as I could, trying to mask my concern.

He nodded, his calm face showing none of the inner turmoil I could feel. 'Sure.'

Hes snorted. 'He's fine, he's a vampyr miracle child. He's had a huge glob of wizard blood and no withdrawal or anything.'

Oh yes, there was an anything. Nate and I were now bound together somehow. He met my gaze; he knew it too, but he hadn't said anything and it didn't feel like it was my place to bust it all wide open. Particularly when I had little clue as to what the hell was going on. 'I'll be heading to Liverpool soon,' I said to Nate. 'Will you be coming?'

'Don't come on my account,' Hes said firmly before he could reply. 'Bite me once, shame on you. Bite me twice, shame on me.'

'Technically it should be "bite me once, shame on Jinx". I was responsible for the first bite and the second one. I gave Nate wizard's blood when I knew what would happen. I was so focused on saving you both. I'm sorry Hes.'

She shrugged away my apology; she didn't blame me, she blamed Nate. I could feel his despair, I also knew that he appreciated me trying to move the blame. He didn't feel like the situation was wholly his fault, but, nevertheless, he was soaked in guilt.

I studied him. 'Would you pop to the shops and get us all some food? I'm starving and I fancy a cooked breakfast.' He needed something useful to do. His hands were in his pockets, he was leaning against the wall. Everything about him screamed that he was totally relaxed and fine, but I knew otherwise.

Hes rolled her eyes. 'He doesn't eat,' she pointed out. 'I'd better go with him or he'll be back with four pints of blood.' Nate's eyes flashed a little at that. He was down, but not out. The pair made their way out.

I was alone and, for the first time in ages, I didn't want to be. I sat down at my kitchen table and stared at my phone. This had to be done. I summoned all my courage, picked up my phone and rang Stone. It rang and rang, my gut churned. It clinked into voice mail. I bit my lip and waited for the beep.

'We need to talk,' I said in a hard voice. 'Call me.'

BOOK 2 – GLIMMER OF HOPE

Don't panic! Despite that cheeky hook...book 2 is coming very very soon. In fact it is available for pre-order now! Book 3 and Book 4 will follow in rapid succession and in a few months you will have a complete series to read again and again. You're welcome.

ACKNOWLEDGEMENTS

I'm so excited that this day is finally here, and I wouldn't have made it this far without a huge amount of support.

My husband was the first to read my books and tell me that they were 'actually very good'! He has supported me through this whole endeavour and even through many evenings alone whilst I was writing away. So the biggest thank you has to go to him.

Thanks also to my editor Karen and my proofreader Steph, and the girls of W and W. Karen told me emphatically not to put my manuscript in the bin, and has held my hand regularly throughout this book and the others. She's been a huge help and I'm so grateful I stumbled across her. Thanks to Mich, my eternal cheerleader. Thanks to my alpha, beta and ARC teams, you've been amazing.

Finally, thanks to my family. To my Mum, for teaching me over and over again that I can do anything if I work hard enough. For teaching me to love reading, and writing, at a very young age. Thanks for inspiring me Mum. And to Dad, for continuing to support my dreams in all ways. Love you all.

ABOUT THE AUTHOR

Heather is an urban fantasy writer and mum. She was born and raised near Windsor, which gave her the misguided impression that she was close to royalty in some way. She is not, though she once she got a letter from the Queen's lady-in-waiting.

Heather went to university in Liverpool, where she took up skydiving and met her future husband. When she's not running around after her children, she's plotting her next book and daydreaming about vampyrs, dragons and kick-ass heroines.

Heather is a book lover who grew up reading Brian Jacques and Anne McCaffrey. She loves to travel and once spent a month in Thailand. She vows to return.

Want to learn more about Heather? Subscribe to her newsletter for behind-the-scenes scoops, free bonus material and a cheeky peek into her world. Her subscribers will always get the heads-up about the best deals on her books.

Newsletter: heathergharris.com/subscribe
Follow her Facebook Page:
facebook.com/Heather-G-Harris-Author-100432708741372
Instagram: instagram.com/heathergharrisauthor
Contact info: www.HeatherGHarris.com
HeatherGHarrisAuthor@gmail.com

REVIEWS

Reviews feed Heather's soul. She'd really appreciate it if you could take a few moments to review her book and say hello.

Printed in Great Britain
by Amazon

80914396R00180